Acclaim for Reece's new novel, *Double Blind Double Cross*

"In *Double Blind Double Cross*, Dr. Robert Reece wields a talented pen. His memorable characters jump off the pages, keeping the reader up late into the night. I highly recommend it!"
– **Steven Manchester**, #1 bestselling author, *The Rockin' Chair* and *Twelve Months*

"In *Double Blind Double Cross*, Robert Reece deftly weaves the devastation of war, the quest for medical discovery and the big business of drugs into an engrossing, unpredictable and ultimately satisfying adventure story."
– **David Kerns**, author of *Fortnight on Maxwell Street* and *Standard of Care*

ACCLAIM FOR REECE'S FIRST NOVEL, *TO TELL THE TRUTH*

"Bob Reece has written a compelling story, addressing an issue familiar to physicians who care for children, but important to all of us. A baby dies, and the question of a sad, natural death weighed against a homicide and who caused the death becomes a quagmire of truth and lies inherent in the justice system assigned to determine guilt or innocence. Characters reflect personal attitudes and emotions, creating glimpses into their humanity as the baby's case winds its way through an all-too-real courtroom drama. The narrative of witnesses in the courtroom and tactics of attorneys brings the reader face-to-face with a startling reality: sometimes criminal cases are influenced by more than "the truth, the whole truth, and nothing but the truth."
– **Robert W. Block**, MD, FAAP, Professor Emeritus, Pediatrics, The University of Oklahoma School of Community Medicine, Child Abuse Pediatrician and Past President (2011-2012), The American Academy of Pediatrics

Dr. Robert Reece's moving novel is fiction based upon non-fiction. We judges grapple daily with the dilemma he depicts, as do jurors. Reece's book, besides entertaining and enlightening, is a tool for all Americans. It helps all know that the world of science has finally established not only that the world is round but also that abusive head trauma in infants and children is a scientific reality-without plausible denial! Thousands of physicians agree. Perhaps a dozen criminal defense medical witnesses would disagree. The latter testify, earning $12,000 a day in court, that infant head trauma has other causes...and presumably also that the world is flat. Reece's book supports the reality of abusive head trauma. Let there finally be justice for all, including children!

– **Judge Charles D. Gill,** Connecticut Superior Court.

"In *To Tell the Truth*, Dr. Robert M Reece shows how seriously flawed our trial system is when it comes to the use of and reliance on the so-called experts who would discredit the Shaken Baby Syndrome concept. Reece's book, while fiction, is based on his years of experience both as clinician and a trial expert. For a lay reader, it was disconcerting to read how defendants buy experts who will, for a substantial fee, confuse jurors with blue-smoke-and-mirror medical testimony aimed at arguing that Shaken Baby Syndrome isn't real and doesn't occur. Such "experts" belong among the ranks of the flat-earth folks, the deniers of evolution, and the climate change skeptics who would ignore solid science because they have a vested interest to do so. To Tell the Truth, in addition to being well written, provides important insights into the judicial system that everyone should know about. The fastest way I can think of to understand why the rules related to medical testimony in trials need to be rewritten, is to read Reece's thoughtful, fictional expose. Maybe then we'll learn how."

I. Michael Grossman, Author/Publisher

"I started reading this book and couldn't put it down! Dr. Reece does a wonderful job of providing intriguing plot lines and captivating characters. This book should be required reading for anyone entering the law or medical professions! It should also be required for anyone serving as a juror. It is both entertaining and informative. I hope that it inspires a change in the way that phony defense experts are viewed by the public and media."

Jamie Kondis, MD

"In *"To Tell The Truth,"* Bob Reece displays his skills as both a storyteller and an educator. An internationally respected expert in child abuse pediatrics, he vividly and in microscopic detail immerses the reader in the world of medicolegal punches and counter-punches in a case of fatal head trauma in an infant. His protagonist, a young Kansas City public defender, is torn between her passionate and idealistic commitment to her job, the expectations of her superstar private defense attorney father, and the growing realization that the conduct of her case, relying principally on mercenary pseudo-experts, is corrupt. This novel is packed with colorful characters, a huge helping of authenticity and plenty of surprises. At its heart, it is a tale of disillusionment and redemption, and a plea for professional integrity, legal punches and counter-punches in a case of fatal head trauma in an infant. His protagonist, a young Kansas City public defender, is torn between her passionate and idealistic commitment to her job, the expectations of her superstar private defense attorney father, and the growing realization that the conduct of her case, relying principally on mercenary pseudo-experts, is corrupt. This novel is packed with colorful characters, a huge helping of authenticity and plenty of surprises. At its heart, it is a tale of disillusionment and redemption, and a plea for professional integrity.

David Kerns, MD

This book is an excellent story and a commentary on those who would subvert our justice system. As a "Law and Order" fan, this book is in that vein. It opens with a tragedy and walks the reader through the issues culminating in a criminal trial. This is a solid character and issue study with a grounding in real life drama and science. I own all of Dr. Reece's books. His other books are outstanding textbooks of child maltreatment science. However like "Law and Order", it is this book that engages your emotions to teach life concepts.

Mary Case, MD

Dr. Reece succeeds at the very hard job of exposing institutional failures of the adversary system of justice in a fictional account full of three-dimensional people who fully engage your sympathy and concern. The flaws of the adversary system spring largely from understandable human weaknesses. Lawyers want to win, fact witnesses are fallible, and expert witnesses can make a fine living issuing opinions that are predictable if not always true. Dr. Reece's lifetime of professional experience in child abuse cases give him clear insight into the shortcomings of the world of criminal justice and what drives the people who inhabit it. I am not sure the shortcomings affect only the defense side, as they do in his book, but perfect balance is not a fair measure of an author any more than it is a fair measure of a trial lawyer. The adversary system of justice encourages adversary excess. It is the worst judicial system in the world, except for the others.

Richard Cohen, JD

"With a gripping plot to draw the reader inside the world of medical expert witness testimony, the author tells it like is and allows the reader to experience a trial in real time. The mainstream medicine of child abuse lives this story every day and has since the defense expert witness industry developed in the early 1990s. This defense expert witness industry has gathered steam in the past 25 years and unfortunately has drawn a number of journalists into their alternative world of belief. Readers may be shocked to learn that such shenanigans occur in real life in the courtroom where child abuse physicians strive to protect and save our most vulnerable patient."

Scott Benton, MD

"*To Tell the Truth* was a great book – I didn't want to put it down until I finished it. It was not only well written (much better than some of the books on the market from very famous authors!), but also very insightful into and provocative of both the medical field and the legal system. It created many different feelings and questions in my mind with regard serious topics and the reality of how our judicial system and medical system probably work in real life. I can't wait to have a discussion with others who read the book. Worth the money."

Marissa Nelson

"Bob Reece's first novel reminds me there are some good reads in the genre of detective/courtroom drama. At the center of *To Tell the Truth* are the workings of the well-defined characters and their complicated relationships. The lawyer lingo in the dialogue is believable--not overdone. The straightforward technical medical explanations of child abuse make a painful subject accessible to the lay person. It all adds up to a great story with a great through line that held my attention from start to finish."

Bill Oglesby

"I just finished Dr. Reece's novel this morning. I already have a long list of people to whom I plan to personally recommend it – including judges. There's great potential for this book to help inform the public at large."

Melissa L. Currie, MD, FAAP

To Charlotte,
Pleasure knowing
you + admire your
artistic talent!
Bob

DOUBLE BLIND
DOUBLE CROSS

Robert M. Reece

ROBERT M. REECE, M.D.

PUBLISHER'S INFORMATION

EBookBakery Books

Author contact: rmreece@gmail.com

Author website: www.robertmreece.com

Cover by Pear Ink Design: http://www.pearinkdesign.com

ISBN 978-1-938517-71-6

© 2017 by Robert M. Reece

ACKNOWLEDGMENTS

No one writes a book without help. My heartfelt thanks go to Tracy Hart, an editor who helped me in countless ways; Tom Kirkman and Richard Cohen, two judges who advised me in the early stages of the writing effort; Dr. Jessica Wolfe, an expert in Post-Traumatic Stress Disorder; Mary Margaret White, whose insights about storyline were helpful; Ray Byrne, whose sharp eye caught a couple of mistakes; my son Scott whose daily work brings him into contact with veterans; Lily Chambers, a fellow pediatrician; David Kerns, author of soon-to-be-released *Fortnight on Maxwell Street*; Marcella Pixley, author of acclaimed novel *Ready To Fall*; my stellar graphic designers Jenny Reece and Tom Lutz; Martha Langer of Pear Ink Design; Michael Grossman, publisher of my novels; and particularly my wife Betsy, whose patience sustains me always and whose editing skills have aided me in my professional publishing and now in my fiction writing.

DEDICATION

This work of fiction is dedicated to the courageous men and women in our Armed Forces who risk their lives in terrifying encounters, some of whom return home with debilitating injuries, both physical and mental.

CONTENTS

"Then Helen, daughter of Zeus, took other counsel. Straightaway she cast into the wine of which they were drinking a drug to quiet all pain and strife, and bring forgetfulness of every ill."

— **Homer's *Odyssey*, Book 4, verses 219–221**

PART I

1

A Chance Encounter

THE OLIVE-GREEN WALLS IN MY apartment are shrouds surrounding me. The bilious color conjures up malignant combat images I can't extinguish. Awake, I'm trapped in this drab cage. When rare sleep comes I'm jolted by chilling nightmares, torn and bleeding soldiers on stretchers pouring in. I'm supposed to put them back together, that's what trauma surgeons do. Screaming. Sobbing. Desperate men and women. These memories have stolen my skills, my spirit. I punch the walls in fury, a rage so deep I can't reach to quell it. I look in the mirror and see a shadow of the man I once was – auburn hair now mouse-colored, blue eyes fading to gray, forehead bearing deep furrows. My mouth is downturned where a smile once dwelled. Too small in college to be a basketball center, my six-foot four-inch height was fine for playing forward. But my formerly fit athletic body is skinny and in decline.

Where is respite? Medicines can't touch it. Therapy focuses my mind too sharply on the horrors of war. I have no god to cry out to. Maybe the dead are better off. The living envying the dead. Maybe I should carry out the act I've considered so often.

No. Get out of this stinking apartment. Go for coffee.

I'd just settled at a table tucked in the corner at Starbucks when I was startled by a familiar voice from the past.

"Tom Barrett, I can't believe it's you!" Akira Yamaguchi said as he spied me skulking in the corner.

Flustered, nearly spilling my coffee as I rose, I managed to croak out, "Uh, hello, Akira. What a surprise seeing you here." Awkwardly I returned his hug, an unusual display of affection from him.

"I heard you were back and wondered how I could get in touch. You living here in Worcester?" Akira asked.

"Yeah, have a little place around the corner from here," I said, hesitant to get into any conversation that might uncover the truth. "How'd you know I was back?"

"Oh, word gets around," he said. "I'm so glad to see you! Why don't we get together for dinner? I'm sure you're busy but I'd like to catch up."

Since returning from the Middle East I was phobic about reconnecting with anyone, especially my erstwhile friends and colleagues. But he'd be offended if I didn't accept his offer.

"I'm free on Thursday," Akira said. "Could we meet for dinner, say around seven?"

"I guess I could do Thursday." It came out more curtly than I intended but I was very uncomfortable. We arranged to meet, largely because of his enthusiasm – not mine – for reconnecting. I'd changed in so many ways since we'd been neophyte surgical residents together ten years earlier. Had he?

Why'd I say I'd meet him? He'll find out I'm incompetent, a surgeon who's lost his skills and a man who's lost all confidence. How can I get out of this? I could tell him I got a bad sore throat or forgot about other plans I'd made. But he didn't give me his number – no way to get in touch. I could just not show up. Nah, can't do that.

On the day of our dinner I worried about what we'd talk about. The taxi driver bumbled around looking for the Asian restaurant Akira had suggested on a side street of a sketchy neighborhood in Worcester. Finding the non-descript storefront, I squinted as I walked through a dimly lit entryway, breathing in the spicy fragrance of Asian cooking. I saw Akira studying a menu near a giant aquarium, well stocked with exotic tropical fish. Looking up, his expression was as I'd remembered: inviting, brimming with a warm smile.

"So glad to see you!" he beamed, shaking my hand and inviting me to take the seat across from him.

"So, what're you doing these days?" I asked hurriedly, trying to divert attention from myself for as long as possible.

"Doing research about memory," he said in the self-effacing manner I recalled so well.

"You mean you're not cutting anymore?"

"Yeah, this memory thing is my passion now."

"Don't you miss surgery…those patients you loved…who loved you?"

"I do miss patients," he said. "But I love this even more. Say, I've got an idea – why don't you come to where I work sometime so I can show you what I'm up to?"

"So when did you decide to do this?" I said, deflecting his question. I didn't want to go to wherever he worked – what was it, a hospital?

"Around the time you went into the military, I joined this bunch of neuroscientists at this place – the Zylinski Institute – doing memory research. We started with animals. We're lucky – we have a wealthy person with interest in neuroscience giving us money to support the research. I work with about twenty other scientists. You'd like them: they're a lot like our old surgical team back at Boston Medical, you know, high-spirited, with a zealous sense of mission."

"So what's your actual job at – what did you call it – Linski?"

"Zylinski. Although my title is Director, I'm mainly a facilitator for a lot of smart people," he said, not really telling me much. "But I'm interested to hear about what you're doing. It's been such a long time since I've seen you."

I didn't know how to respond. Yeah, he was a friend, but from a very different time. Here I am, stumbling around trying to get back into a new life and he's rolling along doing something he loves. He's like everyone else I knew before I was in the service – going on with their lives and careers while I was in the Middle East getting fucked up.

"Well, getting adjusted to being a civilian again is what I've been doing," was all I could manage. I didn't want to talk to him – or anyone – about my tour in the Middle East War. But I had to say something. "I moved to an apartment near Starbucks when Cynthia and I decided to live apart."

"Oh," he said, looking away, his face flushing. "I'm sorry to hear you're not together. Are you still in touch with her?"

"Oh yeah. We're still friends, and we talk often. It's just better this way for now." I didn't want to go into the real reasons for our decision. That would drag open the trap door to my cellar of problems.

"Of course," he said.

As the silence lengthened I shifted the conversation to Akira.

"So, you have anyone?" I asked.

"Well," he said, looking down, slightly embarrassed, "actually, I am seeing someone. She's so easy to be with. We seem to have much in common. She's recently divorced, in her early forties, a couple of teenagers. It could get serious. The problem – a big one – is that she also works at Zylinski. We're in different divisions, but still…"

The waitress came, took our order and we looked at one another, not sure where to go next with our conversation.

"You following the Red Sox?" he asked, going to neutral ground.

"From afar. The game's so slow I get impatient."

"You go to a gym for exercise?"

"Not as much as I should. I do a lot of walking though."

After some typical guy small talk, our waitress returned with steaming dishes of Pad Thai and a basil dish.

This meant I had to pick up the chopsticks to eat. Maybe it wouldn't happen this time. My mouth went dry, my palms were getting moist. The growling in my stomach was not from hunger. I looked around the restaurant, panic rising in my throat.

"Tom, are you alright?" Akira said, noting my nervousness.

"Sure, I'm fine," I said, not admitting I was about to scream.

The plastic chopsticks I held in my trembling hand clattered onto my plate. I grabbed for them, knocking my water glass over, spilling the drink into my lap. "Shit!" I yelled, bolting out of my chair and brushing the water off my pants. A blush rose in my face, the pulse in my neck throbbed.

Akira jumped quickly from his seat, coming to my side, dabbing the table with his napkin. His eyes locked on mine. We both knew I was in trouble. The waitress rushed over when she saw the spill, cleared the mess on the table and then brought us fresh servings. After a while we sat back down, not knowing what to say.

"Well, accidents happen, don't they? I broke three plates this morning just unloading the dishwasher," Akira said with a reassuring smile.

I knew he was trying to put me at ease, but I read concern on his face. Ever the sensitive clinician, empathy radiated from him.

"Yeah." I looked down at the food, my appetite gone. I forced myself to eat, and when we finished, Akira leaned toward me, smiling.

"Remember that night we had all those banged up war protesters come into the emergency department?" Akira said, doing his best to shift attention from my discomfort. "We must have worked all night patching them up. And fixing the cops who also got hurt. Man, that was a wild night."

"Can't forget that – and a lot of other nights with crazy cases. Those were the days, weren't they?" I said, relieved to talk about old times, good times.

"They were fantastic. Seems so long ago." Akira saw that I was smiling as we reminisced. "Say, are you free Saturday? Maybe we could get together again and talk more about those old times. It'd be good for both of us."

Now what? How do I escape this? I have no ready excuse – no patients to see, no plans with Cynthia to claim my time, so how do I get out of this? I'm so exposed, he'll find out. I was in a corner and couldn't get out without blowing Akira off entirely. I couldn't do that. Reluctantly I accepted.

"So, same time, same place?" he said, smiling at the prospect.

"Okay. See you then."

Back in my apartment, gloom settled over me again. I wondered how long I could keep up this charade, how long before another panic attack or violent outburst would show Akira what I'd become. I popped another tranquilizer and slumped into a hazy sleep.

On Saturday I dreaded seeing Akira. But part of me wanted to talk more about our good times together. Maybe that would give me a lift. I got to the restaurant first and sat at the same table. I tried not to think of the chopstick episode.

"Hi Tom!" Akira smiled as he arrived.

"I beat you here this time. How're you doin'?"

"I'm good. I like this time of day. Have a drink?"

"No, thanks; I'll just have some tea," I said, not wanting to tell him I was on strict doctor's orders to stay away from alcohol.

"So how long you been back?"

"About four months." Uh Oh. Knew this would come up.

"I was thinking about how our time at Boston Medical Center must have prepared you well for battlefield surgery over there," Akira said. "We saw so many gunshot and stab wounds at BMC. Guess that was good preparation."

I sat there, silent, looking away from Akira's gaze. When he saw I wasn't picking up my end of the conversation by agreeing, he said, "Tom. Just wanted you to know I didn't run into you by chance at Starbucks the other day. I saw Stan Morrison recently. You remember him? He was a first year surgery resident when you were senior resident. He told me you were back. He told me he's seen you often going into that Starbucks. Since I didn't know how else to get in touch with you, I went there several times hoping I'd run into you. So glad I was able to track you down."

I felt both pleased at his offered friendship and threatened by it.

"I've tried to stay under the radar since I've been back," I said, fearing the direction this conversation was taking. "I haven't felt like making contact with anyone. The more I tried to talk even with Cynthia, the more I was convinced she'd be better off without me bothering her."

"I'm really sorry about you and Cynthia," he said, reaching out, grasping my arm. "Hope you don't think I'm stalking you. I'm only interested in re-connecting with you – for old times' sake."

"I do appreciate that, Akira. I hope you don't think I'm a jerk for not being more receptive. Getting back to normal, daily stuff has been hard." I tried again to turn the conversation back to him.

"Tell me more about what you're doing. It's still vague."

"The work I'm involved in is about memory, as I told you, but more specifically, it's about getting rid of bad memories, particularly in veterans."

8

That perked my ears up.

"Getting rid of bad memories? In veterans? How?"

"Not easy to answer over dinner. Maybe it'd be better if I could show you what I'm doing. Why not come see me at Zylinski? I could explain it all there. Show you around the hospital, maybe introduce you to some people I work with.

"At least give me your phone number so I can stay in touch with you," Akira said as we left the restaurant. "We go back a long way. I have deep affection for you. I want to stay in touch – renew our friendship."

After these dinners, in my suspicious state of mind, I wondered if he would really "stay in touch" and be a friend. He was deep into his work, and in my state of self-loathing, I felt I wasn't worth the effort. He knew me when I was somebody, not just a wrecked human being limping along, draining national medical care coffers.

A couple of days later, though, Akira called.

"Tom, Akira here. Hope this is the right number. Give me a call."

I didn't call back.

"Tom, I know you're busy, but please give me a call."

By the third time he called I decided I had to respond.

"So glad I've reached you," he exclaimed when I finally called back. "I got a little worried when I didn't hear from you. Thought I'd have to track you down again at Starbucks," he said with a chuckle.

"I sometimes don't pick up my messages. Sorry."

"I meant it when I invited you to come over here so I can show you what we're doing. You interested?"

Unsettled at first, I gathered my senses.

"I guess I'm curious to see what you're doing," I said, thinking he'd continue bugging me until I got this over with. "How about tomorrow?" I said. At least this would be a hiatus from loneliness and boredom. He did say the memory research involved veterans. Got me to wondering…

"Perfect," he said. "Come at nine if you can. You know where we are?"

I wrote down the address, surprised he could clear his calendar for me that easily.

What the hell was I getting myself into, re-engaging with this high-achieving guy? Guess I'll find out tomorrow.

2

THE NEXT DAY

AKIRA'S OFFICE AT THE ZYLINSKI Institute was modest, in keeping with his persona. On the walls were reminders of his native Japan: calligraphy and framed silks, colorful vases on small platforms. In one corner was a tatami mat, probably there for his power naps, a habit he'd practiced when we were at Boston Medical Center.

I couldn't sit down. I walked around his small office, looking at the artwork on the walls then hurrying over to the window to look out, to escape the feeling of entrapment. Akira must have wondered what was bugging me as I nervously moved around his office.

He followed my eyes as I scanned the pictures. One photograph caught my eye, and I stopped and stared at it. It was Akira as a small boy standing alongside his father sitting in a carved wooden chair. Akira, a tiny delicate man, grew up on his father's two-acre farm near Kyoto, that Japanese city of shrines. An intense, conscientious, and quiet person, his shyness sprang from an introversion part cultural and part inborn. Surprisingly, for a person who enjoyed solitude, he was not unfriendly. Despite his reticence in social settings, his evident warmth never failed to attract people to engage in conversation

"That's when I was six years old," he said, noticing my interest. "My mother took the picture. She was into photography in a big way. That picture next to it was of our little farm."

He proudly showed me several other photos of his family.

After a few more minutes of my skittering around his office he broke the silence.

"So great you're here. Shall we sit down? I'd like to tell you a little about what we do here. Some tea or coffee?" He walked over to the carafes on the sideboard.

"Got decaf? I'm already wound up tight so don't want to jazz myself up any more."

"Sure. Wanna bagel too?"

"Naw, too jumpy for much to stay down. Stomach's been upset lately."

He handed me the cup of coffee.

"Could you put it down on the table?" I said, fearing if I took it from him, my tremor would surely spill it. Why did I accept his offer of coffee? That was dumb. Why did I even come here?

"Sure." He placed the cup and saucer on the table in front of the couch.

"So what would you like to do?" Akira asked. "Maybe take a tour of the inpatient wards, introduce you to some of our patients?"

Glad to get up and move again – and to avoid picking up the coffee cup – I answered, "Sure, lead the way. I'll skip the coffee."

"Let me fill you in as we walk. We have over two hundred veterans in our inpatient service with post-traumatic stress disorder resulting from their combat service. We're testing a treatment program involving a combination of therapies, including a new medication that damps down bad memories. Here we are at the clinical research center."

We walked into a corridor similar to many hospital halls I'd worked in. Some patients in street clothes were milling about, others gathered in small groups, still others flirted with the nurses. Some were staring blankly ahead. Akira stopped one man.

"Jimmy, this is my old friend, Tom Barrett."

Jimmy turned and I saw his burn-scarred face break into a crooked smile as he thrust a hand toward me.

"Any friend of Dr. Yamaguchi is a friend of mine," he said.

"Jimmy was in his vehicle when a flamethrower blasted through the window. How goes it, Jimmy?"

"Okay, Doc. Gettin' there."

We continued to walk the hall, met a few more patients and some nurses.

We swung by the laboratory where technicians in long white coats were busy pipetting various fluids into containers bound for analysis.

"This is where the blood, urine, sweat, and spinal fluid are processed. Downstairs is our radiology suite – PET scans, MRI, CT, ultrasound, and old-fashioned X-rays are done there."

Akira stopped and turned to me.

"Let me show you our swimming pool. Part of the therapy program. How'd you like to take a swim?"

"Huh? A swim? Uh, well, I didn't bring my swimsuit," I said as nonchalantly as I could.

"We've got a whole locker full of suits. I'm sure we can find one your size," Akira said in a light-hearted mood.

"A swim actually would feel good," I said, surprising myself. "Haven't had access to a pool for a long time. Let's do it!"

Back in Akira's office, he relaxed into a chair and invited me to sit.

"So what do you think of the place?"

"Impressive. Did you say all of your patients are vets with PTSD?"

"Yeah, that's the medical profile of the vets in the program. They vary in all kinds of ways beyond that, but that's what they have in common."

What I'd seen on this morning's tour was gradually settling in. The doctors at the military hospital had told me I had PTSD, but I was not convinced. PTSD? Not me. But I'd been wondering: do I really have PTSD? Would this program help me?

"Akira – I have a question," I began hesitantly. "How did these guys get into this program?"

"Referred from a lot of different places. Some come from the military hospital or other hospitals, some from private referrals. Some just walk in after long time doubts."

"I go to the military hospital," I finally decided to tell him. "But my improvement has been slow to non-existent.

"Guess I should level with you: I've had a damned hard time since I've been back. You saw my tremor the other night at the restaurant. I can't operate with that. The docs at the military hospital say I have PTSD. I was sure I'd get over it on my own."

13

"Tom, I'm your friend, not your doctor," Akira said. "But I can't help noticing things. You seem kinda down. You have that tremor that I don't remember from before. You seem jittery and not as outgoing as you were before your service. If you have PTSD related to military service, you would qualify for our program."

If this weren't Akira talking to me, I'd run out of here. But because it was him I wanted to listen, hear what he was trying to tell me.

"Let me introduce you to some of my colleagues. I told a couple of them that I'd run into a friend I'd trained with at BMC. I'd like you to meet them. Would you like that?"

"What possible interest could they have in meeting me?"

"If you got interested in our treatment regimen, you could make a unique contribution. Because you understand the scientific method, you could provide our team with subjective and objective details of your responses to the therapies that we couldn't get otherwise."

I was intrigued but at the same time spooked out.

"How about I arrange for you to meet with some of my colleagues?" He was getting more animated. "I could get Dr. Patel – she heads up this clinical trial – to explain the rationale of our research, give you a chance to ask questions, make suggestions, or just listen if that's what you'd prefer."

Be the focus of a bunch of scientific investigators? My heart raced. To participate as a subject and perhaps contribute as a fellow scientist… hmm. Maybe my adolescent fantasy of doing something very important – discovering the causes of cancer or devising a new treatment for malaria – could come to fruition in a different way than I dreamed. After med school and residency, that dream had dissolved fast. But now…having been exposed to the sickening visions of war and knowing what a number it's done on me…no way my surgery career will resume anytime soon… can barely function throughout the day…but to be useful again…maybe I won't live a life in shadows after all.

Akira waited patiently, good observer that he was, watching me mull over the offer.

"I hope you'll consider this for a number of reasons," Akira said. "It's a way to use your medical background. More importantly, I think this new treatment could benefit you. It's not because we need you as a subject.

14

We've plenty of subjects. I consider you my friend, not a subject." He paused and leaned toward me. "After our dinners together, I got worried about you. I wondered for several days if inviting you to join our research project would be appropriate – whether you'd see this as intrusive or as a gesture of my friendship and desire to help. The idea of integrating you into our research team while you're a study patient came to me as I was going to sleep the other night. It seems like a win-win to me. What do you think?"

He paused to gauge my reaction. I wasn't ready to answer.

"I hope I haven't offended you," Akira said. "That's the last thing I want to do. If you want to skip all this we can arrange to get together again, another way to continue our friendship."

"I'm sorry." His sincerity touched me. "My reluctance is central to my problem. The whole business of getting back into civilian life. I'm so paranoid and discouraged – I see threats everywhere. I'm like a naked nerve ending. I'll get better in time. I know that. All I really need is some time."

I was playing the same tune as I did that time I argued with Dr. Segal when he ordered me back stateside. Was I fooling myself? Would time really make this hollow feeling go away? Would I wake up one morning to find my symptoms magically dissolved? Resume life as a normal guy, take up my surgical career and be happy again?

I looked at Akira who was waiting patiently for my response. I considered taking up his offer just to get together again. One step at a time. But... if I could just dial up some courage, like in the old days when I made that initial incision for a procedure I'd never done before.

"I suppose meeting your colleagues and seeing what you're doing would be okay," I said absently. "Maybe this new treatment could help me. And maybe I could somehow contribute to the project," I said, warming to the idea. "What can I lose by listening?"

"You can only lose an hour or so of your time. I understand your worry that this is a research study, the treatment unproven. That's the exact reason for our doing the research – to find out how good this treatment is. Patient outcomes have been mostly good. I say mostly, because, I have to admit, there've been a few failures. But you're a scientist – you know that's how it works – positive experimental outcomes and some not.

"Could you come in tomorrow to meet these folks?"

Is this a good idea? What if Akira's changed over the years and become so obsessed with his research he's lost touch with relationships? Maybe I should walk out of this "Memory Institute." Even this building is like something out of a science fiction horror movie – cold, futuristic.

On the other hand, what if this therapy could help me? Nothing else has. Maybe my input would add something.

"Okay, Akira," I said with trepidation. "I'm willing to listen. Tomorrow? What time?"

As I left Zylinski, intensely curious to know what was going to happen the next day, I was short of breath, my mouth parched. Blood was pounding in my ears. Short of panic, but still wound up tight.

3

Ten Years Earlier

"**I** THINK YOU HAVE A TALENT for surgery. I can help you find a good surgical residency if you'd like," Dr. Martin, my faculty advisor, told me.

"Well, I do love surgery. Th–thank you!" I stammered. What? He's going to recommend me? I sure didn't expect this. What a break! "Where, uh, should I apply?"

"I'd like you to stay here at Cincinnati Medical Center, but you shouldn't do your residency where you went to medical school," he said. "I got my surgical training at Boston City Hospital, and in my day the worst trauma cases in the city were brought there. The decrepit hospital buildings that I knew are long gone, but the modernized Boston University Medical Center is still one of the best trauma-surgery training programs around."

"Am I qualified to go to a big deal place like that?"

"Of course you're qualified. You're one of our best students. I'll put in a good word for you with Christopher Rawlings, Chief of Surgery. No guarantees of course, but your record here and a few good words from me will put you in a competitive position. So get cracking on your application."

In the hoary tradition of the old boy network, the path to a first-class residency was cleared for me. Was this unfair to students who had no advocate? No doubt, but with enlightened self-interest motivating me I applied and was accepted. This whirlwind left me with mixed feelings. Guilt, exhilaration. I was also plenty scared. I was going to the city dubbed by some: the "medical Mecca," where three medical schools existed. And another one forty miles west in Worcester. Many familiar names in medical journals conducted rounds, saw patients, did research, and most importantly, taught medical students and residents there. I couldn't wait to test my mettle.

My first rotation was in the emergency department. I was dazzled by the dedication to patient care by the medical, nursing, and ancillary staff. Despite daily threats of closure due to underfunding by the City Council, political wrangling, and a carping media, the hospital persisted in its mission. We cared for patients injured in car crashes, industrial accidents, and vicious personal assaults. The camaraderie of the staff, combined with their talents and indomitable attitude made working there seem more a calling than a job. Sure, there were a few jerks and slackers, but they were in the minority.

I shared the on-call room with Akira Yamaguchi. He'd gotten his medical degree in Japan and came to the United States to do research in neuroscience. Like all foreign medical graduates, he was required to take more training – a residency – before entering the PhD program. And like many American medical school graduates, I was skeptical about doctors from other countries – some of the schools abroad weren't in the same league as American schools. I soon learned my worry about Akira was unfounded. He was the best resident of the group, and we became close friends.

It wasn't only work that captured my attention.

"Who's that?" I asked Alex, a second year resident in the emergency department.

"Cynthia Billings, Head Nurse."

"Isn't she pretty young to be Head Nurse?"

"Not really. She's about thirty, and she's smart as hell. Watch out, she won't hesitate to dress down any resident or attending surgeon if it's warranted. She has her hands full with neophytes of all kinds – student nurses, med students, residents, dietitians. She rules here. But I have to admit, she's fair."

Watching her keep order and minister to patients, I was drawn to her from my first day. A tall, slender woman with a narrow face, her nose had little depressions where her glasses rested. Her large eyes were dark brown, with eyelids hovering half way down. Her hands were delicate with long, narrow fingers springing from small palms and thin wrists. Her handshake was firm, but her touch was as soft as a butterfly when helping patients.

"So you're from Ohio. Around here we pronounce that Iowa," were her first words to me.

Is she kidding or teasing me? I'd had my share of that since coming to the East Coast. In Boston the locals were often provincial in the extreme and believed that nothing worth knowing existed beyond the Berkshires, sometimes even as close in as Route 128.

"Yep, still have the hayseed in my shirt. You from here?"

"Grew up in Dorchester. I was joking about Iowa. I do know the difference. What's a nice guy from the Midwest doing in a place like this?"

"How'd you know I was from Ohio anyhow?"

"Oh, I have my ways. Have you settled in?"

"Well, except for the terrible drivers and rude people, I kinda like Boston: all the history of the city, the grand old architecture. Mostly I like working in this crazy place. You see it all here, eh?"

"Oh, yeah. That's why I stay. Amazing variety of cases. And despite my carping, I get along with most everybody, and I really respect the docs. They work their tails off, and they come from some of the best medical schools in the world to work here."

The chief resident arrived in the corridor. "Time for ward rounds," he said.

I didn't want to end my conversation with Cynthia but had no choice. I saw she had no third finger rings so I was encouraged to ask impulsively, "Uh, are you ever available for dinner or a movie?"

"Boy, you mid-westerners move fast," she said with a laugh. Then, surprising the hell out of me, said, "Matter of fact, I got a few days break after tomorrow. If you can get free, call me."

Jotting down her number, I hurried off to rounds, hardly believing my good luck. Hmm…wonder why she's not attached; is there something wrong with her? This was my usual take on anyone who accepted my invitations. Like Groucho, I'd never belong to a club that would accept me as a member. What the heck, I'll trust my gut.

I called her, and she invited me to her place for dinner on Sunday night.

I found her condo on Warren Street in the South End. Wealthy Bostonians had built these grand, old, red brick homes, sparing no expense. When lifestyles changed, they moved "to the country," largely because they feared the influx of "rabble immigrants." They sold their homes to developers who cut up the interior spaces into smaller and smaller units, and slum landlords rented them successively to Irish immigrants, then to Italians, African-Americans, and Latinos. The landlords gladly collected rents but did nothing to maintain the buildings. Gradual deterioration led to leaking roofs, crumbling stairs, drafty windows, and faulty heating and plumbing systems. Every day poor tenants could hear rats and cockroaches skittering over floors and inside the studs. Small children ate the sweet-tasting flakes of lead-based paint peeling off the walls, windowsills, and doorjambs of these old buildings, leading to a silent epidemic of childhood lead poisoning. In the 1960's it had become fashionable for yuppies to buy these bow-front structures on the cheap and restore them gradually to their original beauty. The poor who had called these buildings home were forced to move. Most of the units retained their apartment configuration and later sold as condominiums.

I gave the brass knocker a couple of taps. Cynthia came to the door.

"Right on time – must be a mid-western thing. Come on in," she said, smiling.

I walked into one of the coolest condos I'd ever seen. It was small but decorated with exquisite taste. She'd painted the walls a dark, glossy Chinese red. The original window frames were painted a deep ivory and the window shades were made of a beige linen weave. Her couches and chairs were built of contemporary stainless steel and dark brown leather, a counterpoint to the antique feel of the building itself. A few scattered small Tabriz, Sarouks, and Bokhara rugs accented the shiny oak floors. Original art, some beautifully framed, some nakedly unframed, covered the walls. Bookshelves declared the owner to be a reader with a broad range of interests, and although a Kindle was tucked in among the real books, Cynthia apparently liked the old-fashioned feel of paper. The compact kitchen had appliances that were de rigueur, and of course the countertop was granite. Copper pots and pans hung from overhead racks and wine glasses slipped into wooden slots above the sink. I was impressed, wanted to move in tomorrow, thinking of my own sterile apartment in the Northampton Street residents' quarters.

"What a great place," I said. "How long have you been here?"

"About four years. When I got divorced, I got a nice settlement, and I got all this stuff. A nurse's salary obviously wouldn't stretch this far, but he was pretty decent when he decided to leave."

Almost anything I could say in response to this would've been foolish. I didn't want to know anything more about her ex and really didn't want to talk anymore about her past marriage.

Dinner was a chicken dish with a rich sauce and capers nestled over white rice. She had prepared Brussels sprouts, a vegetable I usually hated, but after tasting the way these were cooked I changed my mind. We finished the meal with a mixed salad with balsamic vinegar and olive oil laced with garlic and ginger.

"So, how long have you run the ED?"

"Came six years ago, fresh out of nursing school, got my bachelor's during my first year. Then the head nurse quit suddenly, and they asked me to fill in temporarily. Apparently no one wanted the job so they gave it to me, probably laughing at my naiveté for taking it. But I love it – stressful as hell at times but so satisfying.

"What's your story?" she asked in her straightforward manner.

"Well, not too interesting. Grew up in Cincinnati, got my medical degree there and came here to find out if I could cut it in this famous medical center." I took care to reveal nothing about myself before medicine. "So far, medicine here doesn't seem much different than in Cincinnati. Could it be that the doctors here read the same journals we read there?"

"Sure. But I've always lived and worked in Boston and can't imagine being anywhere else. I think we have great medical care here, but I have no idea how it compares to the rest of the country. I'm sure there are good and not-so-good doctors everywhere."

"What do you do when you're not working?"

"You think I have a life outside of the hospital? How quaint!" she said with a big grin. "Well, for starters, I sing in the South End Choral Society. I love music of all kinds – folk, rock, the symphony. Blown away by ballet.

Big time Celtics, Patriots, and Red Sox fan. In winter, I go to Vermont to ski, and in summer I have a favorite place on the Cape where I go for a couple of weeks. It belongs to my ex, and he lets me use it."

"Sounds like a pretty amicable divorce," I said, hesitant to take it any further.

"Yeah, Dirk's a decent guy. We just grew apart. He's a businessman in town, and we had different attitudes about most everything. He's way too conservative for me, wanted me to work somewhere else, like Newton Wellesley Hospital, where he said the patient population was of a 'better sort' – a metaphor for our differing philosophies. He didn't even like to come to the South End – worried about getting mugged or killed."

"How did you get together in the first place?" I asked, unable to suppress my curiosity.

"Mutual friend. Dirk's really okay, as I said, but he's got these blind spots. Well, enough about him and our failed marriage. It's over, and I'm fine with that.

"Now you know about my past, what about yours? You're a pretty good -looking guy – probably a star athlete – so you no doubt had your pick of women friends," she said with a smile. "But you're apparently still single."

"Just haven't found the right person. I focused like a laser on getting through med school. I worried any distraction would make me flunk out. Watching a couple of friends with wives and kids stressed out convinced me not to go that route. Years of training ahead of me before I can even think about a partner. On the other hand…" I trailed off.

"Know what you want to do in surgery?"

"Probably trauma surgery. Repair business. I've never been drawn to cancer surgery or cardio-thoracic surgery. I like to fix people up after they've been hurt. Like when that bus drove off the bridge injuring dozens of people. I was so inspired by those tough people who overcame their injuries. I'd like to be in a position to help in those situations."

We talked for hours. She told me her father had been a plumber, her mother a stay-at-home mom, who lived in a Florida retirement community. Her only sibling, a brother eight years younger, was distant from her geographically – he lived on the west coast – as well as emotionally. They seldom saw one another.

I couldn't help fantasizing about her. I wasn't interested in the marriage thing but having a close relationship was something else. We called it a night around midnight and gave each other a hug as we parted. It crossed my mind that our working in the same place might pose a problem, but dismissed the thought as unimportant as I headed back to my Northampton Street monk's cell.

On my way home, Cynthia became a visceral presence. I was intrigued with this strong, intense woman. Not the most beautiful woman I'd ever seen, but I was attracted to her in a different way; she was mysterious in some undefined manner. Cynthia was made of sturdy stuff, but complementing that was a sensuous tenderness radiating from her like perfume. I'd been conscious of this, watching her interact with patients and co-workers. Her quick wit suggested an ironic view of the world. I could see endless possibilities in a relationship as the stars in my eyes gathered.

I wondered how many lovers she'd had. Surely I wasn't the only one who had noticed her, who's been attracted to her. I was already jealous, a nonsensical emotion. What possible right do I have to be jealous? I've spent the sum total of one evening with her and already I'm feeling possessive. What chance do I have anyhow? Maybe she thought I was profoundly unattractive and uninteresting. I'm a "mid-westerner" and she's "of New England." Still, it felt like she returned some of my feelings.

By necessity we were in the same space at work over the next several months. Observing her deepened my respect, admiration – and attraction. She always made patient welfare job one. I could tell that the nursing staff loved her. She expected superlative effort by everyone on the team but in a way that didn't put anyone off. She was patient with less talented nurses, always helping them to improve. I particularly got a kick out of watching the surgeons with outsized egos try to dominate her.

"Hey Billings, hurry up and get that surgical pack into this god dammed trauma room! We need to get this procedure goin'!"

"Turn to your left, Doctor, and you'll find what you're looking for," she would say.

"Billings, get Room 3 ready – patients coming from the Southeast Expressway crash," Dr. Paxson cried.

"Thanks for the heads up. but it's ready, Doctor. Just take a look."

She was never intimidated, seemingly one step ahead, and she always held her own. Even as she stood up to them, they all respected her.

After that first time at her condo, our time together lengthened as she showed me around Boston. She took me to the Freedom Trail on Beacon Hill and to the Old North Church tower, where in Longfellow's poem, a lantern signaled to Paul Revere that the British were coming: "one if by land, two if by sea." Revere's house in the North End, the Harriet Tubman house in the South End – a tribute to the former slave who was a linchpin in the underground railway – and a tour of The USS Constitution – "Old Ironsides" – were just a few of the sites that made weekends a pleasure with Cynthia.

We discovered shared favorites in music, art, literature, and even architecture. On weekends off, we traveled to the Berkshires or to Portsmouth, and when summer came we spent a weekend in Acadia. Our relationship moved beyond pleasant times together to weekends filled with concerts, gourmet dinners, and lots of sex. We shared stories about our parents. I withheld some important details about mine but she was transparent about her family.

I stored these pleasurable portions of time in my memory, alongside the successes and disasters of clinical care at the hospital. Each day brought broken patients through the portals of the emergency department. One night, three calls of catastrophe blared into the triage desk.

"Ambulance coming in – three people shot in Dorchester. One probably dead, the other two not far behind. Get Room 1 ready to receive," a nurse called out to the Trauma Room.

Shortly after, a call came in from an ambulance on the Southeast Expressway.

"This is bizarre! We're bringin' in this guy from a wrecked station wagon. This steel dowel layin' on a platform behind his head, went like a bullet through the back of his skull, clean through his head with one end sticking out just above his left eye. He was goin' about fifty when he rear-ended a truck. He's alive, but how is one of God's mysteries. Four minutes out. Vitals stable right now. Need everybody on this."

And another call on top of the last one: "Overdose, possible suicide, nineteen-year-old woman. Breathin' shallow, blood pressure barely perceptible. Think it's oxycontin, but don't know for sure. Be there – about five minutes."

The shooting victims died, as did the woman with the overdose, but the guy with the steel bar through his head miraculously survived. Akira got the bar out of his head and except for losing his left eye and some neurological function, he went home three weeks later. What he'd do for a living was a question no one could answer.

Punctuating the steady flow of routine cases were the anti-war protest demonstrations. These supplied our emergency department with abundant cases of traumatic injury and death. Most were protesting government action sending ever-larger numbers of troops to the Middle East War. Beginning peacefully, the protests typically escalated soon after police arrived when emotions took over and confrontations prompted vigorous attempts to restore order. Batons bashed heads and frenzied crowds stampeded, crushing unlucky protestors. Tear gas was sprayed to disperse the crowds.

By my fourth year of surgical training, Cynthia and I were living together in her condo – the one I'd lusted after when we first met. Living together made me want to marry this fabulous woman if only I could convince her that tying the knot with me would be an improvement over her present life. Her previous marriage made her wary, but I felt sure that we would someday be a permanent couple.

4

THE LETTER

A REGISTERED LETTER FROM THE MILITARY High Command lay on my desk for several days before I opened it, trying to postpone the inevitable. I knew what it was; several of my colleagues had already been scooped up. The US military gained congressional approval to conscript at will, and with little advance warning, people in "essential activities." The Armed Forces had a limitless need for doctors, especially trauma surgeons, necessitated by the rising numbers of casualties in the Middle East War, the longest military engagement in the nation's history.

I finally opened the letter and read it to Cynthia.

"You have to go to the Middle East?" she said, with more fear in her voice than I'd ever heard from this rock-solid pillar of the emergency department.

"That's where they need doctors most so that's probably where I'll have the great pleasure of serving my country. This, of course, is the war to end all wars, like all the others. I'll get lots of experience in trauma surgery. I suppose I should look at it that way."

"For how long?"

"Well, eighteen months is the usual tour."

"This is awful. So many others have gone, I know, but this is about you," she groused. "I can't believe it. And for what? What good is it that America is in this stupid war?" she snapped.

"I know."

We looked at each other, our faces mirroring dejection and fear.

I had no choice. Conscription was now part of being an American. Some held we had a moral responsibility to help innocent citizens in the Middle East whose leaders consolidated their power into tyrannies. Recruitment by terrorist factions continued to be perversely successful. Political and religious extremists dominated the other ninety-five percent of ordinary citizens – mere pawns in the conflict.

Within a few weeks, I was on a transport plane for Cyprus, the staging area for NATO forces. Confusion reigned at the base, with personnel coming and going through the revolving doors of assignment and relief. The grim expressions of those returning from Syria, Lebanon, Iraq, and Iran stared blankly into the eyes of men and women about to lose their innocence as we plunged into the unceasing maelstrom of conflict. What lay ahead was incomprehensible but it would be seared into our consciousness forever.

Mobile medical units were on red alert 24/7. The medical teams typically worked eighteen hours each day. During these long shifts as a combat surgeon I saw tableaux worse than Dante, worse than all the things I'd seen at Boston Medical Center. Beyond torn bodies, shattered limbs, and crushed heads due to automatic rifles, grenades, and other conventional high-powered weaponry, wounds from toxic chemicals and horrific burns from fourth generation napalm challenged our skills. We lost more good men and women than we saved.

Our medical units resembled large Legos – plastic interlocking parts that could be assembled within hours. Swedish ingenuity from Ikea had designed operating room tables that snapped together simply. Anesthesia delivery systems were equal to those used in world-class hospitals. Ready-to-use sterile surgical instruments came in shrink-wrapped packages. This superlative equipment was designed to meet a demanding and frustrating mission – to piece together broken bodies from war, the worst recurring plague of mankind.

"When we started out," my Commanding Officer Higgins told me, "these pods were white – huge red crosses all over 'em. But the ISIS zealots used the red crosses as bulls-eyes. ISIS assholes are proud to attack anything belonging to the infidel West. They don't know – or if they know, don't give a shit – about The Geneva Convention Rules of War.

To protect ourselves we covered the pods with sand-colored paint. Some protection, but not much."

I arrived the same time as Danny Mott, another surgeon. Blond, blue-eyed, slim, good-looking and athletic, Danny's rangy limbs cried out "surfer!" Paddling a surfboard had made his shoulders overdeveloped and his tanned craggy features spoke to many hours under the sun.

"Say, any chance you know Ken Carter at County?" I asked, as soon as he threw his gear on a bed. "We were in the same med school class at Cincinnati."

"Carter? Yeah, sure, I know 'em. Small world, eh? Great guy. Played a lot of handball with Carter before I got married. He's now a plastic surgeon making LA women more beautiful. I shoulda done that and I wouldn't be here," he said as he looked around at our dumpy quarters.

"Think we have time for a beer? You as tired as I am from the trip?" Danny asked.

"Yeah, I'm pooped. A beer would be great. We don't have to start work until tomorrow."

"Hey, lemme ask you about a case we had just before I left LA. This guy came in with a hunting knife stickin' out of his left chest," he said excitedly, as surgeons do when talking about their worst gory cases. "It was right beside his left ventricle." He went on to describe in great detail the procedure to get the knife out before it penetrated further into the heart. It seemed we'd known each other for years as we talked about similar experiences we'd had in emergency departments three thousand miles apart. Soon our talk moved into our personal lives. Unlike me, he was married with a couple of boys, two and four years old.

"Here's Katharine," he said, passing his iPhone to me with videos of his wife. "She's a marine biologist at the Scripps in La Jolla." In a wetsuit, she could have been an advertisement for health food as she toted her board toward the Pacific surf.

"And take a look at these two guys. Luckily for them they look more like their mother than me," Danny said. "The four year old – he's Hunter, named after Katharine's father and the two year-old is named Jeff, after my brother."

There were his sons playing with a garden hose in his back yard, giggling, shocks of blond hair falling over their faces. The resemblance to his wife was unmistakable.

"You married?" Danny asked.

"Not married, but living with a woman for several years. Cynthia. Hope to marry her when I get back and finish off my training."

In the days to come I found Danny to be a splendid surgeon – steady, eager, and energetic. We worked together from the first day as though we'd been operating side- by-side for years. Some people just mesh like that, and in this situation it made life bearable.

"Got that bleeder over there?" I asked Danny, during one of our cases.

"Yup, and the other one next to it. Think we'll save this kid's leg?"

"Vessels are pretty torn up but maybe enough collaterals to keep it viable. We'll see."

"You check the kid with the burns on his face? You know, the one with the eye burned shut?"

"Yeah, it's beginning to slough. Doubt that eye'll make it. So sad. Kid's only twenty."

"Speaking of youngsters, I'd like you to take a look at that boy they brought in from the city," I said. "Couple of troopers found him cowering in the basement of a bombed-out building. Must be about eight. He won't speak, but his leg is gone below the knee and despite the antibiotics we're pumping in there's a lot of sloughing dead tissue above the amputation. I don't know what we'll do with him. Guess we get the Red Cross to take him outta the war zone."

We walked from the OR to the ward where this little guy was. Danny looked at him, knelt down in front of him as he sat on a small stool. The boy kept his eyes down while Danny gently unwound his dressing. The smell was pungent as the last layer of bandages – the part glued loosely to the underlying tissue – came off.

"Looks like pseudomonas. Let's give him a sedative, debride this a little more and change antibiotics. I think this'll heal okay, but he needs to be outta here. Major Higgins can surely arrange something."

The boy looked directly at Danny, their eyes locking on each other. The boy's look told me his trust in Danny transcended their age difference and their disparate cultures. Maybe because Danny was a father or some innate humane quality some people have. The child lifted his arms up to Danny and he took him up, wrapped his arms around him and held him tightly for a few moments. Over the next several days the boy improved and he and Danny smiled at each other when we made rounds.

Outside the OR we spent what little free time we had together, talking about life back home. We jogged together when we could squeeze it in. It was during these sessions that we shared our feelings.

"I'm a lucky guy, ya know," he told me after we stripped off our scrub suits and got into our running gear. "Katharine's a woman in full. She's beautiful, sexy, funny as hell and a natural mother. They love playing soccer with her. You'll love her when you meet her."

I knew we'd continue our friendship when we got back to the States and hoped we could team up professionally.

"Tom, come with me. I need you to check on a trooper in the ambulance before we move him," Major Higgins called.

Christ, must be bad. On our way out, we sidestepped a stretcher carrying a soldier, his bloody leg gaping from who knows what kind of shrapnel.

Just as Higgins and I got to the ambulance several yards away, BOOM! A deafening sound exploded from the operating station.

Oh my God! I froze. Looked at Higgins, who stared back, wide-eyed. Time did that weird thing where it stretches and detaches from its typical rhythm. We tore back to the unit.

I slid – nearly fell – when I ran into the room. "Holy mother of…" I screamed. I was sliding on their guts – Danny's or the nurses' or that poor bastard on the stretcher. My puke mixed with blood and flesh fragments on the floor or sprayed on the walls. I retched my way out of the room, gasping for air.

After the acute horror and disbelief subsided turning into numb reality, Higgins gathered us together, offered a short prayer, and took a deep breath.

"This is devastating for all of us," he said in a practically inaudible voice. "We've lost five exemplary professionals – five members of our family, our team. Unbearable to contemplate the grief in their families

31

– their wives, husbands, sons and daughters, parents and grandparents. What we do know is they'll suffer more than we." His voice broke and he sighed, standing up straighter as he continued. "A light's gone off in our spirit – but we have no choice but to press on. To save the lives we can so other families don't endure this kind of pain," He flicked a tear from his eye. "Be good to each other. Keep your chins up and carry on.

"You all know Dr. Segal," he turned to the unit's psychiatrist. "We can all use help coping with this awful tragedy. He's here for you."

A new trauma surgeon and four nurses were transferred in to take Danny and the nurses' places. Some of the old team veterans pulled themselves together and moved on. As for me, it was as though part of me was gone forever. I couldn't accommodate to the void of Danny's absence. He'd become my closest friend, soul mate, a brother I'd never had and now could never forget. I tried to block out the thought of the suffering borne by Katharine, Hunter and Jeff. I stumbled through each hour and tried to shake off the hollow feeling inside. The new crew didn't come close to what Danny, those great nurses and I had.

"For Christ's sake, get that bleeder over there. You want this kid to die?" I said to the new surgeon.

"Get that retractor over outta my way, you dummy," I exploded at Karen, the newest nurse on the team. I apologized later, but their angry expressions told me I was not forgiven.

After seven months of bearing witness to the horror of the war and my inability to get beyond my dark sadness about losing Danny, my tolerance was exhausted.

"Tom," Dr. Higgins said one day. "I want you to report to Dr. Segal. I'm concerned about you. You're no longer coping with even minor injuries to our troops."

"C'mon, Major. Look, I know I've not been myself since we lost the old team. And all the other shit we deal with here every day. But I'm plowing through. I'll be okay. Talking to a shrink isn't going to make it any better. I just need to push through this. Been through stressful situations before and came out fine. I just need a few more weeks."

"Sorry Tom, not this time. You need to talk to Dr. Segal. That's an order."

"I'm sure you know why you're here," Segal said.

"I know I've been on edge," I replied, minimizing the situation.

"When you say 'been on edge' what do you mean?"

"I don't know. Guess I'm less patient with staff."

"My report says that you often shout – or a better term may be yell – at the personnel in the OR."

"These new people just aren't as sharp as our old team. I get frustrated with them."

"They say you're abusive."

"Abusive? That's not true! I get a little pissed, but it's for the good of the patients. I want them to get the best care we can give."

"How're you sleeping?" Dr. Segal said, shifting away from the behavior I was denying.

"Not so good."

"Nightmares?"

How'd he know? "Yeah, some of them shake me out of sleep. I'm probably easily irritated because I'm chronically fatigued. If I could get a good night's sleep I'd be fine."

"Some of your colleagues complain this is affecting your surgical abilities. Do you think that could be true?"

"Hell no!" I shouted. "Some of the new surgeons – the rookies who just got here – may be telling you stuff, but they don't have my experience. Some of them act like they hope they won't have to operate with me, I've seen that. They sometimes crowd me out of the operating room. That's humiliating." I realized how defensive I was sounding. "I admit it does bother me that nurses look away when I walk by," I said, defeat in my voice.

"You went through a terrible loss when you lost your colleagues."

"They weren't just 'colleagues,'" I said, raising my voice.

"Can you say more?"

Is it my imagination or is he sitting up straighter, a little afraid of my losing it?

"I lost Danny, my best friend ever, and I miss him so much." Tears, as if on a timer I had no control over, rushed down my face. "His wife and kids must be so devastated. He loved them more than anything; they were his world."

Dr. Segal pushed the tissue box closer to me.

"Can't you understand I'm merely going through a rough patch? I'll be okay if I can just get some sleep. Maybe some sedatives?"

"Medication is not the answer," Segal said. "I'll be frank with you, Tom. Your senior officers think you're too damaged to function and you need to be transferred before you hurt or kill someone."

"What the fuck you talkin' about? Kill someone? I'm saving lives here. Don't give me that shit!"

"This is a hard decision for all of us. We know how good a surgeon you were."

"Were! Were! Whadda you mean? I'm still a better surgeon than those rookies we have in there now!"

"Let me finish. We know what you've been through – rough times. But for your sake and the sake of the unit we've got to send you to Command Central."

"What for?"

"For further evaluation and treatment. I'm sorry, but we see this happening all too frequently in this senseless war. You may be able to resume duty, but for now you need rest, rehabilitation and therapy. You must appreciate how high the stakes are.

"I'll give you some tranquilizers for the interim. We'll get you out of here in the next few days. Is there anything I can do for you before you leave?" He stood and offered his hand.

"One thing. Can you tell me how to contact Katharine Mott? I need to be in touch with her to offer her my condolences and see if I can do anything for her and her kids."

"I'm sure I can get that for you. Stop by my office before you leave."

I felt like a failure for the first time in my life. I'd always taken pride in being able to set agonizing cases into my out-of-reach places, intellectualize about them. But these hellish injuries were beyond anything I'd ever seen. And Danny was gone, forever, a paragon taken down by a terrorist whose brain was operating at a reptilian level. Added to that was bone-deep fatigue, an unending stream of fractured heads and bodies, and worst of all, the futility of it all. I felt dead inside except for the splashes of unexpected and spontaneous expletives, screaming nightmares, and general irritability.

After further evaluations at Command Central examiners concluded my recovery would be too slow to return to war zone duty. With each evaluation and determination that I was seriously traumatized, my sense of self shriveled. I couldn't even look the psychologists in the eye toward the end of all these repetitive encounters. I was given a medical discharge and sent home for therapy.

I boarded the plane and settled into an uncomfortable seat. The kid next to me – couldn't be more than 23 – glanced over, sizing me up.

"You goin' home?" he said.

"Yeah. You?"

"Yessir. Lost my foot so I'm not any good for the Army anymore. They tell me I can get an artificial foot when I get back to Walter Reed. How 'bout you?"

I didn't want to get into my story. I hadn't been in combat, had no visible wounds, limbs all intact. I felt like a wuss for falling apart. "My tour is up so I'm getting out. Home to Massachusetts. Where you from?"

"Tennessee."

Our conversation ended there and he fell asleep. I envied him. I couldn't sleep, adding to my already numbing fatigue. When the plane touched down in Boston my mouth went dry, my pulse raced and I realized how terrified I was of seeing Cynthia. I slogged my way through all the lines at the International Terminal, almost lost my temper with one of the functionaries behind the passport booth, but emerged into the crowded waiting area. Cynthia was waving her arms at me, tears rolling down her cheeks. We held each other, the warmth of her body strangely unfamiliar.

"Got all your gear?" she asked, with a big smile.

"Let's get out of here. I'm really exhausted." I couldn't return her smile and my mood soon enveloped her like a leaden cloud as she surveyed me.

After getting into her car in continued silence, she looked at me with a worried frown.

"You look very tired. Are you okay?"

"I am tired. Not okay. Just get me home and let me get some sleep."

"Hungry?"

"No! Didn't you just hear me? I need sleep."

We rode in silence to her place, got out of the car and into the condo. I headed straight to the bedroom, sprawled out on the bed, tears and sobbing overcoming me. Cynthia lay down beside me.

"What can I do?" she asked.

"Nobody can do anything. I'll fight this but I'm at a low point. Just leave me alone."

She put her hand on my back.

"I'm not leaving you alone. You need medical attention now. Did they tell you where you should go for care?

I sat up, hung my head between my knees.

"The military hospital in Worcester." I paused. "Maybe I could use a drink."

"What would you like?"

"Scotch," I said without hesitation. Maybe some alcohol would calm me. She brought it to me.

"Tom, I think you need to tell your doctors you're in trouble and need help right away."

"So you think I'm crazy too," I spit out. I threw the glass across the room and it splintered against the wall, making Cynthia, the steadiest nurse I'd ever known, look frantic with worry. This had to change.

"Let's try to get some sleep. We can talk about this in the morning," Cynthia said, after cleaning up the shards of glass. "Maybe if you take a tranquilizer you'll be able to sleep."

"Doc, no matter what, I don't wanna die. Cut off my legs or arms, but don't let me die!" he pleaded, lying in a pool of blood on the operating table.

"He's almost ready for you," Glenn Stockman, the anesthesiologist, said to me. "You can begin anytime."

36

As I raised my scalpel, Glenn suddenly was knocked off his stool, and an ISIS soldier rushed me. I ducked his rifle barrel and slammed into him with all the force that adrenalin brings when the primordial animal is threatened.

"Tom, Tom, stop! What're you doing?" Cynthia gasped.

I woke up and saw her cringing on the floor where I'd slammed her.

"What the–?" With rising panic and alarm, sweat pouring off my body, I jumped out of bed, ran for the light switch. She was holding her pillow in front of her, abject fear in her face. Oh my God, if she hadn't been able to scream I could have killed her. Uncontrollably trembling, I slumped back onto the wet sheets, groaning, "I'm sorry; I'm sorry."

Cynthia tried to soothe me, but all I could do was moan.

When light came, Cynthia and I sat down at the kitchen table. I stared at her lovely body and saw abrasions and bruises welling up on her shoulders where she'd fallen.

"I don't want to be this way. Seeing pictures in my mind of young people being torn apart, gushing blood, arms and legs hanging by threads, the screams, the agony – I can't erase them."

"I get it. That's why I want you to get help right away; I'm not trained in this part of medicine. You're practically a skeleton – dark circles around your eyes, no appetite. You're very depressed and agitated. I'm scared. I love you too much to just stand and watch while you're suffering so much."

She took me to the military hospital in Worcester that afternoon. The duty officer took one look at me and admitted me. My working diagnosis was post-traumatic stress disorder or PTSD, according to the intake nurse.

The next day on rounds the senior resident was trying to be helpful when she described what PTSD was.

"What we know is that the prefrontal cortex of the brain helps resurrect early memories buried in the amygdala, the reservoir of bad memories. While here you'll be offered a variety of therapies including medications," she said. "I'll set up your appointments so you can start getting better."

"You sure of this diagnosis?" I asked with irritation.

"Well, it's a provisional diagnosis but what we see – your signs and symptoms – points to that as most likely. Our mental health doctors will meet with you tomorrow. They'll have lots of questions about what happened to you over there. They'll ask more questions about your early years, your experiences as a child. We know that many people who get PTSD have a history of childhood traumas. These childhood traumas, called Adverse Childhood Experiences – ACE's for short – dramatically change the way critical brain connections work. People who have had more than four adverse events in their childhood are more susceptible to PTSD."

Well, my childhood was sure full of "adverse" experiences.

After a week of shuttling amongst various medical and neurological evaluations, psychological testing, and blood tests, I was ready to begin outpatient therapy. Cynthia came to collect me but by now I'd decided I should live alone.

"Cynthia, I can't ever subject you to what happened last week."

"Tom–"

"No, no, don't start. I'll find an apartment near the hospital until I'm better. I've got to get control over myself. I've made up my mind," I said, looking into her eyes. "I can't risk hurting you badly. I'm a very messed-up man. I don't want to be apart, but it's got to be, at least for now."

We wrapped our arms around each other. She finally agreed to being apart if I promised to stay in close touch, take my therapist's recommendations, and stay away from all but prescribed drugs.

"I'm going to make it easy for you to stay in touch. There's a great job available at a hospital here in Worcester. I'm applying and think I have an excellent chance of getting it. I'm also looking for an apartment or condo so I can be nearer to you. I'm excited about this – I'd be in charge of all ambulatory services of the hospital, not just the emergency department. And the condos in Worcester are a lot cheaper than in Boston."

"You're the best," was all I could say as we held each other.

Neither one of us could have foreseen what lay ahead.

5

THE MEETING

MY SWEATING HANDS OPENED THE door of Akira's office. The door to a small conference room was ajar and the sound of voices drifted out. I looked back at the door I'd come through in case I needed to make a fast flight out.

Were those voices talking about me? I tried to catch scraps of conversations. Get hold of yourself, man. It's far more likely they're discussing what they did over the weekend rather than talking about this potential experimental subject skulking into the room.

Dark thoughts nagged at me: what if the goal of Akira's team is not my welfare but their own career advancement, their hope of some scientific gold medal, a Nobel Prize for the discovery of a breakthrough treatment of PTSD? Filled with apprehension and feeling like an inanimate object for scientists to test their hypotheses on, I imagined them examining me, finding fault with my every move. Should I turn around and run like hell to get outta this crazy place? What was I thinking to come here anyway?

Still. Was there a chance that Akira and his colleagues would help me?

In flashes of unwarranted optimism, I hoped listening to their explanation about this treatment might make me understand how it could work for me. I breathed, deeply, to calm myself. I knew Akira, I trusted him. He wouldn't just treat me like another guinea pig, would he?

Yeah, right. Why did I think my being Akira's friend and surgical colleague would convey some kind of special treatment? But I'll accept any advantage to overcome this misery. Feeling constantly jumpy and not so quietly desperate has to stop.

"Welcome, Tom," Akira called out, standing when he saw me. "Everyone, please listen. This is my old friend and fellow surgeon Dr. Tom Barrett. He's considering entering our clinical trial as a subject so I asked him to come hear about it."

He introduced four people at the table, his polite respect for them apparent. I listened, bathed in self-conscious bewilderment; I might not remember a single name. The performance anxieties of a thousand surgical procedures and case presentations swept over me. Shadows filled the edges of my vision. I reached for the back of a chair so I didn't fall. I looked around furtively to see if anyone noticed the sweat on my forehead, perspiration already trickling down my sides. I could feel the damp circles under my shirtsleeves, my flushed face.

"Tom, have a seat here," indicating the chair I was grasping. "Take your time to get settled. We're not in any hurry. Let us explain what we do here," Akira said as he came to my side, seeing I was overwhelmed. I sat down and reached for some tissues in a box on the table in front of me, wiping my brow quickly, stuffing the used tissues into my pocket.

"After you hear this I hope you'll consider entering this clinical trial with us. I believe the treatment could benefit you – that's the principal reason. Your medical background and knowledge may also give us insights not available any other way."

He turned and introduced a young Indian woman, Lakshmi Patel. I concentrated on her teak-colored face and a bright red spot between her eyebrows, a symbol of her Hindu faith. I'd been told it was called a "bindi" and to some indicated the "seat of concealed wisdom." I hoped Dr. Patel's bindi did indeed mean she was wise.

"And this is Dr. Lyon, one of our psychiatrists," Akira said, turning to a tall, slender man in his sixties with a full head of pure white hair. He stood and extended his hand.

"Pleased to meet you, Dr. Barrett."

"Dr. Starr, one of our internists, is to your right, and Dr. Mohammed, our pharmacologist, at the end of the table."

I nodded to Dr. Starr who smiled back. As my eyes settled on Mohammed I felt a mix of fear and anger rise in me. I tried not to see the embodiment of ISIS in this man – mahogany-colored skin, dark brown eyes, raven-black hair. It took all my self-control to avoid getting up and running out the door.

"So, Dr. Patel, will you begin by outlining what we do here for Dr. Barrett?"

Her pleasant English-accented singsong voice evoked memories of other Indian doctors I'd trained with.

"Dr. Barrett, I'll summarize the scientific underpinnings of our project, okay? Pardon me if it seems elementary but I hope you'll have a deeper understanding when I finish. Of course, ask any questions you have as I go along.

"We know that traumatic events sear into particular regions of the brain, mainly the frontal cortices, implanting indelible memories," she said. "The enzymes in certain brain structures – particularly the hippocampus and amygdala – facilitate this. Research has taught us that memories from emotionally traumatic events are quite hard to treat."

Dr. Patel paused and seeing that I was listening intently, went on.

"The older treatment model is based on the idea that when patients in environments they know to be safe are repeatedly exposed to disturbing memories they become relatively desensitized to these traumatic recollections. We call this 'memory reconsolidation.' The theory is that during this process, the threat associated with the bad memory is reduced."

"Okay, so far, so good, I'm following you pretty well since I've already been in similar therapy," I said. I tried to stop the rhythmic jiggling of my leg underneath the table but this nervous tic wouldn't be tamed until I was out of this room, away from this angst.

A loud ring from an iPhone broke the silence. Embarrassed, Dr. Mohammed groped to turn it off. Frowning, I leaped up from my seat, looking in the direction of the ring, my chair toppling over behind me. The two on either side of me jumped up to steady me and another person righted the chair. They gently eased me back into my seat. Their touch was reassuring and I regained my fragile composure.

"I'm terribly sorry." Dr. Mohammed, said. "I thought I'd turned it off when I came in. Please forgive me."

"I guess no one needs now to be reminded to turn off your cellphones," laughed Dr. Patel. "Dr. Barrett, please accept our apologies. May I continue?"

"Can we take a short break? I need to go to the bathroom,"

"Sure. Would a fifteen minute break work for everyone?" Akira said as he directed me to the men's room. When I got there and looked in the mirror I saw my grim visage staring back at me. Get a grip, man! That was only a cellphone. Not a terrorist. Not a bomb. Not a dying trooper. I rinsed my face off with cold water, drying it with rough paper towels. I took several deep breaths, headed out of the men's room.

When I came back to the conference room everyone took their places around the table.

"As we talk, please interrupt me if you want to add anything," Dr. Patel said, looking at her colleagues around the table. "Even I get tired of the sound of my own voice.

"Dr. Barrett, we're using the older therapies I described with another approach that's been shown to be quite effective. Called EMDR, the initials stand for Eye Movement Desensitization and Reprocessing. Sounds weird, right?"

"Sure does. What is it?"

"Let me have Dr. Lyon explain EMDR. He knows more about it than I do."

"Dr. Barrett, I'll do a down and dirty explanation of EMDR. Sitting face to face, we ask our patient to allow the whole experience – the images, the smells, the sounds – of the traumatic event wash over him. Then he's asked to follow the therapist's index finger as it moves back and forth before his eyes. This causes the fright of the event to come full force to the surface. For reasons we don't entirely understand, after EMDR, patients seem able to put their trauma into a larger perspective and gain some mastery over the event. So we use this maneuver in addition to what you're going to hear about next."

Sounds like psychobabble, I thought. Crap, so hard to keep an open mind. So focus. What he just said is intriguing, though.

Dr. Patel then turned to Dr. Mohammed.

"Ahmed – Dr. Mohammed – will tell you about what we consider to be the central ingredient of our clinical trial, the drug we're studying."

Dr. Mohammed smiled at me.

"My cell phone is off now, so we don't have to worry about that. Sorry again about that interruption.

"Let me give you a little history about this medication.

"Drugs enhancing memory reconsolidation have been under development for several years. Called histone de-acetylase inhibitors, they've been tested in rats, showing that they reduced the intensity of traumatic memories. Recently other drugs have been found that do an even better job of inhibiting remote memories. We call the one we're using 'nepenthe' named after the 'drug of forgetting' in the Odyssey."

Okay, this is getting into esoterica, and I'm feeling like a dumbass. Any reference to drugs makes my palms sweat and my heart rate starts galloping. One big thing my medical training drilled into me is that drugs invariably have side effects. Will this guy get to that issue? Or will he skip that so I'll agree to enter the program?

I shifted back to listening as Dr. Patel resumed her presentation, my fidgeting leg beginning to pump again.

"I'm principal investigator for this study. All the scientists here at Zylinski – geneticists, pharmacologists, molecular biologists, chemists, and so on – contribute one way or another.

"A mental health specialist is designated Case Manager, a sort of chief executive officer of each client's care. Case Managers are with clients every step of the way. Their job is to listen, advocate, and be responsible for their client's general well being. Most importantly, the Case Manager keeps the team informed about the needs and feelings of each client.

"Any questions so far, Dr. Barrett?"

"Well, yeah, lots of things spinning round in my head," I stammered. "Like where in the brain does this drug work? And – uh – how does it do the things you're talking about? I don't know, these theories about inhibiting bad memories – it sounds like science fiction."

I stopped to collect my thoughts so I wouldn't be seen as an ignoramus.

"Why does this drug erase just bad memories? What about other memories? Or all memories? Could it leave you with total amnesia for everything? Scary thought. I'm also very worried about side effects. I guess I need more time to digest what you've said.

"It looks like a steep learning curve to grasp it all," I ventured since no one said anything and the silence drove me to speak. I was torn between being the compliant patient and the skeptical scientist. "But you've certainly got my attention." I glanced at Akira, whose gaze was still on Dr. Patel.

"Before I sign on, I need to study the literature and look at the data you've developed. I'll be a diligent student," I said apologetically, as though I needed their approval. "If I do this, I want to be an informed and cooperative patient. But I admit it's frightening."

If it goes that far, I thought. Am I going forward with this?

"Honestly?" I said, "This sounds like a mix of the ultimate mad scientist approach to a complex area of neuroscience and at the same time, the answer to my prayers."

"I understand your reluctance," Dr. Patel said softly. "A common reaction for someone entering an unknown and experimental realm of medical care. About side-effects: as a physician, you know that any treatment, especially the testing of a new medication, can have side-effects: allergy to the drug; headaches and general malaise; sleep disturbances; induction of bad dreams; possible loss of global memories; unmasking of latent psychosis – all that. That's why we have such a large group of investigators working together in this program."

My God, she's just tapped into all my fears about side effects. Am I going to relive my horror about Danny and the nurses? My childhood stuff? More nightmares?

"Dr. Starr here has been following that aspect of the study since we began. Dr. Starr?"

"Sure, let me tell you about our experience thus far. The good news is that we haven't seen any adverse side effects operating in our study population. The potential always exists and as we activate bad memories, they may seem more frightening at first. But our patients have told us that the early discomfort brought about by the unlocking of old memories lessens over time as the treatment program takes hold."

"That's a little reassuring, but I'm a worry-wart."

"We don't want to rush your decision, so take as much time as you need," Dr. Patel said. "When and if you're prepared to take the next step, we'll set up appointments with members of our group who will explain their roles and how it meshes with others. You'll have many opportunities to question them, and they'll do their best to give you answers. And you can opt out of the program any time."

She looked at Akira. He stood up, signaling the end of the meeting.

"Thanks Lakshmi, Ahmed, Dr. Starr, and Dr. Lyon for your explanations. Tom and I will spend a few minutes talking. Again, thanks for coming."

"Yes, Dr. Patel, thank you very much," I said. I looked around the table. "Thanks to all of you for taking the time to meet with me."

Drs. Patel, Mohammed, Lyon and Starr all shook my hand, saying goodbye as they filed out of the conference room.

Akira looked at me for a moment.

"What do you think?" he asked.

"Well…. still full of doubts. I've been through so many regimens." I looked down. "What if I lose all memories, not just the bad ones? What if it doesn't work at all? What if I get bad side effects? I realize you can't answer these questions, but just so you know – I'm uneasy."

"You're right, I can't answer those questions. If I knew those answers we wouldn't be doing this study," Akira said. "However, I can tell you that total amnesia hasn't been seen in any of our subjects to date. That's about two hundred thirty five cases. Preliminary results tell us this program has been very good in mitigating traumatic memories."

"I wonder if I'll ever get rid of these memories, worried that the treatment could be worse than the disease – although I can't imagine anything being worse than what I've got now." I looked Akira straight in the eye.

"You remember some of those patients whose backs we operated on?" I said. "Those whose pain and suffering got worse after surgery and never went away? The recall of those patients' suffering – and lots of other things – makes me skeptical about new treatments. I know how often there are side effects to any therapy, especially drugs: liver, kidney, neurological. Here, we're talking about messing around with the brain, the last black box of medicine."

I was convincing myself to reconsider going forward with this.

"A few years ago I took meds for depression. They did nothing to lessen my bad mood, but they killed my libido. Even after stopping them I have no sex drive. That's a huge gap in my life. All drugs have side effects; we know that," I mumbled, looking down at the floor.

"All I can say, Tom, is that we'll do our best," Akira said. "And yes, I do remember those surgical patients who got worse under our care. That's one of my bad memories, and I still wake up nights worrying about having done harm. I believe, though, we have better evidence about memory reconsolidation drugs than we had on surgical procedures in those years." He turned in his chair and placed his hands on mine.

"I admit this drug is still experimental. You know biological systems are not uniform. Everyone's genetic endowment and life experiences are unique, but there are commonalities. Outliers will always exist, but statistically you have a good chance of a beneficial outcome from this therapy.

"Clearly, you should learn all you can before you consent for treatment," he said. "The exciting part of this for me is that your insights and wisdom can add a unique dimension to our data."

We both rose and headed for the door.

"I'm glad you came today and listened to our presentation. Mull over what you've heard, read as much as you like, ask questions of anyone here when you can't find the answers in your reading. Let us know your decision when you're ready."

I left the conference room and Akira with a mixture of conflict and gnawing anxiety. Realistically I couldn't get advice from anyone. I especially didn't want to burden Cynthia with my deliberations.

Outside Zylinski a helicopter flew overhead. The whir of the blades chopping the air sent my mind back to the airlifting of wounded men and women coming to the field hospital. In my imagination I was wading again in blood of uncounted young soldiers as they fought for survival – many would lose that fight. I was fixated on these mental images, flashing rapidly across my visual fields. My thoughts returned to Danny, as they did every day since he died, and I cursed myself because I'd vowed I would contact Katharine as soon as I got home – but I hadn't. Tomorrow for sure. I should have done it sooner. Another thing to feel guilty about.

I looked up at the helicopter, wondering what its function was today here in Worcester. Distracted, I crashed into a lamppost, falling hard onto the ground. I threw up sour yellow vomitus, felt arms lifting me off the ground and concerned voices asking me if I was all right. Slowly the fog lifted, my vision cleared. I thanked those strangers who had come to my aid. Reassured that I was okay, they went their way, looking back a couple of times to make sure I was functioning.

I knew now what I had to do. I simply couldn't pass up such a good opportunity to get well. There was more promise in Akira's program than anything I'd tried. No way in hell was I going to miss a chance to be in a break-through treatment program for this crippling disorder. In my current state I couldn't operate as a surgeon or function normally in life. It was the best thing – maybe the only thing – I could do.

6

GET READY

DR. ALICIA KLEINMAN WAS TO be my Case Manager. I expect-ed her administrative assistant to answer my knock, but Dr. Klein-man herself opened the door, smiled, and invited me in.

"Glad to meet you, Dr. Barrett. Sit right over here," motioning me to a chair. "I've heard great things about you from Dr. Yamaguchi. You were residents together, right?" She spoke in a low and reassuring voice as she sat down opposite me.

Looking more like a den in her home than a professional office, the floor was covered with faded Oriental rugs, her furnishings an eclectic mix of antique chairs, a long leather couch, and sagging shelves in a bookcase spanning an entire wall. A huge latticed window framed her desk piled high with journals and books. Her cleaning service must shudder trying to tidy up this packrat's nest.

"Yeah, we were at BU. Good times, then. Many good memories from those days."

"I've heard being a surgical resident is a high point in a surgeon's life, a time when you're more directly involved in challenging cases than ever again. Right?"

"I guess so." A lame answer. I was tempted to say cases I saw in the war were so much more challenging and horrific but didn't want to open that door. She must have sensed that and adopted a more formal tone.

"Let me tell you what goes on here. My role is to be your listening post and advocate. Most people when they first arrive here are bewildered by the mystery of memory research. Before I describe more about our approach, do you have any questions after hearing what Dr. Patel had to say?"

"Well, I've read a bunch of articles about PTSD but there's a lot I don't get. It doesn't seem to be a simple diagnosis. Previous trials seem a mixed bag, very confusing." As I talked to this stranger sitting across from me, my hands were doing as much talking as my mouth. Involuntary jiggling of my leg embarrassed me.

Dr. Kleinman appeared to be in her sixties, a woman with streaks of gray interspersed with her jet-black hair. She wore a dark blue jacket and slacks with a bright red and green scarf at her neck. An attractive woman. She leaned forward slightly as she listened to me. I wondered about her personal life – married, children, maybe grandchildren?

"I'm curious how this drug changes memories, how that was discovered," I said. "What results did they see when it was tested in animals? Other clinical trials? Truth is, I'm really nervous about potential side-effects." There's that bugaboo again – side effects.

Dr. Kleinman scribbled notes as I questioned her. She glanced at me a couple of times, and her answers came slowly.

"All appropriate questions," she said, scanning her notepad, her hand brushing a stray strand of hair from her eyes. "I'll answer what I can. For particular questions related to the study's scientific detail and results, you'll need to ask others on the team.

"Let's start by talking about PTSD. An interesting history. During World War I, psychological scars of battle were called shell shock or neurasthenia," she said in a quiet voice. "Later it was given other names. The commonly used term now is post-traumatic stress disorder, or PTSD. We've stayed with this name although it merely describes a constellation of symptoms. It doesn't identify the anatomical seat, an actual location, of the damage in the brain. The name may change as we learn more.

"A few years ago, several investigators, including some here at the Zylinski Institute, used exposure-based therapies called memory reconsolidation."

"Yeah, Dr. Patel discussed memory reconsolidation. I'm beginning to get the picture about that."

"Good. So, there are several psychological and medication approaches to soften the impact of traumatic memories. We're studying techniques that involve traditional talk therapy, EMDR, and a drug we're calling nepenthe. This medication inhibits certain enzymes in the hippocampus."

She took her glasses off and leaned towards me. "Now, I'm a psychologist, not a neuroscientist, and you as a neurosurgeon must know a lot more than I do about this deep brain structure. I'll defer to others to explain this in more detail."

She settled back into her chair, crossed her legs and put her notes in her lap.

"My role, as you proceed through this clinical trial, is to be available to you for questions and concerns. To hear you and convey your thoughts, feelings – anything bothering you – to the team. I'm your liaison."

Dr. Kleinman rose from her chair, walked over to her desk, and picked up a large manila folder.

"This packet of documents – also on our client website – lays out the therapy regimen. We need you to read and sign permissions for treatment. They're fairly standard, but please look them over carefully as they describe details of therapy. There's a form to capture your family's medical, social, and psychological history, as well as your personal medical and experiential profile."

She handed the packet to me. I could tell by the weight that it would take hours and patience to wade through it. Yuk, so many forms to fill out, one of my least favorite activities.

"Sorry it's so long, but we need in-depth information to understand your problems. We ask this of all our subjects. Your answers will help guide the sequence and modes of therapy.

"Take your time. When they're done, get them back to me. Here's a bibliography of articles on memory reconsolidation along with access to the online medical library," she said, handing me a sheaf of papers.

I scanned the bibliography. I'd already read some of them, but was glad to have this to fill the gaps in my knowledge.

"How long is the program?"

"Hard to say. A few weeks, maybe 3-4 months. Maybe longer."

"What determines the duration? That's quite a range of times."

"PTSD is not a monolithic condition. It's a spectrum ranging from mild to severe and many factors enter into why some patients need longer treatment than others. There's also the complication that some victims have not only PTSD but also destruction of brain tissue from explosions or head trauma, so they're in a different category."

The more I learned the more complex it got. It's an interaction between the patient and a disease. In the case of PTSD, the dose of the trauma interacts with the patient and that determines the degree of disability.

"Will I be living at home, or do I get admitted to some kind of facility?"

"You'll be at home while we analyze the information you provide prior to the actual reconsolidation treatment. Then during the exposure period we'll admit you for observation and data collection. You'll be carefully monitored during treatment both for research purposes and for your own safety."

"So I should suspend my usual activities for some time." It seemed the more I heard the more questions arose. "What about the therapy I'm getting at the military hospital?"

"We'll let them know you've entered our program. We have several patients from there so they're familiar with our approach. They're very cooperative in supplying us with participants' records. A release form is in your packet."

"What about costs?" I asked, since I had no savings and my care had been under the military hospital's veterans' benefits.

"All costs are borne by the Institute. No charges to you."

We stopped talking as this sunk in.

It sounded all very thorough and professional, but I'd be surprised if this helped me any more than past therapy. Probably one more time to feel hope crash. Oh, what the hell. But this'll be my last shot. I don't think I can live like this if it doesn't work.

"Thanks, Dr. Kleinman. When I complete these, how do I take the next step?"

"Call me Alicia," she said with a warm smile. "Here's my card. Call me when you're ready and I'll arrange your first appointment. Don't rush this. We've plenty of time. And so do you. If you want to talk to me before you sign on, I'm here."

Plenty of time? It's obvious she's never experienced what this program is studying. How much longer does she think I can go without sleep, without functioning or contributing? Would I make myself a guinea pig with God-knows-what side effects if I weren't desperate?

Heading home, I wondered if I should call Cynthia to talk all this over. No. I shouldn't. I'd just gotten through the first painful phase of living apart and so has she. Better to let things ride for a while. God, I miss her. I don't know how long I'm supposed to last before I give in to the temptation to call her. This scares the crap out of me. She'd want to help, wouldn't she? But could she?

7

GET SET

BOY, THE VOYEURS WHO CONSTRUCTED this medical history questionnaire…they really need to know these minutiae? What do they expect, total recall of every possible influence on my health since infancy?

I had to concede it was a masterpiece, subject to validation by computer analysis. I spent days making sure my answers were as accurate as possible. I had what clinicians refer to as an "interesting" medical and psychosocial history with a host of adverse childhood events sculpting my mental health. After fretting over whether I'd provided a key to healing in my responses, I figured they were the best I could do. The team at Zylinski would definitely have a spirited discussion about why my PTSD is so bad.

I hit the send button. A few days later Alicia called.

"Hi Tom. Thanks for returning your questionnaire. It's obvious you took a lot of care completing it. I've distributed it to the team and I'll call you later this week to schedule initial interviews. Within a month or so we'll finish our diagnostic analysis and design a treatment protocol."

"Hope everything they need is in there."

"So, how're you doing?"

"About the same. Anxious to get under way but apprehensive. New ground to me."

"Just remember, any time you get nervous, call me. I can see you at a moment's notice. That's an advantage of working in a research environment – limited caseloads and concierge service."

My call-waiting signal went off and we closed our conversation. I switched to the call coming in.

"Hi Tom, please don't hang up! I know you want me to leave you alone, but I need to know you are okay.

"So, are you okay?"

Oh my God, it's her! Crap, what should I do? I don't want to backslide.

"Yeah, I'm fine. Taking each day as it comes. How're you doing?"

"I miss you so much. I think of you when I try to go to sleep and first thing in the morning. Whenever I don't keep busy as hell, my thoughts rush to you. Anything new going on?"

"Well, as a matter of fact, I just sent everything I could remember about my entire life to Alicia, my Case Manager and psychologist at Zylinski. It was a fiendish questionnaire from hell. They have all patients fill it out before treatment starts," I said, as nonchalantly as I could.

"I'll bet you had such fun doing that," she said, and I could visualize one of her eyebrows rise and a grin spread across her face. "So what's the next step? I've heard a little about the Zylinski Institute, but don't know much about it. Seems a little mysterious to me since no one I work with knows any more than I do about what goes on over there."

"Well, I'll see a psychiatrist soon. That'll be the front end of this process. Then they'll start what's called memory reconsolidation. Don't ask me much more 'cause I don't know how this'll play out. But I'm feeling pretty good about things so far."

"Any chance we could have dinner sometime? At a restaurant where we wouldn't be tempted to do anything but talk and eat?"

Why not? Not seeing her probably adds tension to my life; I think about her a lot. Having her near will make that cavity in my chest less cold. But where would it lead? I disrupted our lives together because of my unpredictable rage; what if I lose it in public? Can I trust myself to resist re-engaging with her?

My heart won the argument over my rational self.

"You know I'd love to see you, you evil woman. Where should we meet?"

"There's this little place on Shrewsbury Street where I'm told the pizza's great, and it's quiet enough to actually hear each other's conversation. I'm off tonight, but starting tomorrow I have several straight days on duty. Tonight would be ideal. Can you get a cab?"

Boy, would I love to see her. Her crooked smile, her glistening brown eyes. To hear her laugh and listen to her light-hearted take on events in her day. Man that would feel so good.

"An offer I can't refuse. What's the name of the place?"

She got there first, and when I walked in, the sight of her rocked through my body like lightening. She smiled and waved. Rising, she put her arms around my neck, her soft body against mine. Cynthia's enveloping hugs had always been a grounding force. I'm a goner. I knew this would happen. I decided to relax and let the feelings pour over me.

Taking our seats, we were quiet for a moment. As usual, she knew how to make anxieties melt away.

"I already ordered a Hawaiian pizza for us. I remembered you like pineapple."

"Must be some other guy. I hate pineapple pizza."

We laughed and our hands came together across the table. Had it really been five weeks since we'd seen each other?

"How's the hospital emergency department, now that I'm not around to make sure you're doing the right thing?"

"Since when did you ever oversee my running of an ED?" she said, with a wink.

"I miss those days working with you in that loony atmosphere."

"It's still a hyperactive place and the new residents look like high school students, younger and younger every year.

"Remember Akira? Whatever happened to him?"

I'd shut her so completely out of my life that I hadn't told her anything about Akira and his leadership of the Zylinski Institute. My face flushed, and I tried to make amends.

"Since we haven't been in contact, I didn't get to tell you that, coincidentally, I recently had dinner with him."

"Really?"

"He'd found out I was back and devised a plan to meet me 'accidentally' but as it turned out, on purpose. Are you ready for this? He's the Director of the Zylinski Institute. I'm a dodo that I forgot to tell you that. My mind's pretty muddled."

"Well, I'll be damned. Small world. The Director? Wow."

"He's still a sweetheart, gentle and caring, and as brilliant as ever."

"Is he doing any surgery? What's he working on that has anything to do with you?"

"No surgery, he's completely into research. He hasn't changed otherwise."

The words came tumbling out as I told Cynthia – belatedly – all about the program I was in. Why I hadn't told her these things before astounded me.

"You know that questionnaire I was telling you about? That's part of Akira's program." I unloaded all of my recently acquired information about the program.

"I'm trying to be optimistic. Maybe they can help me."

Cynthia studied my face.

"Can I be with you during this treatment?" she asked, without a trace of hurt at having been left out of these crucial events in my life.

I hesitated, worrying that we were on a dangerous slippery slope.

"I'm not sure about anything right now. After that time I shoved you out of bed I'm scared of flashbacks and the unpredictable stuff I might do. It sounds so corny, Cynthia, but if I ever did anything to hurt you, I'd never recover."

Her eyes softened and a hint of a tear formed in the corners.

"I'm hurting now, Tom. Not being there to help you through this stuff is so hard," she said. "Maybe they can suggest some kind of alarm system we could use to rouse you out of your nightmares so you wouldn't lash out in terror. I'm willing to take that chance if you'll let me."

Looking at her made me so grateful for having her in my life. Her warmth spread into the center of my being. How did I get so lucky?

"Well, some of the early treatment will be in their inpatient unit, so I'll be cooped up there. But before I go in, while they're analyzing my records…I don't know, Cyn.

"I'll talk with Alicia – you know, my psychologist slash case manager – to see if she thinks that's feasible. You'd like Alicia. She's a very wise, warm, maternal type."

My guess was that Alicia would tell me it's my decision, but her body language would tell me "no."

"The idea of getting back together scares the hell out of me though. It's not that I wouldn't want your 'shelter from the storm,' as Dylan says, but I don't want to risk having something happen. Oh, here's that lousy pineapple pizza."

Just in time to change the subject.

"So how's your new condo?" I asked. "And your new job?"

"I miss my old place. A lot. But this one is close to U Mass Medical. It's an antique building like the other one, so it's acceptable. My new job – Head Nurse of Ambulatory Medicine – is fabulous, but I miss the excitement of the emergency department. And of course I'm nostalgic about when we both worked together at BU."

Cynthia picked up on my need to talk about subjects not so charged. She talked about things we both enjoyed: the Red Sox, Celtics, the Patriots.

"One of my new friends at the hospital – her name is Rosalie – and I go to Celtics games and plan on Red Sox games next year. She also sings in the Worcester Chorale with me. She's single and, like me, loves her career. We're both unsure about having a family. We have a lot in common."

"I haven't thought about regular aspects of life in a while, Cyn, you know, sports teams and music. Thanks for the reminder that there are so many good things out there to enjoy." I hated feeling so dependent on her, but I attributed it to my "condition," a term I had come to despise.

"You need to get some sleep," I said. "I'll call you after I talk to Alicia. Just so you know, without raising hope in either of us, I'd love to get back together. I just need to be sure it's the right thing, the safe thing, to do."

"I've already told you that I'm ready to take the chance. Let me know soon," Cynthia said.

"I will."

After a long hug, we pulled apart and headed our separate ways.

Fat chance in hell they'd let me live with her before treatment begins. If I were the doctor in my case I wouldn't allow it, why would they? I still have moments of rage when I punch the wall, throw things around and want to kill. A couple of neighbors have complained of my noise when I'm in one of those periods. No, I'm putting off the prospect of living with her until I'm sure I can control my emotions so I don't have another explosion of rage.

8

Go

"TOM, ALICIA HERE. DR. MARK Lyon, one of our team psychiatrists, can see you tomorrow at ten for your initial interview. Will that work?"

"Sure. I'm just sittin' here staring off. Nothin' on my calendar," I said, surprised I could be seen so quickly and already stewing about this next portion of my life.

Nervously anticipating my visit with a new shrink didn't help lessen my usual challenge of getting an easy night's sleep. Visions of crushed and bleeding bodies of soldiers put my brain into excited overdrive. I woke up drained as usual and crawled out of cul-de-sacs of restless sleep. I gathered myself, got a cab and went for my appointment.

Dr. Lyon opened his office door and greeted me warmly. Reassured by his rumbling bass voice, I sank into a leather chair facing him. His patrician nose was narrow, his cheekbones sharp, and his ears were canted outwards. After exchanging pleasantries, he turned serious and my preoccupation with his features faded.

"You've been in therapy before, so it'll come as no surprise that I'm interested in your childhood. You can start wherever you want, but go as far back as you can remember," he said. "Just let your stream of consciousness flow."

"Okay," I said as my mind went blank. "I'll do my best. I'll probably just sort of ramble."

"Actually, that's best. Use whatever springs to mind that allows your feelings to come out. As one wise neuroscientist said, I'd like you to describe "the feeling of what happened.' Mind if I record you?" Dr. Lyon asked.

"No, I'm fine with that.

"Well, where shall I start?"

"The earlier the better. Reach back as far as you can."

"Well, I grew up in Clifton, a leafy suburb of Cincinnati, in the late 90's." My mind drifted back to those halcyon days.

"Clifton was like a Norman Rockwell picture of unsullied life in Midwest suburbia, you know, where people are nice, dads have good, mid-level jobs, and moms cart kids to after school soccer, swimming, baseball, and lacrosse.

"Is this what you want to hear about? It seems kinda irrelevant," I said.

"Keep going, I'll tell you if you're too far afield," Dr. Lyon replied.

"Life there was well organized. Garbage picked up on time, people followed rules, all that kind of stuff."

As I spoke it was like pulling a warm blanket over myself. I stopped talking as reverie settled over me. Memories came back to life: in that place nobody discussed disagreeable subjects like climate change, starvation or brutal dictatorships in far-off places. The good burghers of this conservative enclave ignored race riots in the "Over The Rhine" and "Basin" areas, looked away from the epidemic of drugs and guns. They repressed anything that might disturb the smug balance in "Pleasantville, USA." It was so safe, so much our birthright. News from a turbulent world never penetrated our little cocoon. There were newspapers and television, of course, but I wasn't paying attention. No one in my family, or in the neighborhood for that matter, ever discussed anything controversial. As I now recalled those days, it occurred to me that life there was boring as hell.

Rising out of my hazy recollecting, I realized Dr. Lyon had patiently waited for me to resume.

"Tell me about your father."

"Ah," I paused as my throat tightened a little. That was quite a shift from what I was thinking about.

"Dad worked at the local bank – a loan officer. Talking all day to people asking for loans trained him to pick his words carefully. This caution carried over to his conversations with everyone. He was pretty quiet."

"So, what was your relationship with him like?"

"My relationship with my father? Lemme think. Fishing trips, sharing a pup tent, camping. Getting a high-five for a base hit in Little League. That sort of sums it up."

I seemed to be peering through gauze. My mind glided into those dim corners that usually came out only in dreams. It was eerie. My father's presence became almost palpable as I talked about him.

"You know, it's funny. I can't remember – at least not now – him lecturing me about how to behave or any heavy words of wisdom. I mean that wasn't his style. He taught by example. Some kids' fathers fed them quotations from great men, held forth on the meaning of life – not my dad. He never went to church – Mother did, so I'd go with her – but Dad never talked about religion. No advice about manners or respect. I didn't need them 'cause I was a nerdy straight arrow."

My voice broke as I recalled my father. I'd pushed my memory of him deep inside the dark places I tried never to visit. That's how I'd coped with losses that came later. But talking about him now made his face, his kindness, the odor of his pipe, seem present in the room. How much I'd missed him all these years.

"Is there any one particular experience with your father that stands out?"

"Hmm. Yeah, come to think of it. When I was nine, he and I decided to get a dog. We found this dog at the rescue shelter – the friskiest one there, chocolate colored – my instant favorite. Dad and I agreed he was 'our dog.' We brought him home without hesitation. Mother had no chance to object. She wouldn't have anyhow.

"He was way too exuberant in obedience school. All he wanted to do was chase other dogs and roll on the ground. The trainer called him his 'worst pupil ever.' But Dad and I were lifted by his good nature and goofiness."

"Your first dog?"

"Yeah, I knew nothing about taking care of a dog. Especially a big breed like 'Chief'."

"You named him Chief?"

"Yeah. We knew he'd always be in charge."

"Go on."

"Well, one day I came home after school. I opened the garage door where Chief lay in wait for me, like Hobbes in the cartoon. He leapt all over me, licking my face and then dashed helter-skelter down the driveway."

It all came back, those moments of panic as I watched him run heedlessly into our busy street.

"He never knew what hit him. A pickup truck lifted him into the air over the cab, catapulting his sleek body onto the pavement behind the truck. Cars squealed to a stop, the drivers horrified to see the ugliness unfold."

"You recall your feelings as you ran toward Chief?"

"I'll never forget it. I hightailed it down to the street, heart crashing into my ribs, lungs burning, stomach clenched. I can still feel my throat dry and closed up. Felt like throwing up. Lightheaded, close to passing out. You know, as I talk, it seems like it happened yesterday."

"That had to be an awful feeling," Dr. Lyon murmured. "Go on."

"I got to Chief lying in a puddle of blood – knew he was dead. I knelt beside him, tears dripping into his blood. I wanted to die on the spot."

"You knew he was dead? You were just a kid. How would you know that? Or was it just your fear he was dead?"

"Yeah, I feared the worst. Maybe I didn't know it, but I sure was afraid that he was dead. I felt so damned guilty. I should've put his leash on before I opened the door."

"Were you scared your parents would blame you?"

"No, they weren't that way. Blaming myself tore me up. I've always been that way. If anything went wrong I figured it was my fault. Don't know where that comes from."

"Go on."

"The siren pierced my ears before I saw the police cruiser. Dan Craig, a nice-guy cop in Clifton, got out of the car. He nodded to me, approached Chief, saw he was dead, and phoned the dog officer. He came over to me, put his hand on my shoulder and looked at my swollen face, snot running down over my lips."

"'Tommy, tell me what happened',", I remember he said.

"I was so embarrassed because I was crying hard as I described how he'd gotten away and run into the street."

"'Tommy, it's not your fault, dogs can't think,' Dan told me. "Is your Mom home?""

"I told him Mother would be home soon, that I'd be okay until she got there."

Dan tapped his report into an iPad, talked to the driver of the truck, and then got the traffic moving around Chief's carcass. The driver of the truck came over to me.

"I can still hear his voice saying: 'Son, I'm so sorry. I couldn't stop; it happened so fast. Please forgive me. I have a dog, too, and know how awful this is for you."

"I told him I knew it wasn't his fault. He gave me his name and number in case my parents wanted to talk with him. I thanked him and told him I'd be okay, trying to put up a good front."

"Everyone told me it wasn't my fault, but I knew better. I'd been careless, and now Chief was dead. I've dreamt of Chief many times since then."

My mind sank into the dream images.

"Keep talking," Dr. Lyon prompted, noting my silence.

"This next part is the hardest to talk about," I said, with my eyes watering. After a few minutes' pause my voice stopped wavering.

"Four months after Chief was killed, I came home from school – it was a Wednesday, I'll never forget that – saw two unfamiliar cars parked outside. When I opened the front door, I heard murmuring voices coming from the living room. Something was wrong.

"'We're here for you, no matter what time of day,' I heard Mary Reckman, our neighbor say. 'You and Fred have always been such good friends.'

"I remember how all heads turned toward me as I walked into the room and can still hear my mother's choked voice saying, "Oh, Tommy, 'Please come here.'

"She was sitting there with her arms extended towards me, her eyes puffy and red. A Kleenex box fell from her lap. I kept staring at her, knowing something awful had happened, waiting for her to speak; it had to be about my father. It seemed like forever before she put her arms around me, her wet face pressed against mine.

"'Tommy,'" she whispered, 'your father passed away just after you left for school this morning.' Both of us by then were heaving with sobs.

'What happened?' I spluttered. I couldn't understand how this could possibly have happened. Dad and I had eaten breakfast together and talked about a stupid math problem on my homework that we both couldn't figure out.

"'We don't know yet,' she said. "'It'll be a few days before we know. He wasn't sick or anything. He just collapsed. The ambulance came right away, but the emergency people couldn't bring him back. They don't know what happened either.'

"We found out after his autopsy – a ruptured aneurysm in his head," I said. "I was ten years old and terrified. What if Mother died too? Nothing was sure anymore. I worried that I'd be one of those orphans I'd heard about."

"Tell me more about your father," Dr. Lyon said.

Wetness cooled my face, tears flowing freely. I grabbed some tissues and dried my eyes.

"He'd always been kind and loving to me. Even though he was a true introvert I knew, in his own way, he loved me deeply. I thought I could always count on him to take care of us.

"I kept thinking the pain would go away. It never really did. I've dealt with it, but time doesn't really heal. Time only lets a person wall off these wounds, sort of like what happens to a foreign body in the skin," lapsing into familiar medical territory.

I stopped talking. Dr. Lyon waited.

"As strange as it may seem, losing Chief and losing Dad were similar in the pain I felt. I know they shouldn't be the same – the sorrow is different, and of course they *are* d-different," I stammered trying to make sense of my feelings. "But those two were…" I groped for words. "I don't know how to express it. I wandered around in a fog for weeks after Dad's passing, not understanding the horrible emptiness I felt."

"Those were terrible losses you were absorbing. Your reactions are perfectly appropriate."

Dr. Lyon shifted in his seat, glanced at the clock.

"We're at the end of our time together for today but I can stay a while longer if you need to. Is there anything else you'd like to talk about?"

"No, I'm pooped. Enough for today."

"Come tomorrow, same time?"

"Okay. This the kind of thing you want me to talk about?"

"Fine for our first session. See you tomorrow."

I felt worse than when I came. Will resurrecting this stuff – those sorrowful years I've repressed for so long and until now, so effectively – trigger even more sinister nightmares? My sense of powerlessness was making my mind spin. I felt unsteady as I walked out of Zylinski. What good is this going to do me? What have I signed on for?

9

GOING DEEPER

"TELL ME A LITTLE ABOUT your friends, how school was during this time," Dr. Lyon said after he took his seat behind my left shoulder.

"Gosh, I don't remember many friends at school. Don't know why. The only close friend I can recall was Michael Bernstein.

"Michael lost his father years before and maybe that was why we got along. Another reason, I guess, was he thought he was an outsider, being Jewish, the only one in our class. After losing Dad my life seemed so different from other kids I thought I was kind of an outsider too.

"I guess I was also drawn to Michael because we both wanted to be doctors. We spent a lot of time fantasizing about what life would be like when we got to be doctors. When we weren't partnering in chemistry lab we noodled around the Natural History Museum and went swimming at the Y. We sort of insulated ourselves from the rest of the students, now that I think about it.

"Is this important?"

"Everything in your childhood is important. Think about these recollections as pixels that combine to shape your current state of mind.

"How was your mother coping?"

Uh oh, new dangerous territory – the Sexton Myers part of my life. I hesitated, not wanting to walk into this terrain.

"Well, she seemed to be doing okay. I mean, she was still sad and all, but wasn't exactly what you'd call depressed, I don't think."

"Were you both still going to church?"

"Well I didn't go anymore, but she went. Church kept her centered, was her network of friends. Because of church, it seemed she was able to get up every morning and go to work. Her day-to-day living was about the same."

"You say church kept her centered. How?"

"Well, she went to social functions there and she'd come back in a good mood."

"Did she make friends at these socials?"

"Yeah, she met some people."

I stirred around in my chair, crossed and uncrossed my legs a couple of times, cleared my throat, folded my arms across my chest.

"You seem uncomfortable. Any reason for that?"

My leg started jiggling. I looked right, left, frowned, said nothing.

"Did you meet any of those people?"

"Yeah, one."

"Who was that?"

"A guy named Sexton Myers," I said, trying not to sound as disdainful as I felt.

"Tell me about Sexton Myers."

This shrink is good. He's almost reading my mind. I decided I had to talk about him, but didn't want to say much.

"Well, Mother was still what they used to call 'in mourning.' She was up and down in her moods. She told me how Sexton was so sensitive and sympathetic when she told him about losing Dad. She wanted to believe he was a good man."

At this point I had to get up and move around. I walked toward the window, looked out, then back at Dr. Lyon.

"You know, I don't get it, even now. She was usually kind of nosy about people. But never once did she seem to know anything about where he'd come from, what he did for a living, any of that. It was like he'd dropped from another planet, an alien being without a personal history."

"What did you think of him?"

"I didn't like him from the start. I didn't say anything because I thought she liked him, got something out of their friendship."

"Go on."

"What he was, it turned out, was a con man. The worst thing is that Mother plunged blindly into marriage with this loathsome jerk. I guess she was looking for security for us. I've often wondered why I didn't tell her I despised this creep."

"Why do you think you couldn't tell her? You were close to her, right?"

"Well, you know, I was just a kid – pretty confused. Mother learned later – too late – about his alcohol addiction. And his other mental problems.

"I really don't want to talk any more about Sexton, okay?" I finally blurted out.

"That's okay."

"Maybe some other time. Just can't do it now."

Another period of silence. I took a couple of deep breaths and had a rush of nausea.

"Let's leave this here for today. How're you feeling?" Dr. Lyon asked.

"I guess I feel sad. And angry."

"I'll see you tomorrow – same time, alright?"

"Okay," I muttered as I left.

I was gloomy going home. I lusted after a drink, maybe a whole bottle. That temptation was always there, now more intense than usual. But instead of going for a drink I grabbed dinner at a fast food joint and avoided the temptation to find a bar on the walk home. Exhausted, I headed directly to bed.

The next day I dreaded seeing Dr. Lyon. Didn't think I'd feel this anxious so soon – Christ, it's only the first stage of treatment. Maybe this isn't the way to go. I pushed myself to get up, get dressed, and go.

"Yesterday you seemed uncomfortable talking about Sexton Myers. Can you talk a little more about him today?" Dr. Lyon said quietly as soon as we were settled.

I knew it. First thing. I wanted to talk about almost anything else.

"I hate talking or even thinking about that bastard!" I heard myself explode. I took a couple of deep breaths.

"But maybe I need to.

"So here goes.

71

"Right after Sexton moved in he started giving me a hard time. I think he was jealous of me – my closeness to Mother – but basically he was a mean prick."

I could still feel the sting of his blows and smell his bad breath.

"It started out with a couple of shoves against the wall but soon ratcheted up to punching me with his fists."

I floated back to that time as though it was happening right now.

"He'd slip his belt out of his pants and whack my back and butt. He had this evil little grin when I could see his face during the whippings. When he was done beating the crap outta me he'd yell at me to get out of his sight, he couldn't stand to look at me, that I was a miserable little pussy."

Why hadn't I told Mother?

"In time I figured ways to avoid him but he still cornered me pretty often. He told me that he'd beat the shit out of Mother or kill her if I ever told her – or anybody else – about what he called his 'punishments.'"

That must have been the reason.

"I guessed Mother never knew – she was at work. I couldn't tell her – if Sexton ever found out there was no telling what he might have done.

"His dark presence came to dominate our lives. He'd yell and threaten both of us. The fuel of alcohol made him even wilder."

As I talked I struggled to understand and articulate why I'd been such a coward.

"I tried to figure out how I could protect Mother from his drunken rants, but you gotta understand" – I was almost pleading with Dr. Lyon to excuse my behavior – "I was only eleven. He was my stepfather, much bigger and stronger. He scared me shitless. I never knew when he'd turn his rage against me. I often wished him dead, but then worried I'd go to hell for thinking that.

"Then a miracle happened. One day before the Christmas holidays, I came home from school and as soon as I hung up my jacket, Mother told me to sit down. This was usually not a good sign.

"'Sexton's gone,' she told me abruptly. 'We'll never see him again.'

"In total disbelief I remember asking 'What? Where'd he go? What happened?' I felt so mixed up – relieved, fearful – wondering what was coming next in my swirling life.

"'Never mind. He's gone' she said. 'That's all that matters. Sometime I'll tell you all about it.' She took my shoulders into her hands, looked at my face, and said, 'I suspected for some time that he was abusing you. I couldn't let that happen anymore.'

"It was a lot to digest. She knew? How long did she know? And I was frightened. What if he'd slither back into our lives somehow, maybe jump me on the way home from school, start beating me up. Maybe intercept and hurt Mother coming home from work or church. Even in his absence I was scared of him.

"She said we'd be fine, that she kept her bank account separate. She still had her bookkeeping job, I shouldn't worry. 'And if you're scared he'll come back,' she said, 'I guarantee he won't.'

"I didn't know until later how she was so sure, but I felt a little better when she told me that.

"Michael asked me why he never saw him at my house anymore. I told him he must've just taken off and that Mother wouldn't talk to me about it. I never told him about my beatings, or anyone for that matter, permanently terrified Sexton would come back and take revenge.

"Sexton's mysterious disappearance lingered in my mind. How could someone just vanish like that? But as time passed, with the tasks at hand in high school I pushed those thoughts away and buried my questions about Sexton's fate in some dark culvert."

"You were doing a good job of compartmentalizing."

"Never thought of it that way, but yes, I tucked things away in separate boxes in my head."

"What happened next?"

"About halfway through my senior year in high school, Mother asked me, 'Tommy, you still want to take pre-med?'

"I told her 'Sure, I always wanted to be a doctor. I didn't think we could afford it.'

"She pulled a face that said 'nonsense.'

"She told me, 'Money's short, but I checked out costs at the university. It's state-supported, less expensive than private schools. Got a good medical school, a national reputation. Plus you can live at home. We'll manage.'

"So that was that. Michael and I became anatomy lab partners, named our cadaver Henry. But always lurking in the background was my mother's sadness. One day Michael said, 'Tommy, what's with your mom? She doesn't look so good to me, and she barely says hello. She's seems really down.'"

"Your friend Michael was pretty perceptive. I can see why you got along with him."

"It was uncanny how much he understood. I told him I worried about her but didn't know what to do. She didn't go to church anymore since that was where she met Sexton. She didn't trust anyone. I tried not to think about it because my studies would suffer. She'd hate that since my becoming a doctor seemed like the only thing that kept her going."

Now the words came rushing out.

"But she got harder and harder for me to reach. She no longer kept up with her friends. We were studying mental illness at the time and my amateur diagnoses were depression and paranoia. I persuaded her to go to the doctor. The medicine he gave her did no good."

"How was school going by that time?"

"Well, using your term, my compartmentalization scheme worked damned well. I pretty much blocked out my worries about her. I had to."

I closed my eyes, not wanting to dredge up the next memory.

"You're taking a long time to continue. What's going through your head?"

"This part's gonna be hard for me."

"Just take it slow and easy."

"One day in my senior year I came home and called out my usual greeting. No answer. I went into the kitchen and heard the car engine running in the garage below.

"I thought, 'Oh she's just back from grocery shopping.' I waited a few minutes, expecting her to come upstairs any time, but she didn't. The car motor kept on running. Then I got worried. My heart was pounding and my mouth went dry as I pieced together what might be happening.

I dashed down the stairs and flung open the door between the basement and the garage.

"I gasped when I saw her slumped figure in the front seat, her fingernails a deep red color – carbon monoxide poisoning. Panicked, I reached over her, fumbled with the key and shut off the motor. I tried to find her pulse and put my ear to her chest. Heard nothing."

Vividly, the memory of my mother's limp body, blank face and scarlet fingernails took over.

"By then I was hungering for air myself and felt woozy. I jumped out of the car and threw the garage door open. I went back to the car and tried desperately to pull her body out of the car, but she was wedged in behind the steering wheel.

"I groped my way upstairs and called 911. I can't recall those moments very well, but the emergency people were efficient, saying little to me as they removed my mother's body from the car into the ambulance."

"That must have been your worst experience ever," Dr. Lyon said. "I'm so sorry."

His sympathy released a flood of tears. I grasped a wad of tissues and slowly regained some composure.

"What happened then?"

"A policeman came and took me to the hospital. The doctor there stalled around and put off talking to me. But finally he – apologetically, as though it was his fault – told me that my mother was gone, asked me about an autopsy, which I adamantly refused."

I turned to Dr. Lyon. "Isn't that something? Here I am a medical student – taught to honor the idea of postmortem examinations for final diagnoses – totally unable to overcome my revulsion at the thought of having my mother's body cut up for an autopsy."

"It's different, isn't it, when it's your mother?"

"Yeah, and I've remembered that moment when I've had to ask family members for permission to do an autopsy on a loved one.

"Anyway, when the cop took me home, Mary Reckman, who'd been with us when Dad died, was there with some other folks living on our street. They'd seen the ambulance. Even though I was in my 20's, neighbors persuaded me to stay with them for the next few days. I must have seemed like a walking zombie. At the funeral service people told me how sorry they were they hadn't been better about reaching out to Mother. One said she felt terrible – she knew Mother was depressed but didn't know what to do. I understood their guilt; I felt it myself.

"The weeks after the funeral were a blur but I managed to keep going to classes and clinics at the hospital – it helped keep my mind off her death.

"She left a note 'For Tom's eyes only.' It was odd to see that phrase, something that I associated with spy movies. I've kept it in my wallet all these years. I have it with me today."

I opened my wallet, pulled the letter out and tried, without much success, to control my voice as I read it. Tears overflowed my eyelids almost immediately.

Dearest Tommy,

I'm sorry to leave you this way, but someday maybe you'll understand it was the right thing to do. You must have known I've been depressed for a long time. On top of other things that made me sad I was diagnosed recently with untreatable cancer. I didn't tell you because I knew it would distract you from your studies. Having you become a doctor is the most important thing in my life, so I chose this way to make sure you finish. I didn't want you to stop your studies and take care of me as I slowly died.

I promised I'd tell you why Sexton Myers suddenly was out of our lives. I found out he'd been in prison for beating up a woman and was out on probation. That was the first thing. Then I kept seeing blood on your t-shirts when I did your laundry. I got suspicious. When I asked Sexton if he knew anything about that he said he'd had to "discipline" you a couple of times. I was furious that he'd hurt you - actually drew blood - and I told him to clear out right away or I'd call the police. We both knew that if I called the police he'd go right back to jail. He left in a big hurry. When I discovered he'd been abusing you I wasn't going to stand for it another day. He threatened me but I stood up to him. He knew not to underestimate my anger and my strength.

Just remember always that I've loved you more than anything else in the world.

Love,

Mother.

"I was then absolutely alone in the world."

Neither Dr. Lyon nor I spoke for a long time.

"I know this has been painful for you," he said finally. "But getting this out has been very important.

"Do you have any questions as we end today?"

"No. I'm wiped out."

"Next time, I want to talk about your experiences in the war."

Don't want to go there, I thought. But that's what this is all about, right? I wonder, should I ask him about getting back together with Cynthia? Nah, not the right time. Who knows what will get stirred up from that dredging up the worst of my childhood and then getting into the worst part, the war.

Cynthia was waiting in the car to take me to my apartment. No way am I ready to move back with her.

10

THE SPLIT

CASUALTIES WERE COMING IN BY the dozens. Mangled bodies, torn limbs, shattered heads, blood everywhere. I stood paralyzed with horror and a crushing sense of futility, trying to repair damage that never should have happened. The medics hoisted body after body onto my operating table. As I looked into the face of one of them, his eyes opened, a glower of hate piercing the space between us. He lunged at me brandishing a knife, going for my throat. I slit his neck with my scalpel.

I awoke covered with sweat, my entire body shuddering. Another nightmare bubbling up from the quagmire that was my nervous system. Groping for the lamp, it clattered off the bed stand. I stumbled to the wall switch and flipped on the lights, the noise of my breathing filling the room.

My tremors subsided as I got my bearings, but my throat and chest burned, and my heart thundered in my chest. I gulped down water greedily, wishing it were Scotch or something even stronger.

What can I do to calm down? Turn on the TV? Try to read a book? Take a run in the middle of the night? Open the windows and have the cold night air chase away these demons? "What dreams may come… must give us pause."

Was that a knock at the door or my brain playing tricks on me again? Am I dreaming? Or hallucinating? I dropped to my knees, crawled to the window to avoid being in the line of fire if there was a threat outside. I warily pulled the curtain aside and peered into the darkness, all the while thinking I was hearing things. A restrained wave from Cynthia greeted my eyes.

Astounded by her presence, in the haze of darkness and in the middle of my nightmare, I screamed through the window, still crouching down, "What the fuck are you doin' here? You shouldn't be here! Don't you understand my body's on full red-button alert? I could kill when I'm in this state. Get outta here!"

Cynthia shrunk back, eyes wide, alarmed at my state. She turned and sprinted to her car.

"Yeah, now you see what a nutcase I am!" I yelled. "What I'm really like."

Get back together? Huh! Fat chance! Who'd want to be with an angry, homicidal lunatic?

At least three hours until daylight. Why the hell did she come? Bet she's sorry she did.

The middle of the night, such an empty time. Shadows play visual tricks and childhood fears take wing. Owls swoop silently down from trees to snatch up and devour unsuspecting prey. Rapists and murderers lurk in deserted lanes, on the sands of beaches, in back alleys. Maybe I should call 911. I'd just end up in Worcester General where they'd shoot me with a tranquilizer, shake their heads behind my back because I was there again…a "frequent flyer."

I paced around the claustrophobic box I lived in, unsuccessfully seeking reassurance from the familiar: a reading chair, books spilling out of shelves, kitchen utensils scattered neglectfully over the counters. Should I eat something? No, my stomach's in such turmoil I'd vomit. I started deep breathing – that sometimes helped.

Alicia had told me I could call her anytime. Maybe now's the time. Yeah, I'll call her. She'll tell me what to do.

"I'll send the emergency team over to pick you up and bring you to Zylinski. I'm glad you called, the right thing to do," she told me, answering after the first ring.

I'd awakened her at home but she sounded like she was fully awake. My panic was already beginning to abate, but I was glad to get help. It wasn't long until the crew arrived followed by a short trip to Zylinski. Intravenous medication made for a rapid descent into sleep.

11

AMBIVALENCE

ALICIA CAME TO THE EMERGENCY department to see me as I came out of medicated sleep. Top thing on my mind was anguish over my angry wild reaction to Cynthia's unexpected visit. My behavior could have been the final straw for her. This brought fresh thoughts of suicide to the surface. Alicia must have sensed my despondency.

"Tell me what happened last night."

"Another nightmare. An enemy soldier trying to kill me and my horrific response. Woke up in a panic and then heard a noise at the door. Turned out it was Cynthia. Why the hell she came I'll never know, but there she was. I was all wired up and I screamed at her to clear out. She left, couldn't get away fast enough, scared shitless of a raving maniac. Now I'm sure it's over for us. I can't blame her – any normal person would run."

"Good thing you called and you're here," Alicia said. "Hard to fathom why Cynthia came last night. Some might say extra sensory perception. I don't know. What I see is how you're feeling right now. But remember Cynthia's a nurse and may understand what's happening to you. Give her some credit for coming. Give her more credit for being wise enough to scram when you told her to leave."

"Think I should try to call her?"

"What do you think?"

"Don't know. If I don't make some effort, our relationship could be done. Even if I call her it may be over. She may think enough is enough. She's got her own life to think of."

"Apologizing for your behavior couldn't hurt."

"She wants to support me, doesn't like being shut out. Like you said, she's a nurse and feels that she can cope with whatever comes up." I sighed. "God, I'm so tired of doing this alone."

"Wanting contact with her is tempting. I understand that. But balancing Cynthia's safety against what comfort she could offer needs to be considered. No question that getting better in therapy is easier when you get support from someone who loves you. But, as you know, there are risks." She looked away.

"Have you ever felt out of control during the day?" Alicia asked.

"No visions like those right after a nightmare, but yes, my emotions can get volatile even during the day. All depends on what goes on around me."

"Want to take this chance? Put her in danger? My guess – your answer is a strong 'no'."

She sure tipped her hand there.

"Then there's no decision to make," I said. "Unless we could have supervised visits. Is that a possibility? Don't friends or families support other patients with supervision?"

"It varies. Supervised visits might be an option. If you call her, you could broach the subject of supervised visits. If she's willing we can probably set it up. Let me know after you talk to her. Worth making the suggestion."

I stared at the curtains in my cubicle where I'd spent the night. Yes, I need to call her. I think – I hope – she'd forgive me. I need to have her in my life, even at arm's length.

"Going on to another subject," Alicia said after a few minutes, "the team has examined your questionnaire and your sessions with Dr. Lyon in detail. They think, not surprisingly, that your PTSD has deep roots in early losses. Multiple adverse childhood experiences are the forerunners to PTSD in many combat veterans. Even though you weren't directly engaged in battle you likely over-identified with the severely afflicted soldiers you treated.

"These traumas-by-proxy got piled on top of your abusive childhood. Your carefully constructed defenses that previously worked for you, failed. Losing Danny and the nurses, on top of your vicarious trauma put you past the tipping point and precipitated your symptoms. Those experiences are as personal as it gets."

The guilt I'd felt about having PTSD without direct combat experience was coming into perspective. Alicia was showing how deeply she understood the vagaries of this syndrome. Perhaps her extensive experience escorting patients through confusing thickets of fear and hyper-vigilance could help in my healing too.

"There are additional aspects of PTSD to keep in mind," she went on. "As I told you it's not a single entity. It's sometimes conveniently – and too simply – divided into internalizing and externalizing forms."

I rolled my eyes, expecting another teaching session.

"I know, this sounds like psychology 101, but hear me out.

"The internalizing form occurs when the patient withdraws from the larger world into his own internal space, avoiding contact with others and brooding about life. Obsessive thinking about the same things repeatedly – called ruminating in psych terminology – takes over. This is flavored with self-loathing, depression, and anxiety. Sadly, these people are at high risk for attempting suicide.

"Should I go on?"

"I'm with you. Suicide has crossed my mind." Often, I thought. "But something holds me back."

"You apparently have strengths insulating you from acting on those thoughts. And further protection is with you now because you're in a supportive treatment program.

"So, to continue with my mini-lecture, the externalizing form is characterized by explosions of anger and aggressive acting-out behaviors. Provoking people with this type of PTSD gets them into frequent physical fights when provoked or if they feel threatened. Domestic violence is a common outcome. Bar fights or road rage may result. But as I said, most people with PTSD are not pure forms of either type."

"I guess I'm a blend," I said. "I've felt both withdrawal and aggression. But I also have short periods of time when I feel almost normal. Any way to know what's gonna happen when I start the clinical trial?"

"We can't predict exactly what will happen in individual patients. That's why it's called a clinical trial. I assume Dr. Patel told you about the hypotheses the study is trying to test. Did she tell you the nitty-gritty details of how the study's organized?"

" If she did I don't remember. Fill me in."

"Well, in broad strokes, there are four groups of patients. The first – forgive me if I oversimplify the study design – is called the 'Drug Only' group. The second is 'Drug Plus Therapy'; the third is 'Placebo Only,' and the fourth is 'Placebo Plus Therapy.'

"With me so far?"

"Sure, sounds familiar to studies I've known in the past. Go on."

"As a physician, you're aware of research parameters, but to keep protocol intact, I'll quickly run through the definitions. The researchers don't know which group is which – called 'blinding' – to eliminate bias in their assessment of the patient's symptoms and responses. Pill bottles are unlabeled to further this blinding. The compounding company delivers the active drug and the placebo in color-coded boxes, and staff who are not involved in the study dispense the pills in trays for the four categories. The color-coded boxes are never seen by anyone working in the study, maintaining blinding.

"So. Any questions?"

"A neat study. How long has it been going on?"

"Couple of years."

"Any idea about outcomes?"

"Nothing that can be analyzed yet. We know some patients are considerably better, but we don't know which group they're in so we don't know which regimen produced that outcome. They could be getting better by EMDR and therapy or from the pill and therapy."

I waited for her to continue, but it became clear that was all she was going to say.

After Alicia left, I felt I had to call Cynthia. This couldn't wait.

"Hello?" she said.

"Hello, Cyn, it's me."

"Hello," she answered, predictably reserved.

"All I can say is that I'm sorry," I mumbled. "I'd just woken up from a bad nightmare and you surprised me. I was still in the mist of that dream. I didn't want you near me while I was like that."

"I've never been so freaked out," she spit out. "By the time I got home I was furious with you. I came to you because I woke up scared and had a sense you needed me. I'd come to try to help. And what I got from you was a screaming rejection. I'm not sure I can go on like this, to be brutally frank."

"I get that and don't blame you. I'm really on the edge right now. I just talked with Alicia. I'm about to enter the treatment phase. That means I'll be an inpatient for several weeks. So that break may be good for both of us. But Cyn, I don't want to give up on us. Please bear with me a little while longer."

"What're you doing now?" Cynthia asked.

"I'm getting ready to go home from the emergency room." A pause. "Are you there?"

"I'm here. Against my better judgment, I'll pick you up and take you to your apartment. What's the next step in this thing?"

"Tomorrow I go in for some outpatient evals and then I'll be admitted to commence the actual treatment."

"I'll be over in about a half an hour."

What's the harm in a ride? I felt pretty relaxed from the medicated sleep.

Cynthia met me in the lobby. We walked to the car in awkward silence.

"I need gas," Cynthia said, choosing neutral ground. "There's a gas station down the street."

We pulled next to a pump, and a man came to her car window. "Fill it?"

"No, just give me ten dollars' worth," Cynthia said.

"That's not much. That won't get you far," the man growled.

I looked at him and quickly decided from his olive skin, black hair and dark eyes, he was Middle-Eastern. I'd seen thousands of them in the war zones, glaring at us "infidels" from the U.S. and Europe who'd come to fight in their interminable war. We weren't welcomed as the saviors our military propaganda promised. In fact, most of them – whether fighting on our side or against us – had little respect and barely tolerated us. I got to the point of hating their guts in return. Anger rose in my throat as I peered at this guy.

"You heard what she said. Ten bucks. Just pump the gas, and shut the fuck up," I snarled.

"Don't talk to me that way or you'll get nothin'," he shot back.

Cynthia's eyes flicked back and forth between us, betraying her fear of escalation.

"He doesn't mean any harm," she said to the attendant, in her nurse's reassuring tone. "He just got out of the hospital. Please just pump the gas and we'll be on our way."

"He owes me an apology. When I get that, you get gas."

At that point, I grabbed the door handle ready to get out and do battle. Cynthia, who hadn't turned off the motor, floored it, burning rubber as we shot out of the gas station before I blundered into a fight I would've lost.

"Son of a bitch! He's like all those 14th century subhuman zealots who blow up our kids and keep this fucking war going. Torturers. Beheading people with knives. Must have been born missing parts of their brains."

"Jesus, Tom, calm down," Cynthia cried out. "Get hold of yourself." She gripped the steering wheel tightly, her eyes narrowing.

"Try to remember how we used to work to control chaos in the emergency room," she said with staccato speech, a deep frown across her brow. "How was I to know a Middle-Eastern guy might be pumping gas there?"

Here was another time since I came home that I'd put her in imminent danger.

"I still have a lot to learn about your hot buttons, but please Tom, try to keep your cool," she said in a tone indicating her own cool had returned.

Still furious, my temples throbbed and my pulse raced. Why the hell did I go off like that? Damn, how can she be with a bullying lunatic? Who am I kidding? I can't be with her unless I get better. I looked over at her. She returned my gaze briefly, probably wondering if I were coming off my adrenalin high.

"This kind of thing is exactly what worries me, putting you in harm's way. I try to control myself, but some things make me explode inside. Sometimes my gut tells me if I don't come out swinging, I'll be wiped out. That I'm always fighting for my life."

"You're safe here in Worcester. You're not in a Middle East warzone. That guy back there – he may not even be from over there. He may just be another guy with a macho pride problem. So try to stay calm."

We both stared ahead at the road, not knowing what else to say.

"I'm thinking about going to therapy to help me understand my mixed up feelings," Cynthia said. "I know you're suffering from a mental health condition that's not your fault, and I hope you can heal, but it's been so long since we've been close. I love you, but need to sort things out."

Shit. Now she wants a shrink to cope.

"Wish you didn't need to do that," I said, turning to her. "But do whatever helps."

"I still want to help you get by all this. Don't know why – I must be a masochist. That's one of the reasons I probably need to talk to a counselor."

"Listen, drop me off at my place. I've got to think. What just happened is a big red flag." Alicia's voice came into in my head, asking if I wanted to take the chance of putting Cynthia at risk.

"I'll drop you off and call you later. Don't blow what happened back there out of proportion," she said.

"Cyn, I'm going to be busy at Zylinski for a while so we have some time to figure this out."

"Oh, sure, so you'll be in that nice cocoon while I'm out here trying to figure out what the hell to do next with my life."

"Now you're hurt. Great. This stinks. I have no idea whether this thing I'm starting will help or not, but let me get into it and then I'll call you. Thanks for the ride."

Without looking back and unintentionally slamming the car door, I quickly got inside my apartment. I leaned against the wall. Damn, I forgot to discuss with her the idea of supervised visits.

12

GENESIS

WALKING INTO THE ZYLINSKI INSTITUTE triggered a fear reminiscent of my first day of medical school: I didn't belong in this place, being here was a colossal mistake. Should I turn around and get the hell out of here? What good would that do? I vacillated between an unfounded faith that the treatment program would work and a dark despair that I'd end up homeless, living in a refrigerator box over a heating vent in a back alley of Worcester. If the treatment worked, Cynthia and I would live happily ever after. I'd resume my brilliant career as a trauma surgeon and live in a grand house in Wellesley raising a perfect little family. This first scenario was surely the triumph of hope over experience. I tried to dampen the dread of the second possibility – a homeless veteran – as I checked in at the front desk, but restless stirrings in my stomach reminded me how terrified I was of failure in this latest attempt to get control over my symptoms.

I'd barely gotten seated in the waiting area when Dr. Patel came to the waiting room and led me into her office. After a warm greeting she told me what to expect next.

"We've integrated your medical and psychiatric history from information you supplied and past medical records," she said in her lilting voice. "What I'll tell you now is all about what will go on this week. You remember those medical student workups? This is kind of like that. You'll get a thorough physical examination and we'll take blood for biochemical, endocrine, and genetic profiles. We'll analyze your urine, sweat, cerebrospinal fluid, semen, saliva, and DNA."

She looked at me and smiled.

"All of us on staff went through all of these procedures. Akira's idea, so we'd understand what it's like being a patient in this protocol. It's really not so bad," she laughed.

"Really? Never heard of that being done before. But I'm glad there's no surgery involved," I said, also chuckling.

"Oh, no surgery. Think we'd have lost half the staff if that were involved.

"These tests will be repeated several times during the course of treatment," she continued "We'll do a variety of specialized MRI's, PET scans and other imaging studies of your central nervous system. We'll get a skeletal survey, a bone scan and a measure of your bone density. These are baseline markers against which we'll compare follow-up studies, looking for potential side effects of the drug on bones."

My eyes widened as she said the trigger words "side effects." She picked up on my reaction.

"Just part of the protocol. There's no evidence the drug does anything to bone but it's one of the many organ systems we evaluate during the study period. It's why clinical trials are so cumbersome and expensive to conduct.

"So, any questions?"

"Not now. I think I'm ready to start."

During this time of deep probing into the confines of my body, I accommodated to it by imagining it was being done to someone else, my personal variation of dissociation. At week's end I felt every cell in my body had been thoroughly squeezed, poked and exposed, giving up its secrets and flaws. When it was over, I was set free while they analyzed the measurements of my body's structure and function.

Should I call her? Oh, why the hell not.

"Cyn, this is me. I haven't started the protocol yet. Wondered if you could meet me somewhere for dinner? Just for dinner and you can drop me back off at Zylinski."

"Um, just pulled out some frozen stuff for dinner." A pause. "Actually, going out sounds better. How about Valerios?"

"Meet you there."

She got there first. Should I give her a hug? A kiss? Or just sit down? OK, just sit down.

"So, tell me about your week," she said with a wry smile.

"Oh, it was a blast. I think I'm radioactive from X-rays and probably profoundly anemic from the bloodletting. I feel my bone marrow pulsating to replenish the blood they took."

My voice rose as I excitedly told her more.

"If I ever have another claustrophobic noisy MRI, I'll probably scream and break the inside of their infernal tube." Oops, stay away from impulses about violent behaviors. "Sorry."

"Let's order some food," Cynthia said, brushing aside my apology.

"Well anyhow, they know more about me than I care to have them know. If it helps I guess they're welcome to it."

"It's odd, I feel exposed too," Cynthia said.

"I know what you mean; it does feel like being naked. But I know these investigators have been carefully screened. I trust them – I think. Akira would brook no nonsense. He may be a nice, gentle fellow but he's hard-nosed as hell about colleagues working for him. Remember, back at the emergency department, how he went after that resident who made fun of a patient? He won't tolerate disrespect or indignity involving a patient, or for that matter, anyone."

"Are you on any kind of restricted diet or can we have a nice dinner?" Cynthia asked, changing the subject.

"I'm on furlough so I can eat whatever I want but no alcohol or caffeinated coffee."

"Mind if I have a glass of wine while you sit there in abject distress?"

"Of course not – but only one," I said, teasing Cynthia who was never a lush. "Next week I go into the inpatient unit, get assigned to a treatment group," I continued, unable to stop talking about this all-consuming experience. "Not sure how they decide who's in a particular group. I hope I get along with the other guys during group therapy. Some PTSD patients can be rough characters with very short fuses."

Cynthia stopped perusing the menu and glanced up at me, grinning.

"I know, I know, I can be difficult, too," I said. "I'm just sayin' I hope I have enough patience to listen to other people's problems without reacting negatively. I suppose I'll get used to it. I'm so self-critical. That can carry over to impatience with other people's faults and complaints."

"You can be very empathetic too, you know. But when you're in one of your moods you get like a schoolmarm – your Calvinism takes over. A good therapy leader will control that," Cynthia said.

"Alicia told me that you and I could maybe have supervised visits while I'm in the hospital for treatment. What do you think about that?"

"God, that sounds like you're in jail. Supervised? What does that mean?"

"I think it's simply to be sure I don't melt down, like I did at the gas station. I don't think I'll have as many anger flare-ups, during the day anyway. They're mostly at night when I have trouble with nightmares. But it's a chance to see each other."

"After I dropped you off last night, I couldn't get my mind off what happened when you shrieked at me to go away, like I'm the enemy," she said with a waver in her voice. "And then that scene at the gas station – could've ended up in disaster for both of us. I talked to Rosalie – probably my best friend at the nursing school, a sponge for my problems. Well, she agreed I ought to get some therapy, so I'm starting next week."

I didn't know how to respond, so I sat silently, waiting for her answer about supervised visits.

"I would like to see you. I suppose supervised visits would be okay, but let's wait until I've had a few sessions with my psychologist, okay?" she said.

"Sounds reasonable."

Hope she can't tell how scared I am. What if I forget who she is? I've got to show her I'm feeling confident this treatment's gonna work, can't let her see how nervous I am.

"Cyn, I feel really optimistic about this treatment working."

"You don't look as positive as you talk," she said, her eyes flitting from side to side. "You know, I really wish you'd level with me. You never let me see what you're afraid of – only your anger. You don't open up about your real feelings – even about us. I wonder if you get over this horrible problem…well, maybe you'll just throw me aside, find someone who hasn't known you when you had these problems."

She looked down at her hands, a tear streaked down her cheek.

"Sometimes I feel I don't know you anymore," Cynthia said. "Maybe you talk to your therapist, but you're sure not confiding in me. And frankly, I'm tired of being shut out."

How can I tell her about things I can't deal with myself – losing Danny and the nurses? The pileup of casualties? How can I tell her how frightened I am of getting stuck in this empty place? Of losing her? God, I hate to be such a wimp, a weakling needing her so desperately. Being that needy pisses me off.

My impulse was to reach across the table and take her hands in mine, but I held back as anger rose in my throat.

"I'm not shutting you out! How can you say that?"

A couple at the next table stole a look at us as I raised my voice. I turned away from their gaze. Cynthia drank some water, trying to ignore the unwanted attention I'd drawn to us.

"Look, I don't know any more than you do what this treatment might do to you," she said in a low voice. "My place in your life – whatever it is – could change as you go through this program. You might come out a completely different person. Any idea how that makes me feel?"

I always thought of myself as a guy who could identify with other people, to "walk in their moccasins." But in my present state of self-absorption I'd failed to think about what her day-to-day existence was like. She was suffering too, differently than I was, surely, but still... She wanted to help me but I wasn't allowing her in the mistaken notion that I was sparing her. I hadn't considered that she might doubt my desire to have her near me or that treatment might change me.

"I guess I didn't want you to see the depth of my illness because I'm afraid of losing you."

"You don't give me enough credit," she shot back. "Do you recall I'm a nurse? That perhaps I have some insights about you? And PTSD? That perhaps I've read up on it and know a helluva lot more about it than you do?" She was steaming. "As for losing me, that would've happened long before now if I didn't love you, want you to get better. But I need you to trust me and tell me things on your mind. And when you're better I still hope you'll need me."

"I can't conceive of ever not needing you."

"Well, we don't know if that will change, do we?" she said.

I wish I could have reassured her, but maybe she was right. We sat back as our time together got down to minutes.

She looked at her watch. "It's ten-thirty. Better be getting you back to your "cell.""

This was not the way I wanted our evening to end, but it was obvious we weren't going to settle anything tonight. Our conversation had sucked the air out of the room. I was feeling short of breath as we left the restaurant. Our ride back to Zylinski was wordless, clouds of uncertainty hanging in the air.

13

INTO THE BREACH

DESPITE OUR UNEASYNESS, WHEN IT came time for me to
go into the hospital, Cynthia and I held each other, neither willing
to end the moment. I knew – and supposed Cynthia knew also – this
was a critical juncture in our relationship. I finally loosened my grasp
and circled through the revolving doors of the inpatient unit at Zylinski.
Looking back I gave her a more confident wave than I felt. She smiled
and held two thumbs up. I wouldn't see her for god knows how long and
already I had a hollow feeling in my chest and a few skipped throbs in
my pulse.

A nurse whose nametag said Diana helped me settle into my small
room, my dwelling for the weeks to come. If I ever had to be lifted out of
bed, Diana would need help. Her light frame and delicate features evoked
lustful fantasies. No matter what else happened while I was here, I'd enjoy
gazing at this gamine as she glided around my room, arranging the tray
table, handing me my medication and my daily schedule. She flashed a
smile from time to time as she performed her duties.

"So you'll be my prisoner since we don't allow visitors during your
stay – you know, research protocol," she said with a wink.

"I've had worse captors. So, you're my daytime nurse. Who'll be my
jailers during the other shifts?"

"Debbie's on the swing shift, and Nina has the night shift. You'll
like them," she said. "I need to tell you a few things." Diana pointed at
a narrow door. "Your bathroom is through there. If you go out into the
hall and turn left, you'll find the rec room. A lot of the guys like to go
there – pool tables, ping-pong, TV, that kind of stuff. You're also free to

wander around in the library, right next to the rec room. There's a gym and a great swimming pool one floor down. You get your workout and swim gear there.

"There on your bed is a blue folder that outlines the protocol all patients are following. Read it over. I'll be back in a little while to answer any questions. Press that button by your nightstand if you need anything."

She slipped out the door.

I looked around the room. Not too unpleasant for a hospital. A bed with reading lights over the headboard, a nightstand with a call cord, a desk and chair under the window that looked out on a pond surrounded by fir trees. The window had no bars but there were stops on the casings to prevent raising the shatterproof glass more than a few inches. I looked for a one-way mirror but saw none. All the fixtures in the bathroom were plastic and the mirror was shatterproof. The showerhead was a rain-forest type attached to a spring so that there was no chance of using it to string your self up. If I had any questions about concerns about suicide among the study population, this was a metaphoric exclamation point.

I picked up the folder. I'd be getting a pill – either active medication or placebo – each morning, administered directly into my mouth by Diana. The rest of the protocol was predictable. Diana came back to see if I had any questions.

"What's this about attaching monitors to my noggin at night?"

"They're like EEG wires but they come on a sort of crown the tech slips on your head. Won't bother you after the first couple of nights. The other monitors are the usual stuff you see in any hospital."

"Okay. Can I read in bed or is lights out a certain time?"

"You can read but we do want everyone's lights out by midnight."

Around nine o'clock and after the attendant attached the electrode crown to my head, I turned out the light and settled into my surprisingly comfortable bed. I wondered what might happen during this night. It must have been a couple of hours before I relaxed enough to go to sleep. I was anxious enough about being in this new place but added to that were noises from other rooms as patients wrestled with their own personal demons during sleep. Mercifully, on this night I had no nightmares.

The next day the medical staff docs came and asked perfunctory questions, making entries on their iPads. After a quick physical exam by one of the medical team, a psychologist talked to me briefly about my night, my mood, noting my affect and making notes of my responses. My day's schedule was handed to me. I didn't have an appointment scheduled until after lunch, so I had time to kill and went down to the rec room.

I wasn't eager to mingle with the genuine veterans of the war, those men and women who'd seen their comrades dying inches away from them. Ministering to people injured in fires or car crashes, falls at construction sites, gunshot wounds and stabbings prepares trauma surgeons to distance themselves psychologically from their patients. My surgical rotation at Boston Medical Center helped numb me to patients' pain so I could face another round of trauma day after day.

But Jesus...how can anyone get prepared to absorb the carnage and barbarism these hapless ground troops witnessed in combat, far worse than anything I'd seen at Boston Medical Center. Even with all my training I ultimately failed to block out the psychic derangement this mayhem created. This left me defenseless. Losing Danny and the nurses was the absolute worst thing I'd ever experienced, so maybe after all I was entitled to consider myself a legitimate veteran with PTSD.

I entered the rec room as unobtrusively as possible. I warily looked around at men playing pool, reading, sitting around card tables, engaged in inaudible conversations. What if something triggers a bad memory in one of these characters, or one is scared by a new face and gets defensive and aggressive? What if one of these guys somehow provokes me and I fly off the handle?

There was no joie de vivre here. There was a heavy undercurrent of irritability and some bickering, but nothing overtly out of control. Pretending to look at a magazine I tried to get a fix on the sensibility of this gathering of psychologically fragile individuals. But no one even seemed interested in me or aware that I'd come into the room. They all seemed to be inward looking and self-involved. Just like me. I saw that interacting with these guys would take time. And that was okay since I wasn't eager to bond with anyone. Besides, my first appointment was coming up.

I sat down in the waiting room for my one o'clock appointment and precisely at one the consultation room door opened. A large man stepped out.

"Barrett?"

"Here," I said and rose as he directed me into his office. About forty years old, his imposing physique was more suggestive of a hard tackle for the Patriots than a doctor. His square head, close-cropped blond hair and cobalt eyes vouched for his Teutonic lineage.

"I'm Dr. Emil Dietrich, geneticist," he said, brusquely. "Just so you know, I consider myself a serious scientist, to be distinguished from some of the mental health clinicians around here."

With that bizarre introduction, he handed me a folder with his credentials – a gesture I found peculiar, but figured maybe this is how new patients are introduced to those about to take care of them. He had a barrel of degrees, from bachelor and master-of-science letters, an MD with three years' residency in internal medicine, and to top it off, a PhD in genetics. He was all business as he studied my record, grunting as he came across items of interest. He glanced at me a couple of times as he did this, making me squirm self-consciously.

"I understand you're a special subject in our study. You were a trauma surgeon when you were still practicing medicine? What led you to that specialty?"

Surprised that he characterized me as a "special subject" and suspecting a question behind the question about my choice of trauma surgery, I hesitated.

"I suppose because I like repairing damage, putting broken things back together," I answered weakly. In an attempt to establish some level of rapport and collegiality, I asked, "How'd you get interested in genetics?"

"My personal choices are unimportant and not why we're here," he said curtly. "Frankly I don't see how your surgical training can be of much use to us in this study. In my experience, surgeons are interested only in cutting and have little interest in real science."

Breathe. Don't say "Well, fuck you," and storm out of the room. "That's a pretty narrow view of surgeons, don't you think?" I said, trying to be reasonable. Shit, this guy is irritating. "If you want to get into a discussion about professional jealousies we can do that," my anger beginning to simmer. "But I'm here because presumably you need as much information about my genetic endowment as you can get. Is that right?"

He glared, seemingly taken aback that I had the temerity to respond in kind to his supercilious demeanor. He then turned to my medical record.

"In the interest of complying with the regulations about so-called 'informed consent' I need to tell you I'll be performing DNA analyses on your blood in addition to the other routine tests. Is there anything you want to add to the genetic history you provided us?"

One of those asses who hides behind his professional armor.

"No, I spent a good deal of time filling out those forms. I've responded to all the questions," I said with more than a trace of annoyance.

"Alright, then, that's all I need with you at this point. You may go."

I've been given the gate before in my life but not quite as dismissively as this. When Sexton was done beating me he'd tell me to get lost, he hated the sight of me. But this abrupt termination of our interview by a clinician in Akira's program astonished me. I felt a blush come over my face, as much a flare of anger from down deep as from embarrassment, the feeling of absolute powerlessness. This felt so familiar. Bastard. Thinks he can put me in my place? I turned around to look at Dietrich. Kicking the chair near the door, I sent it flying into the wall with a crash.

He thinks it's okay to treat me like a piece of shit? My rage rose to a murderous level. I charged back to pummel him. Arrogant schmuck. I'm going to smash your fucking face in.

He jumped up from his chair when he saw me coming. His size made it apparent I didn't stand a chance in a physical confrontation. I stopped and spluttered in my frustration, "I hate your fucking guts, you miserable son of a bitch!"

If nothing else, Dietrich was startled by my anger. He put both hands up in front of him, warning me against further advance. "Don't come any closer or you'll be sorry," he said in measured tones. "Turn around and head for that door. I've never lost a fight and I'm not going to start now."

He'd read my rage correctly and didn't want to anger me further, but he wasn't about to back down either. Grabbing what was left of my self-control I stopped. Wait. What am I doing? Just get the hell out of here.

I turned, opened the door and strode into the hall. Still angry outside the room, I slammed my fist into the wall. Three blares of a siren filled the hall.

Sonovabitch must have pressed some security system. I ran for the outside door, out to a path I'd discovered along a brook behind the Institute, hoping my anger would recede in that calming place. As I walked alongside the stream, my heart rate slowed, and my hyperventilation subsided.

What just happened? No surprise really, I have trouble with condescending unfriendly people like Dietrich. I'd been reassured by the courtesy of everyone else I'd met at Zylinski up till now.

Dietrich was a jolt. His personality was the polar opposite of Akira's and all the other people I'd met. Does Akira know what he's like? Should I tell him? Shit. What if I have future visits with this arrogant ass? Will he act the same way? Was his interview a calculated attempt to expose some aspect of my syndrome? A stress interview? Was he having a bad day or was this the real Dietrich? What if this encounter goes into my record and changes the course of my treatment?

I'll discuss this with Alicia before I mention it to Akira. Until now I've felt comfortable, optimistic. Now, I don't know. Maybe my faith in this program was misplaced. What if unscrupulous people within his program are taking advantage of Akira's good nature? How could he not know about Dietrich's character?

"You sounded pretty upset when you called," Alicia said as I sat down in her office a few hours later. "But I'm glad you did. You must have heard the alarms Dr. Dietrich set off. I called Security to find out why they went off. When they told me it involved you I assured them you didn't pose a threat, that you and I would meet to discuss this. I would've called you had you not called.

"You don't pose a threat, right?"

"No, but I was – am – upset. Who is this guy Dietrich? And is he a jerk with all patients or is there something about me that triggered his hostility? Have you had any other complaints about Dietrich?"

"You know I can't answer that. I can only discuss your case with you. It would be unprofessional to talk about staff. You do understand that, don't you?"

"Yeah, sorry I asked," I said. Guess I put her in an uncomfortable place. "Are there other geneticists on the team I could see instead of Dietrich?"

"He's our only geneticist," Alicia said, shifting in her chair. "You may not be seeing him at all in the future since he's really only a consultant to the research team. We have debriefing sessions each week, so I'll bring this up.

"No, don't protest," she said as I inhaled to start to argue. "Your negative experience is important. The last thing our patients need is to be angry with staff. This needs to be aired. That's why we have feedback sessions."

"I don't want this to poison the well," I said, now feeling some guilt at complaining. "Maybe I'm over-reacting. I've been doing that a lot lately. Maybe he had an argument with someone, or got a paper rejected, or who knows? I sure don't want this to color my interactions with others on the team."

"If he's offensive or intimidating people, acting rudely with patients, that needs to be addressed. It could be affecting others, potentially altering treatment outcomes and our statistics about efficacy."

"OK, just don't let it be known that I'm as upset as I am." I took a deep breath.

"Who do I see next?"

"Let me check," Alicia tapped into her computer.

"You have an appointment with Dr. Malcolm Crocker, a neurologist, tomorrow at 9. He's a real mensch," Alicia said, betraying her partiality. "He'll have the benefit of your X-ray, CT scans, and MRI results. He'll tell you what he's learned from the imaging studies and his exam, if anything. You'll like his bedside manner. After Dr. Crocker, you'll see Dr. Berman, a radiologist and then Dr. Mohammed, our pharmacologist. On Wednesday, you'll see Dr. Starr, an internist, Dr. Davis, a chemist, and Dr. Hug, a molecular biologist. That'll round out the diagnostic encounters. You'll then move on to actual treatment."

The next morning I was shown into Dr. Crocker's examination room by his nurse, who asked a few questions then measured my blood pressure, pulse, and oxygen saturation.

Malcolm Crocker tapped on the door once and came in looking like he'd just gotten off his yacht in Marblehead. Wearing a Brooks Brothers shirt with a rep tie and khaki trousers, his appearance shouted "Yankee" and his accent was Boston Brahmin. His deep voice was friendly and reassuring.

"Very good to meet you, Dr. Barrett. I see you survived all your tests last week."

"Yeah, if you get out another needle I'll run out the door," I said with a smile.

"Not to worry, no tests today. I'm going to do a straightforward neu-rological exam and you'll be out of here pretty quickly. I've reviewed your neuroradiology images, so I doubt the exam is going to tell us much, but for the sake of being thorough we'll go ahead with that. OK with you?"

Alicia was right – Crocker had a great bedside manner. I felt confident he was an accomplished clinician, comfortable in his skills. He got out the usual neurologist's tools of the trade – reflex hammer and pins to prick you with – and went through his examination. When he was done, he spent a few minutes recording his findings, then turned to me.

"You have some soft neurological signs, some difficulty with your finger-to-nose testing, and a mild tremor of your hands." He smiled. "Not to worry. These could be due to nervous system abnormalities but could also be psychosomatic. Not terribly unusual. We'll follow these things once we begin treatment." He paused and looked me steadily. "I'd be glad to answer any questions."

"Just wondering about the neuroradiology images. Anything there?"

"Mild non-specific abnormalities in the MRI's and PET scans – not unexpected, we see this regularly. Nothing significant missing in your brain and nothing there that shouldn't be there. We'll do additional imaging as we proceed looking for possible changes in those functional studies as the regimen proceeds," he said. "It's one of the main parameters we watch. I'd say you're in pretty damn good shape, all things considered."

"So when do I actually start the treatment part?" I said, betraying some impatience.

"You still have a few more preliminary appointments. Three are non-clinicians so you won't be bled or invaded by them," he chuckled. "After that, we'll start treatment."

"Know which group I'll be in?"

"Randomization determines the group you're assigned to. We won't know that until the study ends. Really the luck of the draw. At the end of the study we'll compare outcomes in the four groups – you know about the four groups, right?

"Yeah, Alicia told me that."

"Only at the end will we be able to determine which regimen has been more efficacious," Dr. Crocker said. "As we observe your progress, you'll continue whatever treatment regimen you've been on as an outpatient as long as the inpatient trial goes well."

He tapped a few more keys on his laptop, smiled and turned to me.

"So, Dr. Barrett, what occupied your time here before you came to Zylinski? Do you have any hobbies?"

"Please call me Tom.

"No hobbies to speak of. So immersed in work since medical school I've neglected life outside of medicine. But I've always enjoyed nature and the outdoors. In my short time here I've found a small pleasure walking along that little path by a stream behind the building. I get a dose of Mother Nature there, watching the birds, chipmunks, and squirrels. Gives me a little peace of mind. I do it every day after my sessions. It's become a pleasant habit."

"I know the place," Crocker said. "It's called Vinny's Path, named after a donor who insisted we provide a place for patients to escape the clinical ambiance inside this building. You're right – you can lose the cares of the day when you walk along that little trail. I pass there every day since the staff parking lot is at the end of that path." He glanced at his watch.

"Well, you need to get going for other appointments. Good seeing you. I look forward to working with you and hearing your feedback."

After seeing other team members in the afternoon, answering their questions and giving my body up for examinations, I was exhausted and glad to get back to my room. By nine o'clock I was glad to put my little "crown" on and try to sleep.

14

PROTOCOL

BY THE END OF THE second week I was having fewer flashbacks and nightmares. I didn't feel as depressed. Was this the effect of the medication? Frustrating not knowing whether I'm getting the active drug or placebo.

"All indications are you're improving," said Dr. Crocker, the next time I saw him. He discussed my lab reports and did a quick neuro check. "Something seems to be helping you."

"Whatever it is, I'm grateful. If I'm getting the drug it hasn't shown any ill effects so far," I said. "One of my biggest fears was that I might forget everything. That doesn't seem to be happening. Hate to lose my medical knowledge, what's left of it."

"Your cognition is as good as when I first saw you. Probably better, now that you're not having so many distracting symptoms. Your improvement could be simply that you feel safe here and the other parts of the treatment protocol are working. In either case, I'm glad you feel better.

"Any other thoughts? Questions?"

"Can't think of anything."

"See you next time," he said, slapping me on the back as I left his office.

I headed for the pool for my free time. A whiff of chlorine hit my nostrils when I opened the door to head for a swim. At the gym and pool, contact with the combat veterans was a daily event. Gradually I had connected with two men, Matt Dimasio and George Logan. Matt was short and stout with olive-skin and jug-handle ears. He talked a lot about his big Italian family in Newark. A high school dropout, he enlisted in the

Army just past his eighteenth birthday. He did this over the protests of his mother – a first generation immigrant from Sicily with a second-grade education whose children were her universe. He described his father as a tough Sicilian who ruled his house like Mussolini and worked as a plumber's helper in downtown Newark. He praised Matt's decision to enlist, telling him to "become a patriot and serve this great country."

George Logan was a bulky, thick-featured African-American whose head was neatly shaven every few days in the hospital barbershop. He wore wire-rim glasses he kept on even when he went swimming. He came from a small town in Alabama that he described as "provincial." He said he was twenty-four when he joined the military. As I regarded these two wounded men trying to recover their lives I saw generic faces of American troopers.

"So, Doc, what's a nice guy like you doin' in a place like this?" Matt asked one day as we sat with feet dangling in the pool.

"Same reason as you, I guess. Can't shake the bad memories."

"Where'd you serve?"

"I was in a hospital unit in Iraq. How about you?"

"Syria and Iraq, but I was a grunt," he said, turning away slightly. "My last orders took me to a unit in Aleppo. The place was a total hellhole – houses and buildings…all kinds…caving in; the place looked like pictures I used to see of Hiroshima. I hate to admit it – I was scared shitless most of the time."

"No shame in that. Anyone not scared by the madness of war has something really wrong with them," I said, wondering if I was morphing into the role of therapist when I should remain just another patient.

"But you know how boys are brought up," Matt said. "My dad used to say: 'boys gotta be brave, never give in to fear, always be tough guys, like Rambo.' Or is that just how Italian kids are raised?"

"Don't think that's restricted to any nationality. Seems pretty universal. Main reason we have wars," I said, unable to resist the urge to preach.

George Logan came to sit down next to Matt. Easy to see they were buddies, comfortable in each other's company.

"I grew up hearing all that bullshit about what it's like to be a man," Logan said, "and thought just like you, Matt. But anyone tells you they're not scared when they could get killed or torn apart is either lying or crazy."

Logan looked at me quickly, not knowing me well enough to figure out where I was coming from. Seeing I was listening, he went on.

"But you can't let your buddies down, can you? Same as when I was a cop. Loyalty is priority number one. You can't turn tail and run. If you do, you live with that the rest of your life, and that's worse than dying. Especially in the show, when you see a friend blown to bits right next to you. That's happened to me too many times, and I always wonder – why them and not me?

"That's why I'm here," Logan continued in his low, modulated tone. "How do I forget those pictures? How do you stop dreaming about what happened to those poor bastards? Being afraid that you're the next one to be ripped apart, spilling your brains or guts into the sand? I wanna be rid of these visions, these nightmares. Sometimes I feel like I don't know what's a nightmare and what's really happening. So when I heard about this program I thought it sounded like the balm of Gilead. I needed to join this and have the cure-all."

Wow, this guy's so open. Honest, no shame. Is that from therapy or the pill? How'd he get such clear insight? Maybe it's from his upbringing or just living his life. Is it inherent in some people? But even with his insight, he still has PTSD, just like Matt and me and the others here.

So, how long have you two been in the study?" I asked.

"Six weeks for me," Matt said.

"About the same for me," George said.

"See any change in your symptoms?"

They looked at each other for a moment.

"I'm a lot better," Matt said. "Don't know whether it's the pill, or the talk therapy, a combination or whatever. No flashbacks for a long time, nightmares seem to have gone bye-bye, and I'm much less jumpy."

He glanced at George, who was staring into the water.

"I wish I could say that. I'm no different than when I came here in the first place. I think I got the short straw, the placebo, especially when I see how much better Matt and some of the other guys are. Some of my buddies are in the same boat as me – no improvement. Now I'm not a scientist or anything, but I think I can figure out who's getting the real pill and who's not. I think they should stop the trial and give us all the real pill."

"Well, except that some guys who were doin' good are backsliding lately," Matt said. "How do you explain that?"

"You noticed that too?" George said. "I dunno. Could they be changin' the pills to see if people relapse? That'd be a real bummer for the ones who got better. And I think kinda cruel – even unethical – if they're doing that."

Huh. This was news to me. Improvement seen in some, followed by return of their symptoms. What's that about? Seems these guys are pretty sharp, like a lot of the grunts I knew over there. Vox populi often bring common sense to discussions. On the other hand, as Mencken said, for every problem there is a solution that's simple, neat and wrong.

This news sent a shudder of fear through me as my apprehensions about the treatment flooded into my thoughts. I have to talk to Alicia about this tomorrow.

"Has this happened to many patients?" I asked.

"I haven't done a count, but a few guys are talkin' about it," Matt said.

"Have you asked your Case Manager about this?"

"Yeah, she sort of blew me off, but I noticed she looked a little worried when I asked," George said. "Maybe the docs know something's goin' wrong. Whatever it is, I'm pretty sure they'll get it sorted out. They're a good bunch. On the other hand, maybe we oughtta press them on it."

Agitated by this news, I went back to my room and got in touch with Alicia.

"So what's up? You sound anxious," Alicia said when I sat down in her office. "Is this about Dietrich again?"

I told her about the conversation I'd just had. Her eyebrows went up as I spoke.

"That's curious," she said, looking away. A most unsatisfying answer. I squirmed in my seat. She knows something she's not telling me. She got up from her chair, went to the window and gazed out for a few minutes. What's she thinking?

As I waited for her to turn around and fully explain what's going on, I hoped there's a way to put healing back on track for those guys who're relapsing. It's really a bummer if the meds work for a short time and then fail. I got up. Alicia turned back from the window.

"I'm sure this is unsettling. I'm sorry – I can't explain this. I'll let you know if someone gives me a rational explanation for the changes you're talking about.

"I'll talk to you tomorrow," she said, with a tone indicating this conversation was over. "Try to stay upbeat."

Well, fuck! Yeah, sure, stay upbeat, easy for you to say. I was getting pissed at Alicia. She's no help. But before my anger pushed me into another explosion I fought to control myself, and this time I won.

"What choice do I have?" I put on a brave smile as I left.

Being with Matt and George again dredged up my time in the war, taking me back to my time with Danny. Damn! I still hadn't written to Katharine. I'll do that tonight. Hope the address Dr. Segal gave me is still where she lives. Not sure what I'll say but I've got to do that.

15

REACHING OUT

Dear Katharine,

My name is Tom Barrett. I'm a trauma surgeon and I was with Danny in the medical unit in the Middle East when he died.

I don't quite know what to say in this letter. First I must tell you how sorry I am about Danny. I felt such a strong bond with him and had tremendous respect for him as a surgeon and as a man. I'll never forget him as long as I live. I can't imagine how you've been able to carry on.

I feel I know you, because Danny showed me pictures of you, Hunter and Jeff. I loved hearing about you. He talked about you while we operated, when we were together between cases, and when we went running together. He was so proud of all of you. I envied him having such a beautiful family.

I wish there was something I could say to ease your pain but I know words fall short. I cared deeply about Danny. Losing him challenged me in ways I would never have predicted. I'm currently in a PTSD treatment program in Massachusetts, but if there is anything I can do for you and the boys, please let me know.

Sincerely,
Tom Barrett

I read it over several times. It didn't read well and didn't convey my feelings adequately but it was the best I could do. If she asked me to help in some way, I wasn't even sure I could, but at least I tried to let her know I knew and loved Danny. I dropped it in the mailbox in the rec room.

16

EMERGENCY!

"EVERYONE STAY IN YOUR ROOMS! Keep the corridor clear!"

Huh? What's goin' on? I woke up around seven to shouting and thumping of hurrying feet in the corridor accompanied by sounds of a rolling gurney. I jumped up and looked out my door to a sight reminiscent of my emergency room days – doctors, nurses, and technicians scrambling toward the room where a code blue had been called.

""Please, get outta the way!" a nurse cried as she shoved the gurney down the hall.

Patients then got back into their rooms but their doors were wide open. They peered out as the drama unfolded.

"Christ, there's blood all over that gurney. And he's got a tube stickin' outta his mouth!" someone yelled.

About eight attendants, nurses, and one emergency doctor raced the patient down the hall. It was Paul Walsh – pale as the sheets covering him with the crimson stains of blood making his pallor even more striking.

Oh, man, looks like he tried to end it. Maybe with a smuggled kitchen knife? Wonder if everyone else has the same guess.

Once the chaos subsided, Dr. Billingsley, chief of psychiatry, called everyone to the rec room to hear the official version of what happened.

"I'm sure you all know Paul Walsh was rushed to the operating room because of severe bleeding," he said somberly. "He's going to be okay because of our medical team's quick response. We called you together so you can ask questions and get clear about this upsetting event. Anyone want to start the discussion?"

Twenty-two heads moved to and fro to see who would start the questions. Howie Porter, a guy who was never shy, spoke up.

"The question on everyone's mind is whether Paul tried to kill himself."

"As you're aware, his medical condition has to remain a confidential matter. What I can tell you is that he's all right and will recover."

"Paul was doin' great until a few days ago. Seems to me – and the rest of us – that lately, lots of people aren't doing so good anymore," another patient said. "We been talkin' and wanna know if something's changed in the treatment."

"Treatment continues according to study protocol to assure the results are scientifically valid," Billingsley said in a strong and blatantly programmed voice. "So, no, we haven't changed anything. I don't think this morning's event can be taken as anything other than a coincidence, something that could happen in any study like this."

"This ain't no coincidence, Doc," one man said angrily. "We're all seeing big changes in the way things are goin'. So don't bullshit us. You scientific types gotta level with us guinea pigs," Others joined in and the buzz got louder.

Billingsley hesitated for a few beats waiting for the clamor to die down.

"As I said, the scientific team running this study hasn't changed the protocol," he said stiffly. He then softened his tone and dropped his formality.

"I have to admit the staff has seen changes in some patients. We're working our tails off to determine what's going on. I understand how you men feel, I really do. It's upsetting for everybody to watch positive results turning around, patients and staff alike. As soon as we know something definite, we'll tell you. We're not trying to bullshit you. We want you to feel secure that we're working on this. We feel our responsibility keenly."

That everyone in the room had lost some sense of trust was palpable. They better get some answers fast, I thought. I looked around the group. Billingsley's reassurance only went so far. Their anger was subsiding but I could tell pretty strong doubts remain, with several heads shaking negatively.

After a few more questions and answers, the group fell silent, many stared into their laps, clearly shaken by the morning's event. Dr. Billingsley, seeing no more hands up, headed for the door. Anxiety was as thick as fog. The men rose and began filtering out. Howie Porter stopped Billingsley.

"Something's different. You know it, I know it and everyone else in this room knows it. Why don't you level with us Doc? What's goin' on?

Billingsley looked nervous. This made me nervous. When a psychiatrist shows edginess, you know something's up.

"I've told you all I know," he said wearily. "All of us on staff, from clinicians to attendants, know some patients are going backwards. Please believe me, we're doing everything in our power to figure out why. But until we can pinpoint what's changed we can't give you any factual information."

"Well you guys are like the generals in a war, ya know," Porter said. "Troops depend on decisions you make so we don't get killed. This is like a war zone right now. Guys here are teetering on the edge wondering if this program is like all the others that failed them." Porter moved into Billingsley's space. "So Doc, you guys better get crackin' and solve this. Or else this will be like the charge of the light brigade into the mouth of hell."

Billingsley shuddered and squeezed past Porter hurried down the hall. I hoped he would convey to the rest of the staff how high the level of anxiety was and "the generals" needed to concoct some sort of strategy in a hurry. Otherwise there would be more Paul Walsh's rushed to the emergency department and some of them would not fare as well as Walsh did.

PART II

17

SUMMONS

WHEN TOM GOT BACK TO his room an envelope was on his bed. He tore it open. It was a cryptic message from Akira.

"Please call me on my cell when you get this. Akira."

What the hell is this, he thought. Akira and Tom agreed to keep each other at arm's length during Tom's time in Zylinski to avoid introducing any possible external factor that might influence treatment outcome. So this message was startling. Tom called him without hesitation.

"Hi Tom, thanks for calling. Sorry to bother you but I'd like to get together. Something's come up I need to discuss with you. Are you available, say, for dinner tonight?" His words were clipped, his voice wavering, quite out of character for Akira, whose self-control was always steady.

"Sounds like something that can't wait. Can you tell me what this is about?"

"Oh. I have a report deadline I'm dealing with. Can you meet me at my home tonight?"

The hair on the back of Tom's neck bristled when he heard the words, "A report deadline I'm dealing with" – that was their old emergency room code when a situation looked dire but they didn't want to alarm a patient. And meeting at his home? That seemed strange to Tom. He'd never been to his home.

"Yes, of course. I'll need a pass. Also, I don't know where you live."

"The pass is easy; I'll call the reception desk." He told Tom his address. "I'll send a driver. There's a parking garage for guests, around back, below the condo. I'll tell the attendant to expect you, and you can tell the driver to park and wait there," he said, adding more intrigue to this surprising development.

"Is six okay?"

Tom could tell Akira was deeply troubled from his conspiratorial tone and his clipped anxious demeanor on the phone. He was reasonably sure this summons had to do with the recent sequence of events – a probable suicide attempt, abrupt changes in some patients' symptoms and the emergency meeting Alicia mentioned. He'd find out soon.

"I'll meet you here when I'm done in there," Tom told the driver. "I'm not sure how long I'll be."

Tom followed Akira's directions to his unit, pressed the buzzer on his door.

"Tom, come in, so glad you're here," he said as he escorted me into his living room. "Sorry to be so opaque about meeting, but I think you'll understand after you hear what I have to say. Do you want to eat first and talk later or the reverse?"

"I'm very curious what this is all about, so why don't we talk first and then maybe we can enjoy dinner afterwards."

"That's my preference too. But at least let me offer you some tea or coffee. Which would you like?"

"Some of your delicious Japanese tea would be great." He remembered Akira's special tea from when they'd shared the on-call room back at Boston Medical. "With a little lemon if you have it. And sugar. No milk."

When he returned with the teapot and cups, he sat down and poured the tea silently. He glanced at Tom, his face solemn.

"So here's the dilemma, I'll get right to it," Akira said. "The emergency yesterday was a suicide attempt. I tell you that in confidence, although I'm sure most everyone has already guessed it. This is a sentinel event signifying an enormous problem.

"There've been some alarming changes in some patients' responses to the treatment protocol. It's spotty, not universal, but a number of patients have shown serious signs of regression. Everyone on staff is trying to figure out what's happening."

"I know, Billingsley held an information session. A lot of guys are really worried, scared and some are about to lose control," Tom said, feeling a familiar sensation of this most recent chance of getting his life back sliding away. To hear Akira confirm something was going very wrong was like pulling the trapdoor open to let him fall into a black hole. But his innate scientific curiosity kicked in and he tried to diagnose the problem.

"Could it be that the benefits of the drug aren't sustained over time? Like maybe metabolism plays a part? Or its effects peak, the body becomes acclimated and the drug loses its efficacy? I know I'm reaching, but…how well has the drug's metabolic activity been studied? I've read some of the studies but far from all of them."

"Tom, there have been over 50 studies about all aspects of this drug published. In the few previous long-term clinical trials it's acted like this very rarely. In a meta-analysis of the four best studies, there was a tiny cohort of patients with mild side effects and a still smaller number who became inured to the drug after variable periods of time." He poured me another cup of tea.

"But it turned out those who became immune to the drug's action were different in a very unique way. They had a specific metabolic pathway abnormality. In our study we've screened everyone for that metabolic error and excluded two men from the study for that reason."

"Does anyone on the team have any ideas? With all that brainpower I'd think someone would come up with a viable hypothesis."

"We've considered several possibilities: a mistake in the compounding process making the drug less potent, mislabeling of the drug containers, or some other poorly understood factor interfering with the drug activity."

He shrugged, palms upward in the universal gesture of perplexity.

"You could be right about the idea of the activity of the drug decaying over time, changes in absorption from the gut, some kind of resistance in the subjects' metabolizing of the drug. We just don't know."

"Have you been following blood levels of the drug?"

"Sure, they've been drawn and stored, but the problem here is that since it's a double blind study unless we break the code we can't know what the levels are. We may have to do that, though, if more patients regress."

"If you did that, it would spell the end to the study, wouldn't it? At least it would stop being a blinded study."

"It would undermine the study's methodology. All the work up until this point would be meaningless."

Akira looked away trying to hold his emotions together but with great effort.

"There are other possibilities we need to consider. We can't stop looking for explanations."

He leaned forward and touched my knee. "Yesterday's suicide attempt – the first since we began this program – could have been due to any of the things we've been discussing or –" he looked at me – "an actual cessation of medication."

Tom was confused. How could the medication just stop?

"We haven't broken the code to see if Paul Walsh was on the active drug or the placebo, but we suspect he was on the drug because he'd improved so much. If for some reason he stopped getting the active drug, this could have triggered the return of his severe symptoms."

"The guys at the meeting yesterday are convinced Paul was trying to kill himself," Tom said. "Doesn't help the mood of the group. I assume Paul's other symptoms were typical PTSD symptoms: increased flashbacks, nightmares, irritability, anxiety, depression."

"Right on all counts." He paused, running his fingers through his hair.

Tom had never seen Akira look this worried – a new situation he didn't like.

"You mentioned other possibilities. Such as what?" Tom asked.

"We've wondered if there'd been mistakes in dispensing the drug. Could it be some patients are simply not getting their drugs? We've asked the head nurses to monitor this but it's too soon to tell. That would be a surprise, but we need to check it out."

"I don't see how I can help with that."

"Well, you can't help there. But Dr. Mohammed brought up another possibility. He's our pharmacologist. He's concerned about how the drugs are handled within the pharmacy, the area he's responsible for. He wondered if carelessness of the handling of the drug in the pharmacy could be the answer."

He looked off into the distance.

"I have a thought. Can you come back tomorrow night? I'll get Mohammed here to give you some of his ideas."

"No problem. Same time?"

"Tom Barrett, Ahmed Mohammed."

"Pleased to meet you Dr. Barrett. Akira has told me of your long friendship. Sorry we have to meet under these trying circumstances." An engaging smile spread across Mohammed's face.

"I remember you from the day I heard all the confusing talk about the study," Tom said as he took Mohammed's warm hand into his.

"Ahmed and I went over the literature on preclinical trials in rats again to see if we might have missed anything about attenuation of the drug's effects over time," Akira said. "Nothing. Of course that's in rats, but that's all the information that's available."

"We also looked at the data on absorption from the gut," Ahmed said, "and that was uniform in rats – no deviation over time. And the blood levels in rats were surprisingly constant. I think it's reasonable to assume that absorption in humans is similar."

"Another piece in this puzzle has to do with the precision of the administration of the pills to the patients. So far the head nurses think this is proceeding according to protocol," Akira said. "The patients who are regressing are on different wards. It's hard to believe that nurses on different floors would be mistaking the protocol at the same time and in the same way."

"So I think we have to consider other possibilities," Ahmed said. "These have nothing to do with how the drug acts in the body. We have to ask whether it's possible that something has changed along the pill's lifespan from its synthesis through its journey from the compounding company to its being placed into the patients' mouths."

"We've talked with the CEO of Yankee Compounders – the lab that makes the drug for us – and he's discussed this with his staff there. They have a sophisticated automated quality control system that they're positive assures the compounding process is unchanged and the active drug is the same as ever. They're also adamant that when the drugs leave their plant they are pure and the packaging is being done accurately."

"So do we accept this as proof that the compounding is going perfectly?" Tom asked. "And the packaging? I recall a few years ago there was a drug compounding company in the Boston area responsible for contaminating injectable steroids with a fungus. Investigation showed this was due to poor sanitation at the plant and egregious poor supervision. The prosecutors alleged criminal neglect on the part of the owners and some people were convicted. A bunch of people died from this and contaminated vials sickened others."

"Different company altogether. Yankee Compounding passed all the new regulations and is one hundred percent compliant with safeguards that came out of that experience. The drug compounding industry learned a painful lesson from that case," Mohammed said. "But I still think we need the Department of Public Health to pay a visit to Yankee to double check so we know that link is okay."

"So, for the sake of argument, if we assume that investigation will tell us the drugs are being compounded properly, is the delivery system from them to us at fault somehow?" Tom asked.

"This is where you come in," Akira said. "I think you may be able to help us find out what's happening, where a breakdown may be occurring. You're on the inside of the clinical trial, more than any of us on staff. You have daily contact with the staff and with other patients. The other reason is – I trust you," Akira said, fixing his gaze on Tom.

"How am I gonna be able to find this out? I'm glad to help, but I'll need advice about how to proceed," Tom said as he contemplated what they'd told him. He was being asked to do some amorphous task with no idea of the objective. But this problem intrigued him. As what Akira and Ahmed told him sunk in, several questions surfaced in his mind.

"Let me go over what we know," Tom said, struggling to discern what he'd do to help. "Yankee makes the drugs and puts them in containers, delivers them to Zylinski. Right so far?"

"Yes," Ahmed said. "They package both the drug pills and the placebo pills in identical bottles but they arrive in color-coded boxes so only the pharmacy people know which is which. That is, assuming the color-coding is correct at the time the pills come into the pharmacy. And Yankee is sure they leave their place okay."

"So if you believe and trust the folks at Yankee, and you feel sure the nurses are getting the pills into the patients, in my thinking that leaves at least a couple of places where something could happen: during transit between the Yankee plant or here at our pharmacy. How many people work in the pharmacy?"

"There are six pharmacists working under a head pharmacist, Carrie Brink. Dr. Mohammed oversees the whole operation," Akira said.

"I have to interject here," Ahmed said, "that I'm not there when the pills arrive and I'm not involved in the handling of the pills. That's up to the pharmacy staff."

Is Ahmed being defensive? C'mon, use your head. Get over your suspicions about people from the Middle East. Ahmed is a pharmacologist, not a pharmacist, and not involved in the day-to-day operations of the pharmacy. A researcher and an expert on the way drugs behaved in biological systems. Ahmed was just clarifying his role in the pharmacy.

"Here's how the drugs come to us," Akira explained, ticking off details of the protocol for delivery. "Then, after the pill containers are sorted at the pharmacy, they're distributed to the inpatient service and the outpatient department."

Akira turned to Dr. Mohammed.

"Ahmed, tell Tom about your other suspicion. Tell him about your experience when you worked at that pharmaceutical company in New Jersey."

"Well, this company was doing a study on a blood cholesterol-lowering drug. Funny things were happening in that trial. It came out that someone was meddling with the drug intending to make the results unconvincing. So that got me to wondering – could someone be tampering with our drug somewhere along the chain of supply?"

"Why the hell would they be doing that?" Tom asked, puzzled by this story.

Akira looked at Tom intently.

"If someone wanted this clinical trial to fail, they could sabotage the outcome by tampering with the pills," he said after some time.

Tom stared at Akira.

"Huh? You know, that idea just pisses me off. How could anyone do that?"

"I don't have any evidence that it's being done. But Ahmed brought it up as another possibility, added to the others we've discussed. The idea is anathema to me, as it is to you, but then we're both abnormally moral." He smiled as he said this.

"But my question is – why? Why would someone do this?" Tom asked, still incredulous.

"So that's the second problem: the motive. If you accept the hypothesis that this is what's happening then I think the motive is the commonest of all – money," Akira said.

"Someone getting paid to screw up this study?" Tom said. "Now you've lost me. Who'd pay someone to do such a thing?"

"Okay, let me throw out a theory. Here's one way we can look at this," Ahmed said. "Competing pharmaceutical companies know we're conducting this study. They're also well aware that the potential profit for a successful drug like this is enormous. Think Valium or Zoloft or the statins for high cholesterol. If our study proves our drug efficacious, it represents a major breakthrough in the treatment of PTSD. That means unbelievable revenues for the drug company that has the patent. So it would be in the interest of a pharmaceutical company that already has a big-selling PTSD drug to make sure this clinical trial fails to show this new drug useful. The most effective way to do this is to sabotage the clinical trial."

"Jesus Christ," Tom blurted. "This can't be happening. I can't believe a reputable pharmaceutical company would do such a thing."

"So here's the thing," Akira said, picking his words slowly and carefully. "We know there are only a couple of drugs being widely used for PTSD. The most commonly prescribed one is made by Laxalta Pharmaceuticals. Even though it's used a lot, studies have shown that it's had only limited therapeutic success."

Tom interrupted Akira.

"Yeah, I took that crappy drug. It did nothing but make me drowsy."

"It's selling well because of the aggressive Laxalta sales force and their lavish advertising – in medical journals, popular magazines, on television.

You know the kind of ads – showing happy people enjoying life with the tag line of 'ask your doctor if XYZ drug would be good for you.' If our drug turns out to be highly effective for any number of debilitating conditions caused by adverse experiences, Laxalta stands to lose a large market share. So, in my analysis, Laxalta Pharmaceuticals is the prime suspect. I know that seems like a stretch of inference, but that's how I see it."

"Any other pharmaceutical company working on a breakthrough med? Especially when there's a high demand?" Tom asked.

"No," Ahmed said. "We'd have read about animal studies which pull in research dollars or we'd know about clinical trials starting up. Same way that information on our own study got out in the field. Specific details about protocol and the results are what's kept confidential."

Akira stared into his teacup, the fingers of his right hand drumming on the table.

"It's sabotage. And to carry it out requires someone working to torpedo our efforts," he went on. "If it's inside Zylinksi, that means we have a traitor or traitors who are motivated to disrupt our study. Why would they do that? Financial gain is again the most likely cause. I have no idea who on our professional staff would do such a thing. They've all been carefully selected, have impeccable scientific backgrounds, and seem to be committed to our research."

But there's that prick Dietrich, Tom thought. He'd be suspect number one in my book. My blood pressure goes up whenever he comes to mind.

"Guess I'm naïve," Tom said. "Of course I've heard the usual bad-mouthing of the drug industry and know they do some borderline unethical things to get people to buy their drugs. Billions of dollars spent on advertising, overstating benefits of their new drugs – all that. Change a few radicals and then call the altered drug 'new and improved.' But I didn't think they'd actually engage in – what would you call it – corporate espionage?"

"That's the term, and the fact that there's even a term for it makes it seem more real," Akira said, warming to the argument. "Greed is driving some of these companies and the competition is brutal. Look at what some of the pharmaceutical companies are doing with drug prices – they're going into the stratosphere. Making huge profits on drugs that people must have if they're to survive. It's inhumane, unethical, and immoral. But greed is a powerful incentive. Look at what the tobacco companies did to push their nicotine delivery systems. And they're still doing it, making carcinogens wrapped in paper or as electronic cigarettes, marketing to children and advertising all over the world to make new captives to nicotine addiction."

Akira paused, realizing he was getting overwrought.

"Sorry, but this infuriates me. We worked so hard to bring this drug to millions of people whose lives will be so much better without demons from traumatic experiences chasing them."

He rose from the couch, walked over to Tom's side and sat down.

"Would you be willing to help uncover who's doing this? I can't ask staff since any one of them may be in on this. I hate to consider that, but it must be true. I'm essentially asking you to be my mole, reporting only to me. I simply don't know how else I can get to the bottom of this. What's happening now could destroy everything we've worked to accomplish. And there's urgency, Tom. We only have a week or so to figure this out. I won't put every participant who was taking the med in jeopardy for any longer. Actually, the safety of all participants – and staff for that matter – is in question."

Akira was staring at his clasped hands, his face downcast and his shoulders slumping. Tom had never seen him so deflated. Ahmed had stayed quiet during Akira's rant.

"I'm not sure how, but I'm willing to do whatever you want, my friend. So what should I be doing in my new role as undercover detective?" Tom asked with a half-smile.

"I have no experience in this sort of thing or advice either, except to ask you to be observant," Akira said. "Put your thinking cap on and see if you can come up with some kind of approach. Look at it as a diagnostic problem. Where's the lesion? That's what we have to find out. If you notice anything out of the ordinary – anything – let me know. I'll get a couple of cell phones with numbers known only to you and me. If you see anything suspicious call me. I'm not sure what I'll do when you call, but I'll record them to use in future decisions."

"As patients we're not supposed to have cell phones, according to Diane, my nurse," I said, beginning to like my new role as undercover agent. "I guess I'm going to have to hide it carefully so she doesn't blow my cover. I'll just have to be circumspect about keeping the phone on me or under my pillow at night."

"Of course, you can go about this any way you wish. You have carte blanche. Just be careful and don't do anything to get in harm's way. The people behind this must have no scruples and could be dangerous."

"What about hiring private investigators, you know, real professionals who know what to do?"

"I considered that, but outsiders would be noticed right away and raise a big red flag to anyone involved. So I want to keep this here, in this room, at least for now. This is new territory for me, too. I'm playing it by ear. You and Ahmed are the only ones I've discussed this with and I'm going to keep it that way for a while."

"What about your Board of Directors?" Tom said. "Don't you think you need to let them know of this threat? They're ultimately responsible for the Institute's welfare. They certainly have fiscal and ethical responsibility."

Akira looked out of the window at the ebbing light as the sun dipped below the horizon, weighing Tom's question.

"I suppose I have to let them know, sooner or later. Right now I just don't know whom to trust. Could be someone on the Board is implicated. Well, that's really paranoid. Why would anyone on the Board participate in sabotaging a drug trial in their own institution? I suppose if they held stock in a competing company they might. I don't know," his voice trailing off.

"The staff is aware of the changing clinical picture so we're putting safeguards into place, heightening security, ramping up therapy sessions in order to prevent further self or other harm," Akira said. "Let's see what you can find out, then I'll go to the Board. Don't have anything conclusive at this point anyway. "

"When the time comes, I'd get the advice from the Chair of the Board," Tom said, his newly found mission making his mind work in ways it hadn't for a long time. "My guess is that he or she will want an urgent board meeting. The Board's gotta know about this. You'd be jeopardizing everything – the study, your position – what would this place be without you - by not keeping them fully informed. Besides, you need advice on how to proceed. They might not want me, a patient with psychological problems, to undertake the task you've laid out for me."

"That's why I needed to talk to you first, Tom. Trust is hard to find these days. I'll get in touch with Mrs. Hollingsworth, the Chair of the Board. She's been Chair from the beginning of the Institute and I trust her. Good advice. I'll do that first thing Monday morning. For now, let's eat!" he said, seeming more encouraged now than when I arrived. "There's a variety of sushi – made it myself – a hobby that's been invaluable for keeping my mind off work. And would you like sake?"

"I'll stick with the tea, thanks," I said.

"Ahmed, what about you?"

"I don't take alcohol – you know, religious reasons. I'll also take tea."

After dinner he served a delicious dessert while Tom and Akira reminisced about their time together as surgical residents. Ahmed smiled as he listened to their stories and told a few of his own about his training in Pakistan when the company he was working for supplied HIV drugs to Africa for one-tenth of what the U S pharmaceuticals were charging for the same drug. It may have been the reason he suspected sabotage as the explanation for what was happening at Zylinski. He'd seen bad behavior by pharmaceutical companies before. Because he saw a renewed purpose in life, Tom felt more optimistic than he'd felt in a very long time. He had a mission. He was needed, no longer a lost soul.

Tom woke the driver up and went back to the Institute. At ten o'clock he checked in at the admissions desk. The clerk seemed disinterested, even annoyed that he bothered to show him his pass. He slipped into his room as unobtrusively as possible, but Debbie came into his room, not in a good mood.

"Okay, Dr. Barrett, I know you had a pass tonight, but you're late and we have to attach your sleep monitors. You keep doin' stuff that can get me into trouble. Just sit tight there for a minute and I'll call the techs to wire you up."

"Sorry Deb. Didn't mean to get you into trouble." She wasn't placated, but the tech came right away.

Tom settled into bed and stared at the ceiling. Sleep was hard to come by, with a jumble of worries spinning behind his eyes. Distracted, he got up, detached the monitor wires and went to the ward kitchen, ate some cereal, always a sure soporific for him. When he went back to bed he reattached the monitor but still couldn't fall asleep. This detective work was all very exciting, but the specter of his own pathology hovered around his head. He was sure the monitors would record a lot of agitation this night. Tom's mind was in overdrive.

What if this whole endeavor goes down the drain and I'm left with nightmares, explosive outbursts, and all the other baggage of PTSD? What'll happen to my fantasy of recovery, reuniting with Cynthia and recapturing my professional identity? This is truly an existential threat.

He got up, carrying his monitor wires, and roamed around the room.

Am I more agitated today than yesterday because I was on the meds and now I'm not? Or is this just the terror of thinking that hope is crashing and burning? The sushi that had gone down so pleasantly a few hours before was burning in his throat, and he was getting short of breath.

Should I go over to the emergency room? Get a tranquilizer shot so I can sleep?

"Deb, I need to go to the ED," he said after she responded to his call.

"What's wrong?" she said.

Tom told her how anxious he was feeling.

"I'll get an attendant to accompany you," Deb said, concerned.

At the emergency room he saw eight other guys pacing around like caged animals. Matt was one of them.

"Where the hell you been? You having trouble too?" he asked.

"Nervous as hell. Have you seen George?"

"No, he's not here. But he thinks he was never on the real stuff so he's not relapsing, he's never gotten any better. Some guys here are like me – got better, now the bottom dropped out. I think we were on the pill, and now the pill's not working."

They got shots of Valium and within a few minutes Tom was drowsy. He headed back to his room. Once there he fell into the trough of medicated sleep.

18

MOLE

IN THE MORNING TOM THOUGHT: it's a brand new world, so…how am I going to behave in my new role as Hercule Poirot? Where to begin? Maybe I can get Matt and George to help – without their being aware. Maybe if I present a hypothetical mystery as a game, paralleling what's going on here, they'd offer ideas about solving this riddle.

He went to the gym after the morning medical rounds and found them at the pool, talking.

"Morning," he called out.

"So where the hell were you last night before I saw you in the emergency room?" Matt asked.

"What are you, my mother?" Tom laughed.

"We wondered if you and Diana had decided to get it on," George said.

"I should live so long," Tom said. "Besides, she's got a boyfriend. And I have a girlfriend."

"So, that where you went last night?" Matt persisted.

"How'd you know I was gone?"

"The jungle telegraph is always buzzin' here."

"Well, I did have a date. But it's none of your business," Tom smiled. If they're this good at tracking my movements, maybe I can use them in my new spy game, he mused.

"So what do you think happened to Walsh?" Tom asked.

"Well, everyone's pretty sure he tried to meet his maker," George said. "It's just one more sign something's gone weird."

"Any more thoughts about the pills?"

"Well, a bunch of patients are bitchin' something's changed. The other thing – we heard staff had a big meeting yesterday. So something's up," George said.

"So, let's say you guys were hired as outside consultants to investigate what's goin' on. How would you go about it?" Tom asked, probing for an opening.

"My guess is that whoever's makin' the pills is screwin' up," said Matt. "Bein' careless. Puttin' the wrong chemicals in the bottle."

"Yeah, but that assumes everyone's on the up and up," said George. "My bet is someone's on the take, getting a bunch of money to put sugar pills in place of the enzyme pill."

Jesus, Tom thought. Is he a conspiracy theorist, cynical or does he know something?

"Who'd pay them to do this?" Tom asked.

"Well, it'd have to be someone who didn't want the world to know this pill works. To me this means an outfit making a competing drug that would tank if this pill was better," George said.

Holy cow! Tom thought. George seems to have this whole thing figured out. It's as though he was in on my meeting with Akira and Ahmed last night. Did he know? If so, how? I doubt that he'd be talking this way if he were involved somehow. He's evidently given this a lot of thought. Pretty sharp tack. But he'd been a cop once.

"Interesting. How'd you come up with that?" Tom asked, trying to mask his surprise at George's intuition.

"Seems pretty obvious. When I was a cop I was interested in the investigative unit that seemed to have all the fun. I've read mystery stories by the barrel and think I'm pretty good sniffing out the motives of the bad guys," George said. "But then things happened and I went into the service instead."

"Cool," Tom said, nodding, thinking I could probably learn something from this guy.

"I've also been around. Know a little about human nature."

As they left the pool George headed to his locker to change. Matt went in the opposite direction, so Tom followed George.

"Can I talk with you a little more about this pill thing, maybe later this afternoon? Been worrying about this. What you said gets me thinking – maybe you're on to something."

"You mean my theory about bribes? Hardly original, but why do you want to talk about it? To what end? We can't do anything about it. What's goin' on in this place only reinforces my gloomy outlook on the world."

"Better to think about this than a lot of other things…"

"Yeah, gotta point there, man. Sure." George said.

"Great, how about the library, after lunch?"

"Catch you then," George said and walked away.

Tom wasn't exactly sure how to proceed with George. He didn't know anything about him. What were his beliefs, his attitudes, his propensities? Was he honest? Tom didn't even know why he was a patient at Zylinski instead of the Military Hospital. Of course he had PTSD or he wouldn't be in this program, but what were the origins of his condition, where'd he been? The problem for Tom was that he didn't have time to be sure George was trustworthy. He might just have to take a chance and trust him.

Tom got to the library early to reserve a carrel, little outcroppings in the third level, overlooking an atrium. Perfect, he thought. Shades you can close for privacy. I definitely want that. When he saw George come in below, he went down and intercepted him, leading the way upstairs.

"You're making this like a clandestine international spy operation," George laughed.

"Hey, whisper, will ya?" Tom said, joking, leading him to the carrel and closing the door. "So, how'd you get here?"

"I walked over from the unit," he grinned. "Just kidding, I get what you're asking. You want to know about why I'm at Zylinski. About my war experiences.

"Well, I had the standard horror show over there, you know, guys blowing up, splattering their body parts over me, staggering around with their flesh on fire after getting napalmed, skin falling off their face from mustard gas. You ever see someone get gassed with sarin? Convulsions, agony, then relief in death. You name it, I saw it. I'm a pretty tough customer, but the stuff I saw no one should ever have to see.

"It was when I got hysterical and charged into a mob of those yahoos, spraying bullets into them, killing about a dozen of 'em, screaming like a crazy man, that my captain realized I'd had enough combat and took me out of service. He knew I would've been dead meat by wading into another bunch of those bastards if he hadn't pulled me out."

"You said you were a cop before you came into the military, right?"

"That's one thing I did, but that came after I got my degree in Black History. I wanted to go to graduate school at 'Bama, but ran out of money. My parents were bad off, one with diabetes, the other with cancer, so they couldn't help. So the best job I could get was with the local police. They needed a token African American cop so I sat for the police exam, got high marks. They had no choice but to hire me. Daddy and Mama were going downhill health-wise and I worked my shifts so I could take care of them. They died within a week of each other, Mama first and then Daddy. So after they died I joined up with the Army, mainly to get veteran's benefits to come back and finish my graduate degrees. Man plans, and God laughs," he said with a wry smile.

"What about you?"

Tom told him his story, confessed his guilt about being a non-combatant, having only seen and treated the wounds and counting the dead bodies. As they talked Tom felt more confident that George was honest. But could he trust him? Hard to know, but time was short and Tom had to decide. He couldn't pull this whole operation off without help and George seemed a good bet. He wished he could feel one hundred percent sure but he decided he'd have to go with his gut.

"When we were talking about this messing around with the pill, you said your guess was that someone was getting paid to screw them up. What would you do if you were a detective trying to find the person doing this?"

George crossed his arms, looked up at the ceiling before he answered.

"You have to find out first – assuming I'm right – where the dirty deed gets done. And then you'd wanna know who, working wherever that might be, is susceptible to a bribe – in other words, who needs money real bad?"

"How the hell do you find out who's liable to accept a bribe? They say everyone has a price."

"True enough, but crossing the line needs a motivator. Like a desperate need for money."

"Well, say your theory's correct, couldn't it happen at any point along the chain of the pill's life – from the compounding of the drug, the delivery of the drug to the Zylinski pharmacy, to the distribution to the end-user, the patient?"

"Yeah, right. Process of elimination. Start at the source. Unless there's some real bad actors at the manufacturer, they have all sorts of controls over the production of the drug."

"Unless the compounding company is getting lax in its controls."

"Well then you need to know whether the pills arrive pure and unadulterated at the pharmacy. So you'd have to check the pills before they get to the pharmacy."

"Looks more and more like a complicated mess. How would we find out who needs money?"

"That's a problem you and I can't solve. You'd need someone on the inside of this place who knows a lot about the people working here. Like someone in personnel, or what these highfalutin organizations call Human Resources."

They talked a while longer but Tom wasn't ready to take this any further with George until he'd talked with Akira. They walked back to the unit.

"Thanks for talking about this with me, George. Can we discuss this some more, maybe tomorrow?"

"Sure, man, kinda interesting getting my mind off my own problems. Still don't know where we're goin' with this, though."

"Neither do I, but it's almost as good as reading a mystery story."

As soon as Tom got back to his room, he called Akira. He picked up after the first ring, knowing it was Tom.

"Tom, what's up?"

"Um, I need to ask you about something."

"Sure, fire away."

"Well, I've been talking to a fellow patient – he used to be a cop – about the pill dilemma. Like all of us, he's suspicious about what's going on. So I asked his opinion. His explanation was so brilliant that I wondered if he had inside information. But he'd not be telling anyone if he were involved, right?"

"Go on."

"Well, I think I trust him. Detective work isn't my expertise, but I think it's his. Can we recruit him to help me?"

"Who is this?

"Name is George Logan."

"Let me check him out and I'll get back to you."

"OK. And Akira? We need to move fast. The natives are really restless."

"I know. I'll get right back to you."

About an hour later, Akira called Tom and gave him the okay to bring George onto the case. Tom swung by George's room, poked his head in his room and asked him to meet him out on Vinny's path.

"So here's the thing. Someone on the professional staff wants me to help figure out what's going on. He thinks what they're seeing has to be due to a change in the drug. You seem to have guessed a lot of this." Tom picked up a couple of stones and flung them into the stream, watching them skip across an eddy. "I'm no expert in detective work. I know how to put people back together when they've been hurt, but this detective stuff isn't my thing. It seems to be yours. I need your help. Interested?"

"Who's asking you to do this?" he said, looking skeptical. "What the hell would we be doing? Where would we start? What kind of personal risk are we looking at?"

"We have carte blanche. The guy asking me to help is a higher-up at the Institute and totally trustworthy. But we need a strategy right away."

We sat down on a park bench near the stream. George stretched out his long legs, put his hands behind his head and gave out a long sigh.

"I don't know why I let you talk me into thinking about this. Not sure I want to get more involved. Still don't know what we can do."

"Hear me out, George. The way I look at it is that there are several possibilities: the pharmacy receives all placebo pills, so the compounding company or someone who transports the pills here is doing it; or, someone in the pharmacy substitutes placebo for the real drug. It seems to me that the distribution of the pills from the pharmacy to individual patients involves too many people – mainly the nurses who give us the pills on all the different floors – to make that a reasonable path to follow."

"So," George said, now warming to the task, "it's pretty simple what we could do. I must be nuts to play this game with you, but seems what we need to do is grab some pills as they come to the pharmacy – without anyone knowing we're doing it – get someone to test them to find out if they have the active ingredient, right? Easy, huh?"

"Yeah, not so easy, but that's step one. If legitimate pills are being delivered to the pharmacy then something must be going on after they get here. In the second phase, we'll need somehow to get inside the pharmacy to see if we can finger a culprit changing the pills."

"Can you find out from your 'higher-up' when the pills get here, you know, what time of day do they come in, what kind of truck brings them here, and all that?"

"I'll find out what I can. Let's meet tomorrow morning, here, say around 10?"

George groaned.

"Don't know why I'm such a sucker to go on with this. But I have to admit, it gets my juices flowing. Kinda exciting. After all the boredom of this place, something to do."

"Okay. But remember. Don't talk to anyone. Can't raise anyone's suspicion. We have no idea who's involved."

19

THEFT

"AKIRA, HOW CAN I FIND out when the compounding company – what's its name? – delivers the pills to Zylinski?" Tom asked on his phone. "What's the protocol when a delivery is made? There must be a tight system for the transfer."

"Yankee Compounders. I'll find out what I can about the delivery procedure. Problem is, I don't want to arouse suspicion by direct inquiry. Maybe I'll go down to the loading dock where the shipments come in, chat with one of the workers. It's hard, though, to be sure of anyone." He paused. "I never thought I'd say something like that. This turn of events is making me crazy."

"Patients know something's up. Some are getting their old symptoms back. They're angry, anxious or depressed – or all three. We sure don't want another suicide attempt. When Walsh made his attempt it stirred up a lot of people.

"The other thing is that I've successfully recruited George Logan."

"I can't say I'm 100 percent comfortable with that, but if you think you can trust him – and he has some talent in this area – go ahead, but be careful. We still don't know what's happening. If this is corporate sabotage – and that's not a sure thing – we don't know how far these characters – whoever they are – will go. "

A couple of hours later, Akira sent a text message.

"The drugs come to the dock precisely at 10:00 PM each night. As soon as they're off the truck, they go directly to the pharmacy."

"What he didn't tell me was who was involved in the unloading and the transporting of the shipment," Tom told George when they got together.

"Well, one way to find out – go down there around 10 o'clock and watch," George said. "From the shadows. We'll have to dress like Ninja's." He winked at Tom. "Well, you will," he said, flexing his dark-skinned arm.

They met in the sub-basement tunnel at 9:45, and headed to the loading dock. A couple of rats scurried by as they found their way to the loading platform. The smell of cigarette smoke greeted them along with a murmur of two male voices. They paused, looked at each other, and decided to hold back since there was no truck visible.

A few minutes later a small white unmarked van backed into the middle bay. A short fellow jumped out and gingerly hopped onto the dock, opening the van's back doors in a single move. A small forklift slipped its prongs into slots of a palette holding boxes of pills, backed out, and swung it onto the loading dock floor. The van driver spoke to a man on the dock, had him sign a paper, closed the van doors, jumped back into his truck and was gone. The men whose voices they'd heard cut the shrink-wrap off the boxes of pills, readying them for transport on a black metal cart. They joked around and seemed disinterested in what was in the boxes. It was apparent their only goal was to get them on a cart bound for the pharmacy and get back to their iPad games. Tampering with the pills clearly wasn't taking place here.

Hustling back down the tunnel, George and Tom ran up a stairway, and peeked through a door opening onto a hall. There they saw an athletic African-American messenger pushing the cart carrying the pills towards the pharmacy, his unique foot-long, thick braid was encircled with two white bands. Exchanging a quick look, George smiled and gestured for Tom to follow him. They now were in an area in the hospital used by staff and patients alike. They'd worn non-descript clothes so they drew no attention while they nonchalantly fell in behind the messenger pushing the cart.

I hope we can pull this off fast, Tom thought. That messenger's so tall and his strides are so long, I don't know if we can snatch a box off the cart before he gets to the pharmacy window.

"That's a real cool hairdo you got, man," George said to the messenger, who stopped walking, and turned around to see who was talking. Seeing it was another African-American cat, he said: "Took me eight years to grow my hair that long. It's my signature. So you groov'n on it?"

"Sure am. Get any smart-ass comments about it?"

"Look at me," he said, grinning, pulling himself up to his six foot eight inch height. "You think anyone's gonna mess with me?"

"Would you call that a braid? Sure ain't dreadlocks," George continued.

As he distracted this enormous man, Tom quickly swiped two boxes from the cart, one color-coded blue and the other red. He slipped them under his jacket.

"Enjoy your day, man!" George said as they strolled away. The messenger waved and pressed a call button at the pharmacy window.

"Hold up," George whispered, pretending to tie his shoes. "Let's see who's taking delivery."

Casually, Tom glanced around. A young woman's face appeared at the window, smiled and exchanged a greeting with the messenger.

"Here you go," he said, passing the boxes to her.

"Nothing suspect in either of those two as far as I could see," George said later as they compared notes. "Seems to me the pills arrive at the pharmacy with no interference. So my feeling is that between these two places – loading dock and pharmacy window – the transfer process looks clean."

"Yeah, agree. And we know who receives the deliveries – smart to get that piece. We still don't know whether Yankee is properly formulating and labeling them, but we will as soon as I get them to Akira – whoops, forget you heard that name. Anyhow, he'll get them analyzed to see if those boxes are correctly color-coded. If the pills are okay, then we gotta trace what happens to those boxes inside the pharmacy."

"Awesome job jawing with the messenger, by the way."

"Thanks, man. I do believe I've got some talent in police work," George grinned.

"I hope no one's counting the numbers of boxes before they're distributed. Maybe after we get a couple pills out of them we should take them back to the pharmacy and say we found them on the floor. Think they'll buy that story? Or would they get suspicious?"

"Think we ought to just set them on the counter and vamoose, hoping that pharmacy gal will think she overlooked them and neglected to put them in her tray.

"So," he continued, "if one of these has the real medication, can we assume Yankee Compounders are delivering valid stuff and a switch is being made in the pharmacy?"

"That's only an assumption, but it's what we have to base our next steps on. We've got to get information from someone inside that pharmacy, and I'm not sure how we're gonna do that," Tom said. "First things first. I'll get these pills analyzed and we can go from there."

Tom called Akira and took the boxes to him.

"How long will it take to get results?"

"A few hours. I'll use an outside lab for obvious reasons."

"Do you need to keep both boxes or just a couple of pills from each of them? I'd like to get them back to the pharmacy so no red flags pop up. I'm worried someone might discover two boxes are missing."

"Just some pills from each color-coded box. I'll have to assume that the pills in each box are the same and a spot check is sufficient. I agree you need to get them back. Hope no one actually counts the pills in the vials."

"Another thing – can we get an inside pharmacy person to cooperate in this investigation? We need to scope out any funny behaviors there."

"I've been thinking about that, trying to figure how to find that out. There's a woman– Melissa Jenkins – who's been around since I came here," Akira said. "I've called Human Resources explaining that I'm considering giving her a commendation for her good work. The manager of HR considers her highly reliable, so I'll talk with her, very discretely. It'll be pretty tricky without tipping our hand. We'll see."

"When you're talking to HR, would it be possible to find out if anyone working in the pharmacy is having serious money problems?"

"I can ask. They might not know anything about personal financial problems."

"Are you going to tell Melissa Jenkins about George and me?"

"I don't know yet. I need to know first if she can be trusted. Don't want to reveal any more than I have to."

"At the same time we're doing this, maybe I'll ask Cynthia if she knows anyone at Yankee Compounders. Her hospital uses them for some of their experimental drugs. It's possible she may know someone there. Could be a way to look into that end of the chain. What do you think?"

"Well, if you can't trust Cynthia, who can you trust? It's a little risky. Be sure she understands that. I'm worried we could be dealing with some dangerous players if they sense we're sniffing around."

"Okay, I'll feel her out carefully about it."

Tom shut off his phone and stared at the floor.

Do I really want to involve Cynthia, he wondered. But if she finds out later that she might have helped, she'd be disappointed – probably angry – that I hadn't asked her. I'm only guessing she even knows anyone at Yankee. Maybe she couldn't find out anything even if she did. All we could expect her to do would be to nose around to see if she can learn anything. That shouldn't put her in any danger, right? Tom's internal dialog with himself spun round and round. He decided to call her.

"Hi Cyn. How are you?"

"Tom? Is it really you? I thought you weren't supposed to call during this phase of the treatment. What's up?" she said, her voice at least one register higher than usual.

"Well, I needed to call you because there have been some interesting developments. I wanted to update you."

"Really? What kind of developments? Sounds ominous."

"I'll get a pass this evening and tell you the whole story. Are you available?"

"Well, I guess I'll have to cancel my date with this fantastic guy I met," she teased. "Of course I'm available. I'd love to see you. You can fill me in on all the things you've been doing at that evil place," she said, with excitement in her voice.

Best conversation I've had with her in weeks, Tom thought. Wonder what her recent thinking has been. Just no telling what's next in this strange thing called love.

"So I'll get over there around eight. Okay?

"Eight it is. Can't wait!"

Tom's pulse clicked up. Her response was unbelievably positive. He wondered if this was due to her therapy sessions.

20

REUNION

NOTHING BUT GOOD MEMORIES FLOODED Tom's senses as he walked to her condo. He knocked twice with the familiar brass knocker she'd brought from the old place. As she opened the door his heart pounded as her presence washed over him. They wrapped their arms around each other, kissing like a couple of adolescents. The familiar scent of her shampoo and the musky fragrance of her skin made Tom light-headed and, for the first time in months, he was aroused. She could tell. They stumbled into the bedroom and he forgot what his mission was until they had made love.

"So, whatever they're giving you over there at that Institute is fantastic," Cynthia said with a wink. "Reminds me of the old days when you were just a hayseed from Ohio."

"Yeah, well I think I'm in the cohort getting the real drug – at least for now. That accounts for my feeling better generally. Could be it's the next big thing for depressed libido," he laughed.

"What do you mean, for now?"

"That's the reason I'm here to talk to you. Some funny things are going on. Right to the point, we think there's some hanky-panky going on somewhere in the delivery chain of our magic drug."

Tom told her the whole story about trying to find out where the dirty tricks were.

"So where do you think?"

"We don't know, but Akira asked me to help find out. So my question for you is: do you know anyone at Yankee Compounding?"

"Where? Yankee Compounding?" She looked at him quizzically. "I don't think so. Why would I know anyone there?"

"Well, I vaguely remember you helped in some drug studies at Boston Medical with medications formulated at Yankee."

"Oh, those trials with neuro conditions." She pushed up on one elbow. "Come to think of it, there is one woman I remember talking with during research they did on Alzheimer's disease two years ago," Cynthia said. "I could still have her name in those old files. I can dig them up and maybe find her name."

"See, we need to narrow where we look. If we can eliminate Yankee then we can focus our attention on other areas. But we've gotta do this fast before any more patients go into a tailspin."

"I'll root through my records. I think I know where to look," Cynthia said, as Tom rose to leave.

"Christ, it's past ten. Gotta get back so they wire me up for the night. Wish I could stay here with you but my jailors would send out a posse. Call me if you have any luck with your search. And," as he opened the door, "thanks. I love you." They came close to ending their visit in the same way they started it, but Tom knew he had to race back or he'd catch hell from Debbie.

Tom got back to his room and Debbie came in.

"You're getting to be a major problem. I need to get you hooked up for sleep," she said with an edge. "You know I could get into trouble because of you. The powers that be are already giving us all a hard time about giving out the meds. My nurse supervisor has been watching us all like an eagle. I'm surprised she's not in here now to see if I've done my job."

"Sorry, Debbie. Don't want to get you in trouble. Call the wire guy."

Tom lay down on the bed when the tech came and put on his crown of wires. The last thing he remembered before he went to sleep – another benefit, he thought, of getting the real medicine – was the lingering fragrance of Cynthia's perfume.

His phone rang around six in the morning.

"I found the name of that woman at Yankee," Cynthia said. "I'll call her after nine and see if she remembers me. She'll probably wonder why the hell I'm calling her. Don't know exactly how I'll interest her in meeting. Maybe I can lie about some aspect of that Alzheimer study Yankee was making pills for. Maybe make her curious, I don't know. I'll get back to you later, okay?"

"By the way, how're you this morning?"

"Feel okay, but not great. I'm wondering if I'm off the real drug now, like a lot of other guys. I feel a little down, but it's early.

"Cyn, thanks for this. Right now I think the problem lies in our pharmacy. Not sure – just intuition. Call me soon as you know anything. And," he said, "be careful. We don't know what's goin' on or who we're dealing with."

Tom went down to the swimming pool and found George alone in the pool finishing some laps.

"What's new, man?" he said as he dried his face and head.

"Well, Cynthia's gonna talk with a woman at Yankee, find out how that place functions. Probably a dead end but worth a try. Told her I think our pharmacy is the place we need to focus on."

"Why? We don't have evidence yet."

"I don't know why, I just do. Proving it is another thing."

"I agree right now it seems like it. We need the pharmacy's floor plan to see if there's any place we could conceal ourselves inside that window. Some place to watch what happens to the pillboxes after they're pushed through that window."

"I'll ask Akira if he can get us a floor plan of the pharmacy. He must've been involved in the building plans for the Institute."

Tom called Akira, told him George's idea.

"Yes, I know where the original blueprints are – still in my file cabinet. I'll pull them out. Everyone's gone for the day, so come up to my office."

Tom hustled up to his office. He saw no one in the corridor so he figured he was unnoticed.

"That was quick," Akira said as Tom walked into his office. "How much have you learned? Anything new?"

"Well, I asked Cynthia who knows a woman from Yankee. She's going to call her. I doubt she'll be able to tell us anything useful. Any success recruiting Melissa Jenkins from the pharmacy?"

"No, I decided against that. Too risky for us and for her. We need another plan."

"Actually, George and I have another plan – to sneak into the pharmacy tonight to watch – you know, it just occurred to me, we could video record – what goes on inside the pharmacy when that transfer happens from the loading dock to the pharmacy. Can you lend us a smartphone?"

"The conference center has a ton of smartphones. I'll get one to you," Akira said as he sidled over to his desk. He picked up a sheaf of papers and handed them to me. "Here's the blueprint of the pharmacy. I think you can go in this door," indicating an opening at the back end of the facility. "No one will see you slip in there – it's an emergency only exit, essentially never used. It opens onto a field outside. Oh, and don't worry, it's not alarmed. I'll get you a key. You say you want to go in tonight?"

"Yeah, we've gotta move. It's important for everyone in the study and it's personal for me. I think I've been on the real drug and in the last twenty four hours I'm feeling different – sort of a backsliding sensation. So I have skin in this game."

"Take a look here. There's that window to the hall where you said they bring the pills in," Akira said, pointing to the blueprint. "There's this large room inside the window– probably built to accommodate equipment we never got. For some reason there's this balcony overlooking the whole room with this stairway going up to it. The balcony has a little room behind a glass – there," his pen resting on a spot on the blueprint. "My guess is that it was built for surveillance, but I don't know why. Couldn't have been more well designed for what you're trying to do.

"Good luck with this. We've seen about another dozen patients with a similar deterioration. We've got to get back on track – soon – or this whole clinical trial will go down the drain."

"Did you talk to the Chair of the Board yet?"

"This morning. She concurs with what we're doing but only for the next day or two. If we can't solve this quickly, though, she wants to call in the FBI, local cops and the State Police. I admire her for taking this chance." Akira said. "I want to find out who these bastards are and prosecute them, make them pay and go to prison."

Surprised at Akira's anger and his uncharacteristic language, Tom took the blueprints and headed for the door.

"Oh, another thing," Akira said. "We need to be especially careful, so coming to my office is unwise. You could be under surveillance. We need to communicate only by phone or in person at my condo – not here in my office. Okay?"

Hearing the rising tension in Akira's voice and manner, Tom simply nodded as he left and headed back to where he and George had agreed to meet. They examined the blueprints then went to practice their way to the back door to the pharmacy they'd use after dark. It was not hard to find, but very exposed, with no trees or bushes around it.

"Boy, this door is really easily seen. Think that'll be a problem?" Tom asked George.

"After dark we should be able to get in without being seen. I'm not concerned."

Akira sent the smartphone, the key to that back door and a couple of flashlights in a plain sealed box to Tom's room. Debbie the evening nurse looked askance at Tom when he went into his room.

"Okay, Dr. Barrett, who's sending you presents and what are you up to now?"

"Probably from Cynthia, the love of my life," he lied.

"I have to check what's in the box to make sure it's not prohibited food or drugs. I just don't know what to make of your behavior lately."

"Be my guest," Tom said, worried that when she saw a smartphone she'd confiscate it.

She watched as he opened the box.

Tom got inventive. "This is to record our group sessions," he said, hoping she'd buy the story. "Actually, it's from one of the biggies in the Institute. It's a new wrinkle in the research protocol."

"Really?" She looked skeptically at Tom, then at the smartphone. "Are all the groups going to be recording their sessions?"

"Nope, we're the guinea pigs for this. Just our group at first. If it works out then all the groups will record them." He was getting to be as good as a politician at prevarication.

"Interesting. I wish they'd let us know these things. We get blamed if anything goes wrong. They're already hovering over us like drones to see that we're doing our job."

They must really be bearing down on the nurses, Tom thought. First Diana, now Debbie complaining about tight supervision of their work.

"Okay, see you later. Hope the recording helps in your group discussions."

Tom exhaled when Debbie left hoping she truly accepted his story and didn't talk about it with the head nurse, the one who was under strict orders to check on all the pill administration and probably also anything else untoward. He was also relieved she'd not noticed the flashlights or the key. But he'd be done with all these things after tonight if all went well.

At 9:30, darkness settled around the building. George and Tom went outside so their eyes would accommodate. They wanted to get through the back door in plenty of time to get to the ideal vantage point to see and record the vial transfer.

"This may be our only chance to watch and record what goes on here," George said. "If something doesn't go right here I'm not sure what our next step might be."

They crept through the back door, found the stairs to the balcony behind the glass window, and climbed them soundlessly. They were glad to see good lighting at the place the vial boxes would be transferred. Below them and in perfect viewing they saw the same young woman they'd seen last night from the corridor. She was perched on a stool by the window where the vials would be handed over. She was fiddling with her phone and seemed oblivious to everything else, but then she turned abruptly and looked in their direction. They froze in place, fingers crossed they'd not been spotted.

"Who's there?" She stared for what seemed like five minutes, got up from her stool and walked towards them, squinting as she left the lighted area. Tom and George were both breathing in short shallow intervals.

"Guess I'm hearing things," she said to herself, apparently satisfied that what she'd heard was nothing. She returned to her window to await the bell telling her to open the window for the delivery.

George and Tom got into a good position to record. At just after ten o'clock George turned on the smartphone video. As they watched, the woman opened the window to the corridor and the same messenger with long hair lifted the tray of boxes onto the window's platform. She signed for them, turned and placed them on a cart. Another woman came into view and the two spoke a few words, and the first woman left. The second woman – one they'd not seen the night before – waited a few minutes standing by the cart and watched the other woman leave.

She then did an extraordinary thing: she opened the boxes and dumped half of the red-capped vials into a plastic bag and put that under the cart. She then pushed the cart into another room out of sight. George moved quickly and silently away from their position to follow her movements, the smartphone running all the while. Tom didn't know whether he should follow George or stay put but finally decided to try and stay close to George in case he needed assistance. By the time Tom caught up to where George had moved to follow the woman's movement he was headed back, signaling Tom to head for the door. He gave Tom a thumbs-up. They descended the stairs in total silence and slipped out the back door, carefully shutting it behind them. Outside the building, George smiled.

"I know at least one person messing with the pills," George said. "She may not be the only one but I recorded her dumping pills from the red-capped vials into an incinerator. Have to find out who she is. I couldn't risk getting any closer to her to read her nametag, but I know I got great pictures of her."

"Not a bad night's work, eh?" Tom said as he called Akira hoping they could get together right away. He answered promptly, as always.

"Boy, have we got news for you!" he exclaimed, unable to contain his enthusiasm. "We want to look at these pictures right away."

"Come on over to the condo. I can't wait. This is exciting. Maybe we'll crack this!" Akira said.

This time George went with Tom.

21

REVELATION

WHEN THEY GOT TO AKIRA'S condo Tom introduced George to Akira and they wasted no time before looking at the recording.

"That's Carrie Brink," Akira gasped as he watched. "How could she do such a thing?"

He jumped up and paced around his living room, his hand raking through his hair.

"I can't find words to describe how angry and upset I am she's mixed up in this. What poor judgment I have."

"What does she do in the pharmacy?" Tom asked.

"She's Head Pharmacist. Great credentials," he said, still on his feet, walking aimlessly in and out of the kitchen. "Why would she want to do it?"

"I don't mean to be crass, Dr. Yamaguchi, but money makes the world go 'round," George said. "Am I being too cynical when I say everyone can be bought?" He looked at Tom and Akira for an answer to his rhetorical question. Getting none, he turned back to the evidence.

"No question about her ditching the pills. I saw it plainly and the video captured it. As much as you'd rather not think she's involved, this is pretty plain."

"I don't doubt it," Akira said in a quiet voice, finally sitting back down. "I wonder who else is involved. And, following what you said, who's paying for this?" Akira burst out. "How can we ferret out the contemptible miscreants bribing people to disrupt something that could help thousands of patients?" He fell silent for a few seconds as George and Tom looked at each other, not knowing a way to console Akira.

"One thing we need to do right away," George said, "is put a tail on Carrie Brink, to follow her every movement and see who she's in touch with, both inside and outside Zylinski. What's your guess about the inside person she's working with?" George asked, looking from Akira to Tom, but finally fixing on Akira.

"I can't imagine who it could possibly be. Who would stoop to this?" Akira said, looking bewildered. "I know them all well, at least until now I thought I did. I've worked with most of them for several years. Impeccable credentials. This is just inconceivable. I'm not naturally suspicious, so I guess my radar doesn't pick up latent deviousness. I certainly didn't suspect Carrie.

"I suppose it will come out so I'll just tell you. I have a personal relationship with Carrie Brink," Akira said sheepishly.

Tom looked astonished. He knew nothing about Akira's personal life, either now or in the past. He couldn't recall ever seeing him with a "significant other," either male or female. Akira never discussed his feelings or thoughts about friendships or intimate relationships. The closest he'd ever come to confiding in Tom back in their BU days was when Tom once invited him for dinner and asked if he had a partner he'd like to bring.

"I'm much too boring a man to have a partner," Akira had said.

There was no rational reason why Tom couldn't imagine Akira with a life outside of work. Tom always had considered him to be an ascetic man who, unlike other human beings, didn't have an inner psychic life or a need for an intimate relationship with someone, or even a sex drive. Tom was simultaneously pleased Akira wasn't all work and nothing else, but sad his relationship turned out to be with a now-exposed treacherous woman. Turning back to face Akira, Tom brought the conversation back to considering other staff involvement.

"My guess is one potential culprit is that prick Dietrich," Tom said, still smoldering about his encounter with him. "I haven't liked that son of a bitch since the first time I met him. He's my number one suspect."

"Emil Dietrich? What happened with you two?"

Tom told Akira the story of his encounter with Dietrich. Then George broke in.

"Whoa, Tom, just because you had one bad visit with him doesn't necessarily make him a guilty party," George said with a smile. He turned to Akira.

"Dr. Yamaguchi, I think now's the time to get outside help. What's needed is a professional with investigative skills and unlimited time. Someone who can move around outside the Institute, follow Carrie Brink wherever she goes to try to find out who she's working with. I'm talking about a real private eye. Tom and I did a pretty good job identifying the main actor but she can't be acting alone, just can't be," George said, warming to the theorizing. "Gotta be at least one other inside operator and people outside with big bucks. We need to know where the money's coming from, that's the big question. As I said before, I think it must be a worried pharmaceutical house."

"And that, to my mind, points directly at Laxalta. They've the most to lose from our drug being proven successful," Akira said, facing George. "I agree about an outside investigator. I'll move on this first thing tomorrow morning."

We rose to leave and Akira stood up at the same time.

"As saddened as I am to learn about Carrie's involvement, I'm still very grateful to you guys for all you've done. I don't know how to thank you."

George and I both shrugged without saying anything as we left.

My phone rang as we left Akira's office.

"Tom… I struck out with the woman from Yankee" Cynthia said. "She doesn't have a clue about anything. I didn't get far into our discussion before I could see she couldn't be helpful. Sorry. We knew it was a long shot."

"Well, it turns out we know where the problem lies – as I suspected, right here in the pharmacy. Akira's gonna hire a private detective agency to go forward."

"How'd you find out it's in the pharmacy?"

"Tell you all about it when I'm with you."

"And when, pray tell, will that be?"

"Soon I hope, but I'm not feeling so good. I'm sure I'm off the real drug. I'm going back to my room, try to get some sleep. Call you tomorrow."

22

TOM

EVERYTHING AROUND HIM WAS RED. Blood rose over his ankles as one body after another hemorrhaged on the operating table. Nothing he tried staunched the flow of blood. He looked over at the next operating table where Danny was fighting to stem the red flood, but all he could see was an infinite repeating mirror of dead bodies all around them, on the floor, stacked up in the corner, sprawled out the door. The fixed stares of the eyes in the dead were trained on Tom, the one who'd failed them in their fight for life. The anxieties and shortcomings of his life and surgical career collected around him as he sank deeper into the pools of blood, moving toward suffocation by drowning.

He woke up choking, in another tooth-grinding panic, worse than all the previous frights. This convinced him he was off the active drug, his pills having been switched – like many others – to duds. He was one of many who'd reverted to pre-treatment symptoms. The research portion of his brain – that small part that continued to work – considered this convincing evidence that the drug had been effective. To think that it had actually done some good was heartening, but he knew he had to resume real medication quickly or he'd end up like Paul, unable to cope and headed for relief by suicide. Tom wondered how many of his fellow patients were experiencing this kind of reversal.

When the gray night gave way to shafts of morning light he waited until Diana came on duty and pushed the call button. She came in right away.

"What's up Tom? It's real early."

"Nightmare again. I'm really jittery. I know I'm not getting the pill anymore."

"I've been giving it to you right along. Why do you think that?"

"It's a long story and I'll tell you later. I need to talk to Alicia. What time is it?"

"A little after seven."

Tom knew Alicia would answer his phone call even if she weren't in her office.

"I need to see Alicia. I'm going to call her and see when she'll be coming in."

"Ok, I'll do your morning pill now. Do you want some breakfast?"

"No, skip breakfast. I'll be out of here as soon as I can get a time to see Alicia."

Diana left and came back with the pill. He swallowed it down in what he knew was a charade.

"Alicia, it's urgent that we talk this morning. I'm having a major relapse and have a good idea why. I need to see you to discuss this."

"Come over now. You're not the only one in trouble. The whole damned place is in an uproar."

"You start," Alicia said as soon as she closed the door. Tom told her about the phantasmagoric nightmare he'd had.

"The whole staff is on alert because we think there's been a widespread medication error," she said. "We're trying to find out where the problem is. But for now we're in damage control mode hoping we can put a stop to this."

"It's no error," he blurted out without thinking that even Alicia could be under suspicion. "It's sabotage. We know a lot about it."

"What are you talking about? Who is 'we'?" Her eyebrows were high and her eyes wide open.

"You sound like you think I've gone 'round the twist. I'm upset, sure, but I'm not crazy. I've said more than I should've," Tom said, jumping up and waving his arms around his head, nearly stumbling over the furniture. "I'm telling you someone's substituting placebos for the real drug. That's why I'm relapsing. It's the reason the place 'is in an uproar' as you put it."

Realizing he'd just told Alicia everything, failing altogether to consider her possible involvement in the plot, he stood in front of her, confronting her in a way he'd never done before. His heart was thumping against his ribs, his vision blurred. He was on high alert. Alicia was staring at him, her pupils widely dilated, her arms crossed defensively across her chest.

"Listen carefully to me now," he said with clipped precision. "Whatever I've told you has to be in strict patient-doctor confidentiality. You understand? I'm trusting you not to disclose this to anyone."

"Of course, Tom," she said, her voice calm but, her discomfort apparent as she crossed and uncrossed her legs and moved back as far as she could in her chair. "Can you tell me what's happening to you now?"

Tom felt some reassurance from her voice and was able to back away from his aggressive stance.

"My nightmare was like I used to have regularly. I'm scared shitless, to tell you the truth," he said, with sweat pouring off his forehead, his palms and armpits following suit. He reached for some tissues, his intention tremor nearly knocking the box off the desk.

"I'm getting more jittery and jumpy as I speak, l can't hold myself together. I need SOMETHING NOW to calm me down! Do you have any Valium? Give me something quick! Right now!"

Alicia jumped up, glad to be out of her chair, away from Tom's threatening posture. She went to the sink for water and grabbed some pills from her cabinet. She handed them to Tom silently, waiting for him to swallow them.

"I just heard about this crisis when I came in," she said, after it appeared Tom was under slightly better control. "A number of patients are like you, agitated and racing around the wards. An emergency meeting has been called in about fifteen minutes. All staff members, except the emergency department, have to come. I hope what I just gave you will tide you over until we have a plan to deal with all of this. Go to emergency if you get no relief from the pills I just gave you."

Alicia paced around her office, fumbling as she gathered up patient record folders, glancing repeatedly at Tom, wondering what his next moves would be. She knocked over a water pitcher on her desk, cursing as she wiped up the spillage. By now Tom had spent some of his agitation and recognized how threatening he'd been to the person who had been so helpful to him over his course of treatment.

"Look, I'm sorry I've been such a pain," he said as he wondered if he should tell her the whole story. "You should know what's been happening so you can help.

"Another patient – George Logan – and I, found out at least one person in the pharmacy is discarding active pills. We don't know who else is involved. I'm suspicious of almost everyone here since we don't know who's colluding in this sabotage."

Alicia stopped mopping up the water and froze in place.

"I'm not involved, I swear. I have no idea who is," Alicia said defensively. "I must say I'm not glad you told me. Now I'll be looking in all directions to see who might be guilty, an uncomfortable position to be in," she said irritably, walking to her window, focusing on the finches and the chickadees down at her bird feeder. She then turned back to Tom. "But it is what it is. I know now and have to carry on. We've got to fix this problem quickly and get back to the clinical trial. In staff meetings up until now everyone thinks we're on the right track." Her hand went to her forehead. "Poor Akira. This must be so hard for him. He's so dedicated to this research. It's his life.

"I've got to go to the meeting," she said, resuming her professional demeanor and stuffing her files into a satchel. "Stay here in my office if you'd be more comfortable here. Call Dr. Crocker to get more Valium if that seems to be helping, and to let him know your symptoms. Do that today. He'll be at the meeting for the next hour or two, but go this afternoon. If you need to go to the emergency room, leave me a note."

She touched Tom on the shoulder as she left. He sat there for a time waiting for the Valium to work and headed back to his room, dove into bed and lapsed into a deep medicated sleep.

Around three he woke up, glanced at the clock, bolted out of bed and hurried to Dr. Crocker's office.

"Alicia told me you might call. I'm so sorry you're having symptoms again. Come in and tell me what's happening."

Still drowsy from the Valium and the nap, Tom shuffled into his office and climbed onto his examination table. He described his nightmare and the return of his tremor, and general dysphoria. Crocker listened attentively as always.

"You may know this is a problem several patients are having right now," Crocker said. "There seems to be some kind of response change to the medication. Some of us think patients are becoming inured to the drug – the positive effect is wearing off. It may be it has a shorter half-life than we expected, like some other drugs, and some patients have passed that half-life point. We just don't understand all of the nuances of this new drug."

"That's not it," Tom exploded. "Someone's messing with the drug. It's being thrown out and placebo substituted for it." Acting on impulse he told him about the iPhone recording in the pharmacy.

Crocker's face flushed red, worry lines on his forehead deepening.

"Jesus! Have you told anyone else about this?"

"I haven't told anyone," Tom lied, without mentioning Alicia. "What we don't know is what the next steps should be. How can we get the real drug back to the patients?"

"This is really distressing news. I'm glad you let me know. It sure puts a different face on the problems. He unlocked a wall cabinet, took out a vial and handed it to Tom. "More Valium tablets – one every four hours – you can use until we get this sorted out. I know it makes you dopey, but better than the dreams and the tremors."

"Thanks. I hope you get this straightened out in a hurry." He left Dr. Crocker's office and went to Vinny's path, hoping to calm down.

23

VINNY'S PATH

DAYLIGHT WAS FADING AS TOM left Crocker's office and headed for some relief on Vinny's Path. He hoped the serenity of this gentle glade would allay his apprehensions. The autumnal air was sharp and bracing against his face as he gazed up into leafless trees then down to the stream's flickering reflections as it trickled over pebbles in the creek bed. The purity of nature reassured him that someday he'd be whole again and life held promise.

There was no sound when everything went black.

Rough fabric scraped over his head and shoulders. Gasping for air, he was back in Sexton's grip, his movement forcibly restricted, imaginary walls collapsing around him. Sinewy arms first crushed his chest then slid to his feet, sweeping them off the ground as though some videogame character had snatched him up.

Within seconds his feet were bound together, ropes twisted around his chest and belly. He struggled for air as he was tossed like a grain bag into a truck that sped out of the staff parking lot.

Two male voices, one from the driver, the other near his head barked in guttural bursts. A knee crushed his chest pinning him to the floor of the van. The speech of his captors flipped from an unrecognizable language – was it Russian? – laced with broken American slang and profanities. To Tom it was like one of his nightmares, but this was no product of sleep and dreaming. Sure that he was going to suffocate, he struggled in vain against the restraints, sweat soaking the material covering his head.

After what seemed like hours, the van lurched to a halt, throwing his assailant forward off his chest.

"Hey! Shit for brains up there! Tell me when you're gonna stop like that!" he screamed, and scrambled back to open the van's rear door.

The two goons dragged him out, bouncing his head against the rear bumper, all the while cursing at one another. They hauled him inside a cold building. Maybe a deserted warehouse? Tom was tossed onto a hard cement floor. They pulled off the encircling bindings and yanked the sack from his head. Tom sucked in large gulps of air, grateful to be alive but confused and fearful of what would come next. After they slammed the door leaving him alone and shivering in a small, windowless room, he heard only muffled echoes of their voices from a cavernous nearby room.

What the fuck's going on? Who are these guys? Is this about what George and I were doing? Could George have blown my cover? Was I wrong to trust George? Or have they shanghaied George too?

As Tom lay there confused and panicked, he thought what all prisoners think: how can I get away? He tried to put the pieces of this puzzle in place. Why have they taken me? What do they want me for? How long will these guys hold me captive? What are they going to do to me? Is this the end? How do I keep from going berserk? What was it I'd been told about visualization and imaging to bring anxiety down?

He tried visualizing Cynthia, their vacations in the Berkshires, the time they went to Italy. Momentarily he was in a zone of detachment and quietude. This must be what Buddhist meditation gives people when they substitute internal for external reality, he thought. This could be how prisoners can live from day to day.

Abruptly a door opened and Tom saw a gigantic menacing figure silhouetted in the opening. He stooped to duck through, turning sideways to maneuver his bulk into the room. He hovered over Tom who saw nothing but a looming shadow in the dim light.

"Where's the smartphone?" he growled.

"The what?" Tom said, surprised by this abrupt question coming completely out of any context. A sting spread across his face as this hulking figure backhanded him. Blood gushed down his cheek. It quickly dawned on him this guy was asking about the video George had taken in the pharmacy.

"Don't play dumb with me, you pathetic creep. You know what I'm talkin' about. If you want to play this game, fine. I love beating the shit out of people, seein' them scream in pain. I love seeing wusses like you cringe and blubber as I break their teeth and pull out fingernails. I'll make you blind and deaf, you hear? I'll cut off your balls! You wanna do it that way, I'm all for it. I can't wait to start. I must break you."

As Tom's eyes grew accustomed to the dark, he could make out a square face on a hairless head. His cauliflower ears bore witness to many blows. Piled up scar tissue ran on either side of the gash that ran from his right ear to his upper lip. The back of his neck was a ripple of thick folds. His hands would need extra large gloves, his misshapen knuckles bearing knobby scar tissue. His hands felt like coarse sandpaper as they struck Tom's face. His sickening pungent body odor, a mix of sweat and alcohol, swept into Tom's nostrils.

"I don't know where it is," Tom croaked, sure of what was coming next.

His clenched fist struck Tom's right eye, which began bleeding and swelling.

"We know about the video you took in that nutcase hospital. We know all about it. So where the fuck is that smartphone?"

"Don't know."

Another shot across his jaw, an audible sharp crack and another gush of blood. Tom spit out a tooth.

"As I said, I got lotsa time. When I get tired of making you scream and hurt I got a backup who's even meaner than me." He laughed. "We got this contest goin' to see which of us can break you. So sooner or later you'll tell us what we wanna know. Sooner you tell us where that fucking phone is the better off you'll be. I'm gonna leave you here and let you think it over. We ain't got much time so when I come back you better give me answers."

Tom was nearly unconscious. Blood was all over him, one eye was closed, his jaw – certainly broken – hung loose on his chest. He struggled to spit the bloody saliva out of his shattered mouth.

What's next? Get a grip. Where'd this mad beast come from? I heard that giving a name to oppressors sometimes makes it easier to deal with pain. I'll call this reptile Igor.

For Tom, the unfortunate truth was he didn't know where the iPhone was. Did they leave it with Akira, he wondered. I think so. But I can't tell that to this psychopath. They'd go after Akira. Apparently no one is safe, beyond reach. Did Akira turn the phone over to the cops? Did George keep it? If he did, he's in danger too. Maybe they already have him, in another room. How much do these guys know?

Footsteps drew closer to the door, then paused. Tom braced for another assault. Both Igor and the other guy whose knee had been in Tom's chest during the ride in the van came into the room. Tom had to pee and had no choice but to let it go in his pants. They laughed when they saw the stain spread down his trouser legs. Igor put his hands under Tom's arms and lifted him up, turned him around and the other one began pummeling Tom in his midsection.

"Ready to talk yet, piss ant?"

Tom couldn't answer, rapidly losing consciousness. "Igor" slammed his body against the wall, his head striking the concrete with such force that Tom slumped unconscious to the floor.

"You dumb shit, why'd you do that? We can't get answers from a dead guy!"

"Shut up, he'll come to and he'll be so terrified he'll answer our question. So chill out, asshole."

Mazarov and Rusker were their real names. They went to another ramshackle room in the abandoned warehouse, arguing about what to do next. Mazarov was an overbearing Russian whose vodka consumption was legendary among his fellow Russians in Worcester. He glared at Rusker who had the temerity to challenge him. If he hadn't needed Rusker to carry out his nefarious assignments, he thought, he'd get rid of him in a convenient way. Rusker, almost as big as Mazarov but only half as mean, hailed from rural Mississippi and had about 40 IQ points on Mazarov. Why he put up with Mazarov was a question he'd asked himself many times, but this big Russian bear of a man did provide him with work and money.

"I'll go check on him and see if he's ready to talk yet," Rusker said.

He went back to the room where Tom still lay unconscious on the floor that was now more slippery with coagulated blood. Rusker kneeled down to check him. His breathing was shallow, his heart rate slow and his skin a putty color.

"Jesus Christ, this doesn't look good," Rusker said out loud. I've done a lot bad things to people to get them to talk, but I've never killed anyone, he thought, and I don't want to start now. He went back to where Mazarov was swilling down more vodka.

"Our boy ain't lookin' too good, Maz. He's pale as a sheet, breathin' slow. Have a hard time feeling his pulse it's so weak and slow. Think we oughta get out of here before he croaks?"

"And not get paid for this job? You chicken-shit, he'll come around and then we'll pull what we want outta him. I'll throw some cold water on him in a little while, work him over again, get his dirty little secret, and then clear out. Have a drink?"

"You know I hate vodka, I drink rum," Rusker mumbled, still worried that their hostage was about to die.

As Mazarov downed the last of his vodka, they heard noises outside the building. The sound of vehicles sliding to abrupt stops and the gallop of shoes on macadam pierced the silence in the empty warehouse. Mazarov and Rusker rose as one, looked at each other with alarm as they recognized the sound of a police team being assembled outside.

"This building is surrounded by police officers," the voice on a bullhorn blared. "Come out with your hands up. You have no chance of escape. Don't be foolish and try to run. We have orders to shoot to kill."

Mazarov and Rusker thought they were prepared and well-armed, ready for such a standoff. Both had AK 47's, plenty of ammunition and a box of World War II hand grenades. They scrambled up to the second floor and took positions on opposite sides of the building, hoping to blast their way out. Their van was still in the same spot they left it and getting to it would be tricky, but they knew a footpath through the woods behind the warehouse in case they had to leave the van behind. They fired into the circle of police shields from their separate vantage points.

A volley of gunfire from the police team responded to this fusillade. An eerie silence followed.

"Come out with your hands up! The building is surrounded. SWAT Team is in place. Come out now," the bullhorn voice blasted. Mazaroff and Rusker's desperate AK 47 shooting from the second floor did nothing but prompt a barrage of missiles crashing through the windows. It wasn't long until their eyes began to sting. Mazaroff and Rusker knew teargas – they'd run into it before, but in their rush to capture Tom they forgot to prepare for this possibility by bringing gasmasks.

"Jesus, I can't see! My eyes are on fire! I can't breathe!" Rusker screamed.

"Close your fuckin' eyes and keep pumping shots into those assholes! I'm tossing the grenades. We're gonna get outta this, so quit whinin'!"

Mazarov threw the grenades one by one but his pitching arm wasn't major league and the grenades landed and exploded too close to the building to do any harm. Shrapnel scattered but the shields of the teams repelled the fragments with little damage. Rusker emptied his clip but couldn't see to reload, his eyes now bright red and full of tears and Mazarov was staggering around blindly in the other room. He realized he'd tossed grenades that had no effect on the police siege. Even he, with his limited grasp on reality, realized they were goners. Either they'd die resisting or surrender and live.

"We're coming out!" Mazarov shouted from the second floor. Mazarov and Rusker's feet stumbled as they groped their way downstairs, still blinded by the teargas. The standoff had lasted only several minutes. Police officers, looking like space aliens with gas masks over their faces and Kevlar suits, rushed into the building, handcuffed Mazarov and Rusker and shoved them into a cruiser.

"There's a room down here. See if he's in there," one of the cops said. They opened the door and saw Tom lying on the floor.

"Good God, is this guy dead?"

One of the troopers knelt beside Tom, putting his fingers on his neck to check his pulse. He bent down to put his ear next to Tom's bloody nose checking for air movement.

"Get the EMT's and paramedics in here pronto," he said. "Guy's damn near gone. Barely a pulse. Color stinks, barely breathing. Hope they can revive him."

The EMT's hustled in with their equipment and a gurney, assessed that Tom still had a weak pulse but hanging on to life.

"Get a tracheal tube in, I'll get the IV goin'," the paramedic shouted to her assistant. "He's lost a ton of blood." She turned her head to speak into her collar mike to the hospital emergency department. "Alert UMass Emergency. Bringin' in critically injured man. Blood pressure in shock territory, 60/30. Pushing vasopressors now. Needs mucho fluids. Will need blood soon as we hit the hospital. If we make it."

"So let's move it, get him outta here."

The ambulance screamed into the bay at the emergency department and the emergency crew rushed Tom inside.

"Boy, someone beat the crap outta this guy. What the hell happened to him?" one of the residents said. "Are his vitals stable? Yeah? Need an emergency CT scan. Got this mushy area on his head so probably got intracranial bleeding, brain damage and big time raised intracranial pressure. Get neurosurg and general surg down here stat. Facial bruises and slack jaw look like both maxillary and mandibular fractures. Might have intra-abdominal and intra-thoracic lesions as well – a bunch of bruises on his chest and belly. Rib fractures for sure. Maybe a punctured lung. We also need skeletal x-rays if he's stable. Whoever beat him up did a number on him. Lucky if he pulls through."

24

A Delicate Balance

"CAT SCAN SHOWS BLOOD IN the epidural space, early brain swelling," the neurosurgery resident said. "Get him upstairs fast. Gotta evacuate the blood or it'll push the brain further across the midline – the end for this poor guy. Let's get cracking."

Tom was hurried to the operating room and both the neurosurgical team and the general surgeons went into action, an unusual dual surgical approach because of his multiple life-threatening injuries. His fractured jaw would have to be repaired later.

Dr. Battersby, chief of neurosurgery and lead surgeon, quickly laid back the scalp over the site of his skull fracture.

"We'll take a generous hunk of bone out to get to the blood clot." The smell of sawed bone filled the operating room. Beneath the removed fragment of bone were two ounces of blood trapped in the epidural space.

"See, the pressure from this blood compressed those torn arteries inside this closed box of the skull," Battersby schooled the residents as he worked. "That, combined with his shock-induced low blood pressure compressed the hemorrhaging. But we gotta be careful here when we suck out the clot. Need to find and clamp those broken blood vessels. Now that his blood pressure's restored, bleeding could start up again."

Working below, Dr. Carter, the general surgeon, inserted a needle into the abdominal cavity.

"No free blood in the belly," he reported. "When you're done up there in the head we need a chest and abdomen CT to be sure there's no organ damage in either place."

"Bottom just dropped out of his blood pressure," Dr. Weinstein, the anesthesiologist, said in the calmest voice he could muster. "You about done? I'll shoot in some pressors but then we need to get him to recovery."

"Okay, we'll close and leave the bone fragment out. Probably better that way anyway. Can we go five more minutes?"

"Make it snappy, I don't like the look of this," Weinstein said.

Battersby hurriedly closed Tom's incision and the circulating nurse hung another bag of blood, pumping it in fast. After Weinstein added pressors to the intravenous infusion, Tom's pressure began to rise.

"Get him down to recovery quick. Need to start meds to avoid more brain swelling," Battersby said. "And the general surgeons need to do more diagnostics on the chest and abdomen."

Akira arrived at the hospital around midnight, shortly before Tom came to the recovery unit. The police notified him about Tom's abduction and rescue right after the police scooped him up in the warehouse and brought him to Memorial. Akira called Alicia to go with him. After Tom was in Recovery and the nurses had secured all his lines and monitors, Dr. Battersby came out to talk with them.

"It's touch and go. His blood pressure plummeted while we were operating so we had to close quickly. Dr. Weinstein managed to get his pressure up before he left the operating room. He seems stable now, but much depends on how much brain swelling he has."

He turned to Akira.

"You know the risks in these procedures. We're trying to keep the swelling down by the usual methods, but they're not great. We have problems balancing therapies – keeping his blood pressure normal with enough fluids but not over-hydrating him making the brain swelling worse.

"I know you're doing your best. We'll keep hoping for a good outcome," Akira said, knowing what he was mouthing were empty platitudes. He looked at Alicia.

"Alicia, you know how to reach Cynthia? In all the confusion I don't know whether anyone told her Tom's here."

"Oh God, no. I have her work number somewhere. Maybe in Tom's file. I'll find it and get in touch with her right away."

Cynthia was in a deep sleep when she picked up the phone.

"Cynthia, Alicia Kleinman here. I'm at the surgical recovery room at Memorial Hospital. Tom's here, just got out of surgery for traumatic head injury. Can you get here? Akira's here with me."

"He's where? What? Traumatic head injury? How'd he get that?" she mumbled, shaking off the confusion of deep sleep. "What the fuck's goin' on? Did he jump out a window? Try to commit suicide?" she sobbed. "How could that happen?"

"Sorry to be so blunt, but I'll fill you in when you get here. Nothing like that, but it's too complicated to tell you on the phone. The best I can say right now is that he's in stable condition after neurosurgery. Come soon. He'll want to see you when he wakes up."

With trembling hands Cynthia tore off her nightgown, slipped on her slacks and threw on a sweatshirt.

She picked up her phone, dialed her office number and left a message for her secretary.

"I have to go to Memorial Hospital. Tom's there. Won't be in tomorrow. Call Rosalie and tell her." She rushed out the door.

At the hospital she ran frantically to the desk nearly knocking over an elderly woman talking to the clerk behind the desk.

"Where's Tom Barrett? Where can I find him?" she demanded of the startled clerk.

"I'm sorry, ma'm. Who are you?"

"I'm his wife," she lied. She looked around the room and saw Akira slumped in a chair. After four hours of waiting, Akira had fallen asleep but he awoke abruptly, seeing Cynthia.

"Cynthia, glad you're here," Akira said, leaping up from his seat. He turned to the clerk who was staring wide-eyed at this agitated woman. "I'll take care of this.

"Tom's still asleep from anesthesia. Alicia went down to the cafeteria for coffee. Come over here, sit down and I'll try to bring you up to speed."

Breathing deeply, with tears streaking down her face, relieved to see Akira but still confused and scared, she sat down on the cold naugahyde couch.

"It's my fault, Cynthia," Akira said, the fingers of both hands on his temples. He told her everything, ending with his abduction and beating. As she listened she stood up, paced back and forth, her arms wrapped around her chest, shaking her head, incredulous that this could be happening.

"He told me he was trying to solve this pill mystery when he asked me about knowing anyone at Yankee Compounding. Is that what got him here in intensive care? In coma? Shit! This is so awful!"

She strode to the window looking out, trying to gather together the flight of thoughts, trying to ground herself, confronting this latest emotional turmoil.

"Cynthia, I'm Alicia Kleinman, Tom's Case Manager," a woman said, coming up behind her.

Cynthia took a deep breath and turned around to regard Alicia. "I feel like I know you, even though we've never met. Tom's very fond of you. I don't know what else to say – this is such a shock," Cynthia said as they all sat down.

Akira allowed some time to pass until he thought Cynthia was able to hear about Tom's injuries. When he saw she had composed herself, he turned to her and told her about his status. He said nothing about what Battersby had told him about Tom's prognosis. Cynthia set her jaw, her eyes narrowed, her heart raced and her face reddened.

"Who the hell are the ones who beat him up? Where'd they come from? How'd they take him out of the Institute with nobody noticing? This is just beyond belief!"

"He was outside when they grabbed him. His buddy Matt DiMasio saw what happened and thanks to him got the police involved early enough to rescue him. The two psychopaths who beat him up are in custody. We know who they are but not much else."

Akira didn't know what more to say. His guilt about involving Tom in this debacle was profound and now Tom was barely holding on to life. All his fault. He knew if Tom survived there was no way to know what deficits he'd have. In Akira's experience with brain-injured patients they were seldom the same as before the injury. Even without paralysis or loss of mental capacity, their personalities were often different.

Dr. Battersby came out of the recovery unit, still in his scrubs. Akira introduced Cynthia, telling him of their relationship so he'd keep her informed about Tom's progress.

"Alicia and I have to go back to the Institute to help with the turmoil," Akira told Cynthia. "The two men who took Tom are being questioned. There's a lot more to this, and when things calm down I'll give you a more complete picture. Call me anytime you need to. Will you stay here?"

"I'll be here. What else can I do?"

Cynthia sat at Tom's bed impatiently, willing him to wake up so she could see him, talk to him, give him a reason to live. But by dinner he was still unconscious, continuing on life support. His vital signs were stable so he was transferred to the intensive care unit. The ICU team tried to remove his breathing tube twice to see if he could breathe on his own, but both times he failed and they had to reinsert the tube.

Around ten, she got a call.

"Cynthia, this is Akira. How are things going?"

"Still asleep. Dr. Battersby told me his vital signs were stable, but he's still in coma. No one knows how long that'll last. Battersby told me I should go home, not much I can do here. He'll call me if anything changes. I'm really tired so I think I'll go."

She left reluctantly but knew Battersby was right. She went with a sinking feeling, having seen these kinds of cases before.

At home she ate a bagel with little interest. She knew she had to eat or she'd feel worse. She went back to bed, hoping she could fall asleep. It didn't come easily. She couldn't turn off her brain.

I had such high hopes that this new PTSD treatment would bring Tom through. Now this. Goddam Akira for getting him into this mess. Why didn't he just hire some cops? And Tom – what the hell was he thinking? A detective? Must be his knight on a white horse syndrome. Shit, shit, shit.

What happens to me now? I'm almost middle-aged, a divorcee, and the man I loved is either gonna die or be severely impaired. Interesting I thought "loved" in the past tense. Do I take care of him the rest of my life? Or visit him daily in a nursing home? He may never even know me. What about me? Parents in Florida, brother in San Diego. No relatives around, no kids, no nothing. At least I have Rosalie. And my therapist.

Pretty slender support system. Maybe I shouldn't have left Boston to be out here close to him. I've worked so damned hard to have a good life, to be competent in my profession.

I guess I have to look at the good things in my life – my career, my good health – think I'm in good health but I'm really tired these days. Probably stress. Guess I should get it checked out. I'm still pretty good-looking so maybe there's a chance – stop that! It's not over. Tom could recover. Stop thinking about yourself, you miserable wretch. But still...

25

INVESTIGATION

DETECTIVE DAN MCCORMICK WORE HIS Worcester Police Department badge proudly for twenty-seven years. Near retirement, he had the usual array of bodily complaints – bad back, creaky knees and 30 pounds of excess baggage around his midsection. His team had picked up a couple of thugs who'd abducted a patient from the Zylinski Institute and nearly killed him. McCormick thought he had seen it all, but this took the prize.

"To abduct a former military surgeon, a veteran who served his country, beating him to a senseless pulp, that's near the top of my list of evil crimes. Comes right below sexual abuse of kids and raping old women," McCormick said to Tim Cogan, the captain of the SWAT team as they sat in McCormick's office at police headquarters. "I'll question these two degenerates myself, if the Public Defender's office would get their friggin' lawyer to come."

Cogan gave McCormick explicit details of the rescue by his police force and identified Mazarov and Rusker.

"These two goons are well-known to us. You know them too. Involved over and over with locals and cops in Blackstone Valley," Cogan said wearily. "They always squirm out of convictions. Sometimes it's our own damned fault – sloppy police work, lost evidence. Sometimes it's inexperienced or just plain dumb prosecutors. Most often it's because no witnesses got guts enough to testify against them. Everybody who's heard of them are scared."

This time these guys are goin' to serve serious time, McCormick stewed. Grievous bodily harm, abduction, a bunch of other crimes. Could be murder charges if the guy dies. We do careful police work by the book and we'll finally nail these two scumbags.

"How'd the call for rescue come in?" McCormick asked.

"A guy named DiMasio – one of the guy's fellow patients at Zylinski – called. Saw his friend get sacked and tossed into a panel truck near the employee parking lot over at Zylinski," said Cogan. "DiMasio could read the plates – van had lights on, plates were lit up – when this went down, even though it was gettin' dark. That was about all we had. We sent the scene team to see about tire tracks in the parking lot but way too many tracks there. So that was a dead end.

"We put an APB out for white vans. Wasn't long before a patrol car called in – found one parked in front of that abandoned warehouse on Burnside, you know, that place always got some kind of criminal activity goin' on, mainly drugs, but a murder there couple of years ago. These two morons left the van in plain sight out front. If we'd moved a little faster maybe we could have prevented what happened to that poor devil."

"DiMasio describe the assailants?"

"Nope, he couldn't.

"How'd you figure they were in there? Didn't just ditch the van there and change vehicles, go somewhere else?"

"One of the cops crept up to the building, heard yelling and moans coming from this small room in back. Said it sounded like someone getting beat up – really loud.

"Got our team together, moved in, surrounded the building. Used the bullhorn to tell 'em to come out. The dumb fucks started firing automatic weapons and tossing out some old hand grenades. We thought we shouldn't waste time – you know, there's this hostage in there, so we threw in teargas canisters. Flushed them right out. Two reprobates. They're in their cells out back – well separated so they can't talk to each other."

"They talked to their lawyers yet?"

"Yep. Wanna talk to them now?"

"Can't wait."

McCormick and Cogan went to the interrogation room and waited for Rusker to be brought in. After they were all seated, McCormick went through the preliminaries and then got down to business. He knew interrogations were old hat to Rusker – he wouldn't be cowed. But he'd give it his best shot, try to scare him into some answers.

"You know the guy you two shitheads beat up – Dr. Barrett – is near death, at Memorial hospital?"

"Don't know no Dr. Barrett."

"The guy you nearly killed. A doctor. And you're nothing but a miserable sonavabitch. You and Mazarov nearly killed him. If he dies, I'll see you get the max."

Rusker shrugged, said nothing.

"Did that prick Mazarov do most of the beating?"

"I don't know what yur talking about."

"Maybe I'll offer you a deal. It's against my instincts, cause I'd rather see you in prison for the rest of your fucking life."

"Nope. No deal. I ain't done nothin'."

"Just so you know, you moron, if Dr. Barrett dies there'll be murder charges – first degree, if I have anything to say about it. A capital offense. Life in prison. If this turns into a federal case for any reason, gas chamber. I'll be there to watch you seize up as you take your last breath."

He stood up, moved toward Rusker, one arm across his chest, positioned to backhand Rusker. Cogan jumped up, got between them.

"I should beat the shit out of this guy right now!" McCormick shouted as he backed off.

Rusker shrunk back, blinked, shrugged again, said nothing.

Cogan grabbed McCormick's elbow and they left and headed down the corridor.

"You knew that was all an act, right?" McCormick said to Cogan when they were settled back in the office.

"Wasn't real sure. You should go to Hollywood."

"Anything to gain from getting DiMasio to come in?" McCormick asked.

"We got his statement. He saw the abduction, so we have that. Maybe you should talk to him."

"The big fly in the ointment is the doc. If he dies, or is incapacitated and can't identify these guys, we won't have much for the assault part. Course they resisted arrest and fired on police officers – we'll get them there. Best hope is we can scare the shit outta Rusker enough to make him panic and turn on Mazarov. Let's talk to that Neanderthal."

After a few minutes with Mazarov, McCormick knew he'd get nothing. His menacing grin and a "fuck you" attitude told McCormick this was a guy who wouldn't crack. They left the interrogation room, swung by the coffee machine.

"Tell the docs at Memorial we need to be notified when Barrett wakes up and can talk to us. I should say 'if.' Poor bastard.

"Need to talk to DiMasio. Maybe he'll remember something about Rusker or Mazarov. Let's run over to Zylinski. Call their legal department to clear it and have someone meet us to arrange a place we can talk."

"Well, I just happened to wander down to Vinny's path and saw the whole fuckin' – oh, sorry officers, pardon my French – kidnap thing," Matt said to McCormick and Cogan. "I couldn't believe my eyes at first – thought someone was pulling a prank on Tom. When I got it this was real, I called you guys right away."

"Go on, Matt," McCormick said.

"So…Right after that I called George and told him."

"Who's George?"

"George Logan, another patient. He and Tom and me are friends."

"He's here at Zylinski?"

"Yeah, his room's next to mine."

McCormick leaned over to whisper to Cogan. "Get George Logan here. I'm almost done with this guy." He turned back to Matt.

"Thanks Mr. DiMasio. Here's my card if you think of anything else."

"Not much help there. You get Logan?" McCormick asked Cogan.

"The Zylinski lawyer's tracking him down. Should be here in a little while."

When George got there McCormick introduced himself and they got right into it.

"Mr. Logan, tell me what you know about Dr. Barrett's case."

"Before I start, know how Tom's doing?" George asked.

"Not much. Still in coma far as I know."

George looked up at the ceiling, struggling to hold himself in check.

"This whole thing sucks. I feel responsible for not keeping a closer watch on Tom. He's a good guy, but so naïve. Shit! I'd like to get my hands on those bastards."

"Well, that's our job and we're gonna make sure they pay for this," McCormick said. "With help from you. Think you can answer a few questions?"

"Ask away. Not sure how much I can help."

"How close were you to Barrett?"

"We got to be pretty good friends. We were trying to find out why patients were goin' downhill. We doped out that it was due to someone tampering with the pills."

He told McCormick about watching Carrie Brink trashing the pills.

"We videotaped her....Jesus!" he shouted. "It's the iPhone they were after."

George slapped his forehead. "But Tom didn't have the phone. He got snatched up and he didn't even have what they wanted. We gave it to Akira – Dr. Yamaguchi. I think he turned it over to the investigators from the FBI and the State Police. He told me they had this big argument over who had jurisdiction over the frigging phone.

"But how did they know what we did? Someone else had to know about the recording, that Tom had something to do with it. Otherwise why would they take Tom? How'd they find out?"

George closed his eyes.

"If Tom comes to, we'll ask him if he told anyone," McCormick said. "We're gonna question Carrie Brink about how she got into this. I wonder if she's the one who told those two to grab Barrett," McCormick said.

"If she didn't arrange the abduction, then someone else had to know about the recording. But only that person and Tom know who it is," George said.

"So you think it had to be someone Tom talked to?"

"Had to be. Who'd he see in the time between when we took the pictures and when he was jumped? Wonder if his room nurse knew where he went."

"Cogan, go ask the head nurse who Barrett's nurse was and could we talk to her – like real soon."

In a little while, Diana was sitting where George had been.

"You saw Tom Barrett in the morning of the day he was kidnapped, right?" McCormick asked after some preliminary questions.

"Yes sir. He told me early that morning he'd had a bad nightmare and didn't think the pills were working anymore. He said he needed to talk to Alicia – that's his advocate – as soon as he could. He was pretty agitated."

"Did he leave to go see her, as far as you know?"

"Yeah, about 7:30 he left the floor. I assume he went to see her. Don't know where else he could've gone at that hour."

"What's Alicia's last name?"

"Kleinman."

"And she's got an office here?"

"Yes."

"Was that the last time you saw him?"

"Yeah, he didn't come back."

"Anything else?"

"Well, the only thing I can think of is that the day before, Debbie, his evening nurse, told me he got an iPhone delivered to his room. She told me he said it was for the therapy group and took him at his word. I really wondered about that. Does that have something to do with all this?"

"That's what we're working on. Did you tell anyone about it?"

"Um, I don't remember if I mentioned it to another nurse. It was a crazy night, a lot of patients in distress."

"Thanks Diana. Appreciate your help. If you remember anything else, please let us know."

"Cogan, we got another one to talk to. Her name is Alicia Kleinman, She's Barrett's advocate, whatever that is. Check it out and see if we can see her while we're here. Otherwise set up another appointment."

26

LAST SEEN BY...

"SO ONE OF THE LAST people to see Barrett was this woman Kleinman. That definitely makes her a person of interest. We need to find out what went on when they met," McCormick whispered to Cogan as they were led to Alicia's office by the paralegal from the law department. The two cops strolled into her office awkwardly, taking in the décor and wondering if this woman actually lived here, it seemed so homey.

"Thanks for seeing us on short notice, Dr. Kleinman," McCormick began. "We understand you may have seen Dr. Barrett early on the day he was abducted. Is that right?"

"Yes, that's true. But before I answer your questions, can you tell me how Tom's doing?" Alicia asked.

"Only know he's still in coma. Sorry I can't bring better news."

"Did I see Tom that day? Is that what you asked?" Alicia said, after she motioned for the cops to sit. "Yes, he called me early that morning – about 7 – to tell me he'd had a bad night – another awful nightmare. I arranged to see him as soon as I got in."

"So what went on when you saw him?"

"He was really riled up. He was angry about having a nightmare and the return of his old demons. Then he exploded, telling me about the spying he and George Logan had done. I was stunned and even more astonished they'd seen the study pills being ditched."

"You say he was 'riled up.' What do you mean by that?"

"He was dangerously agitated. I feared he might assault me he was so furious. He demanded that our conversation be part of our professional confidential relationship, an unnecessary request. Under these new circumstances, I'm sure he'd want me to tell you what he told me.

"He calmed down after a few minutes, having spent his anger. I had to leave for an urgent staff meeting, so I gave him a Valium, told him to get in touch with Dr. Crocker later if he needed more."

"Dr. Crocker? Who's he?"

"Dr. Crocker is our neurologist."

"Do you know if he contacted him?"

"I don't know if he saw him or not. When I left for the day I still worried about what he'd told me and how he was doing, but I assumed, since I hadn't heard any more from him – he always got in touch with me when he needed me – that he was good for the moment. He always called when he needed me," she repeated, looking down at her hands. "Maybe I should have followed up and this wouldn't have happened."

"So that meeting was the last you saw or heard from Dr. Barrett?"

"Yes."

"One more thing: can you arrange for us to talk with Dr. Crocker?" McCormick said.

"I can call his office and ask him."

She punched in his number. Their conversation volleyed back and forth.

"Well they're here in my office now. They want to talk to you," she said.

Another long pause and some garbled noises from her phone.

"I think you should talk to them." A longer pause. They could hear his voice on her phone, tinny and indistinct.

"Tomorrow? Why not now?"

Alicia stared at McCormick and Cogan as she listened. They could barely hear Crocker's voice, talking rapidly, but they couldn't make out what he said.

"Okay, I'll tell them."

She turned off her phone, looked directly at McCormick.

"He says he can't see you now. He's busy. You're to call him tomorrow."

"Okay, where's his office?" McCormick said.

"On the ground level, number 112. Turn left off the elevator."

"C'mon Cogan. We'll hustle down and wait til he's not 'busy' anymore," he said sarcastically. "Dr. Kleinman, we'll need to talk to you later. Stay available."

"I can't believe Dr. Crocker had any role in Tom's abduction, but he sure is acting strangely. In case he heads for the parking lot, it's over there," she said, pointing out the window before the two cops raced out the door.

"Thanks, we're on our way," McCormick said. They hurried toward the parking lot, deciding Crocker probably was hightailing it out of his office. Smelling a catch, Cogan started running. Once outside the building they saw a man in a hurry, heading for a car. When he saw Cogan sprinting in his direction, he broke into a run himself.

"Stop! We need to talk to you," Cogan shouted, assuming the man was Crocker.

He kept running and Cogan raced after him. It was no contest.

"Whoa, there big fella," Cogan said stepping between Crocker and his car. "Are you Dr. Crocker? We just wanna talk to you. What're you scared of?"

"What's this about?" Crocker demanded, breathing heavily, his face crimson.

"Dr. Barrett. Are you Dr. Crocker? We wanna know if you saw him in your office the day he disappeared."

Crocker said nothing. He glanced around furtively, his agitation increasing.

"Again, are you Dr. Crocker?"

"Yes, I am. So what?"

"Just wanna ask you some questions so we can understand what happened to Dr. Barrett. Do you wanna answer our questions here or down at the station?"

"You can't do this. I have my rights!" he barked.

"We guarantee your rights. You can call your lawyer if you want. You don't have to answer any questions until you consult with your lawyer."

"How dare you? You can't just question any citizen without their consent!"

"Sir, you must not be listening. I just told you that you don't have to answer any questions until you have counsel. You know, if you hadn't run we wouldn't have to do this at all. But you did – not a good thing when police officers only want to ask a few questions," Cogan said. "Now where would you like to do this?"

"I'm not doing this anywhere!"

"Okay, have it your way. You're under arrest in connection with the abduction of Dr. Thomas Barrett," McCormick said having caught up with them and having heard the argument.

State Police Detective Tony Ruggerio and the Investigator from the FBI, William Hodson, had an uneasy relationship. It wasn't clear yet that what went on at Zylinski was a state or a federal issue since the drug-tampering involved a medication developed by grants from the federal government but the criminal act involved a state-based facility. So these two were circumspect about sharing information. After discussion, though, they had reached cautious respect for each other. They were set to interview Carrie Brink together.

"Detectives, can I have a word with you both before you begin?" Gwen Reardon, Carrie Brink's attorney asked before they went into the interrogation room.

"I'd like to meet with the prosecutor."

"Give me a few minutes."

They waited in one of the rooms outside a courtroom for Kate Quaid, the assistant district attorney. The DA's office was in the same building so it wasn't long before Quaid strode into the room. Ruggerio and Hodson excused themselves and waited in the hall.

"Hello Kate," Gwen said when she walked in.

"Hi Gwen, how're you doin'?

"You know this case? The one from Zylinski?"

"Yeah, got the file yesterday. You represent Carrie Brink, the pharmacist?"

"Right. I've talked with her the last couple of hours. What I can tell you is that there's a bigger fish here. What kind of consideration can you give us?"

Kate and Gwen emerged from the room later, chatting about a mutual friend's upcoming wedding. Ruggerio and Hodson looked at each other.

"Lawyers are amazing. They can be all buddy-buddy even though they slash and burn in the courtroom. They're able to put their cases in a separate place from their daily lives. A good trait. I wonder why we cops can't seem to do that?"

Turning to Gwen Reardon, Ruggerio asked,

"So what's going on?"

"We're entering a guilty plea. My client sees no hope of winning in court considering the evidence."

"Get a bargain for that?" Ruggerio grinned.

"None of your business."

"She ready to talk with us?"

"Yeah, but please go easy on her."

Ruggerio and Hodson frowned at Reardon as if to say "fat chance." They went into the interrogation room to begin questioning. Carrie admitted to doing what was clearly seen on the video.

"Why the hell did you do it?"

"I needed money."

"What money?"

"Dr. Crocker told me I'd be paid well to do this."

"Dr. Crocker? Who's he?"

"He's a neurologist working at the Institute."

"Where'd he get the money?"

"I don't know for sure. Some pharmaceutical company. Never told me the name. He just told me I'd get $100,000."

Ruggerio looked at Hodson with a look in his eyes that said "Holy Shit!"

"Do you know if others are involved in this?"

"No. I only know Dr. Crocker approached me and offered me money. I don't know of anyone else."

"We'll need to speak with you some more, later." He nodded to the attendant who rose and accompanied Carrie back to her cell.

"We just got a big break," Cogan told McCormick. "Just heard from Tony Ruggerio at the State Police. Carrie Brink confessed and named Crocker as the one who got her into it. She doesn't know why Crocker was involved but she needed money badly. Why? She's drug-addicted, owes her dealer a pile of money. Divorced, a single mom with a high school senior who needs money for college."

"This is an ace in the hole when we talk to Crocker. Looks like he's beginning to come around anyhow. Much less belligerent than when we brought him in. We checked him out. Turns out he – like Brink – is also in a financial bind – gambling debts and a bitter, costly divorce. When we asked him who his lawyer was he said he couldn't afford a lawyer, already owed a lawyer a lot for his divorce case. Asked for a public defender. In fact, he's bankrupt."

27

Two Months Earlier

"HELLO, THIS IS DR. CROCKER."

"Good morning Doctor. My name is Job Glazer. I understand you're working at the Zylinski Institute on an exciting new drug to treat PTSD. Right?"

"Um, yes, that's correct," Crocker said. "Who did you say you were?"

"Job Glazer. I'm a senior manager for Google Pharmaceutical in New Jersey."

"Google's in the pharmaceutical business?"

"Oh, yeah, we're into everything. And this being their latest venture, they're very interested in this new drug."

"Okay," he said, perplexed about the call. "Why are you calling me?"

"Well, we know that you're a prominent neurologist, and we'd like a chance to talk to you about this drug. There could be some potential for future cooperation from our company."

Crocker was puzzled but curious. Is this an appropriate thing to consider? Google has billions. Maybe they'd pony up some money for the study? If I could land funding in support of the research, I'd be a hero to Akira and the rest of the crew. Maybe even get a raise. Sure could use more money. Having a conversation with this guy shouldn't be a problem.

"No harm in talking with you, I suppose. You know where my office is?"

"Well, we're camped out here in a hotel and would appreciate it if you could come here. The hotel is only a few minutes from where you are. We'd even spring for cab fare," he laughed.

"How long you going to be in town? I'm tied up today with patients."

"We're leaving day after tomorrow. Could you meet us tomorrow?"

"Who else? You said 'we.'"

"My partner – a great guy named Kevin O'Toole. A handsome Irishman," Glazer, whose name was really Job Martin, laughed as he looked over at O'Toole, also an alias.

Seems like a nice guy, Crocker mused. Sure is charming. No harm in meeting with them, I guess. And someone has to manufacture and market the drug if it proves to be effective. Someone with solid financials, why not Google?

"Well, tomorrow would work for me," he said, curiosity rising. "What time and where?"

Martin looked over at Flannigan after they'd made the arrangements.

"Told you he'd be easy. My background check on him was right on target."

"Nice you kept my name Irish. My dad will appreciate that. What'd you find out?"

"Yep. Easy. In all the papers. Well-known neurologist going through a nasty divorce. I knew he was in deep doo-doo. Later he declared bankruptcy – also in the paper."

"Well, we'll see what we can do with this guy."

The next day, Crocker told his secretary he'd be at lunch for a couple of hours, he had his phone in case of emergency, but to hold routine calls. He took the offer Glazer had made and took a cab to the Hotel Metropole near Mechanics Hall downtown.

"So glad you could come and meet with us," Glazer said, thrusting his hand into Crocker's. "This is Kevin O'Toole, my business partner."

O'Toole was indeed handsome. His wavy blond hair was unruly, projecting an image of a carefree and fun-loving man in his late thirties. His blue eyes were incandescent and he would be the sort to command attention entering any room. As he and Crocker stood side by side, O'Toole looked down at him. Crocker, not a small man himself, winced as O'Toole mashed his hand, a handshake intended to announce that here was a sincere and sturdy man whose word could be trusted. His smile revealed a set of teeth that must have given his orthodontist an extra week in the Bahamas.

"So glad to meet you Doctor. Job has told me what a nice guy you were on the phone. We were both anxious to meet you in person."

Crocker was swept off his feet. Raised in a Boston North Shore Yankee family, he was not used to unabashedly friendly people at first meeting. In his tight culture it was expected to take at least two years to warm up to new people. Even in his neurology residency at the "World's Greatest Hospital" where he was thrown together with medical graduates from all over the world, he'd not lost the reserve that was epigenetic in his world. It wasn't that he was unfriendly, just reticent. This coolness did not extend to his bedside manner. Inside the medical community he was famous for his warmth with patients.

"I got a meeting room off the dining room so we can talk without any noise interference. Are you ready to eat?" Glazer asked.

"Yes, lead the way."

They walked briskly to a small room where a table had been set up and there were a couple of bottles of wine that had already been opened to breathe. Menus were on the bone china plates. Once they were seated and had time to peruse the bill of fare, a waiter came and took their orders.

"To success!" said Glazer, raising his glass after wine had been poured. They all took healthy sips.

"So Doctor, how's the experiment going at Zylinski?" O'Toole asked. "We're so impressed from what we've heard. What's your take on the progress with this important new drug?"

"Well, so far it seems to be highly successful," Crocker said, pleased that these two successful businessmen were interested in his opinion. "We don't know, of course, who's getting the real drug – it's a double blind study. But we sure can see improvement in some patients. One would have to be a fool not to guess the ones improving are getting the new drug." Crocker drank some more, registering that the wine was full-bodied and must be costing them a fortune.

"So tell me about yourself, Doctor. How'd you come to be on the professional staff for the study?" Glazer asked, as the waiter poured more wine for them.

"Well, after medical school, I was a neurology resident at Boston Medical Center followed by a Fellowship in movement disorders," Crocker said. Usually a modest man, he warmed to talking about himself to these receptive men.

"I'm proud to say I've gotten awards for my teaching and five years ago the Massachusetts Neurological Association presented me with the 'Neurologist of the Year Award'."

"Boy, that's impressive!" Kevin exclaimed. "And how did you say they were smart enough to get you to sign on at Zylinski?"

"Akira Yamaguchi – he's the director of Zylinski – and I knew each other when we were both at Boston Medical Center. When he was looking for a neurologist for the research study on nepenthe – that's our name for the drug – he thought of me. He knew I'd gotten interested in changes in the brains of patients with PTSD while I was doing research on Parkinson's disease. I'd published a couple of papers on the subject."

"Well, you seem to be the ideal candidate for that job. No wonder Dr. Yamaguchi chose you."

After what he'd been through recently he absorbed the flattery greedily. His ex-wife had been merciless in the divorce settlement and got most of his assets since it was shown during the proceedings that he was a compulsive gambler and had lost all of his life's savings. That had colored the settlement substantially in his wife's favor. He was glad to have some positive strokes.

"It's good to hear the clinical trial is going well. Kevin and I are both big contributors to the VFW and the Wounded Warriors project. We're so hopeful that your drug will benefit all veterans who come back with these terrible problems. You're doing God's work!"

"Well, thanks, I agree it's important," Crocker said. He glanced at his watch.

"Boy, time has slipped away. I'm sorry but I've got to get going. I have patients. Thanks so much for lunch. It was good to meet both of you."

"Likewise, Doctor," Glazer said. "We'd like to meet again to talk more about this breakthrough drug. We're sincerely interested. Maybe Google Pharmaceuticals will be interested as well. Can we get together, say, in a week? Same time, same place?"

Crocker hesitated, wondering if he should be talking to someone outside of the Institute. But why not? Nothing to lose. And again, the prospect of this big pharma company taking on the manufacture and marketing was exciting.

"Sure, I'll clear my calendar. Thanks for lunch. Appreciate it."

Their next meeting followed the same pattern: same hotel, same private dining room, good food and wine. At this meeting, however, they asked more about the methodology of the study and how the pills were dispensed. Crocker ignored what he had to have known – that what they were doing at Zylinski was confidential. Sharing this information with Glazer and O'Toole was justifiable, he rationalized, because, within an academic culture, one is expected to share information – to move science forward. And by this time the three of them were on a first name basis. He was learning about their wives and kids, where they went on vacation, and the clubs they belonged to. They were clearly good people.

At the third meeting, Glazer and O'Toole seemed more serious and less animated.

"You must realize this drug will be a blockbuster. Anyone with a connection to it will be famous and rich from the sales," Glazer said. "Do you have anything in your contract with Zylinski that would reward you financially if and when the drug is proven to be effective?"

"Well n-no," he stammered, "I don't believe I have. I doubt any of the investigators at the Institute have such an arrangement." But I don't really know that since no one would talk about it, he thought.

"So all you're getting out of your work is your salary?" O'Toole asked, eyebrows raised, his incredulity showing.

Crocker thought about this for a few moments, gnawing at him as resentment crept into his thinking. They're right. I'm getting nothing but my salary out of this. I bet Yamaguchi will get a big cut of the profits on this drug when it comes to market. And me – man, I need money in the worst way. Here I am, fifty-five years old, stripped of my assets by that bitch of a wife, who I've pampered and given to all those years. Yamaguchi could even get a Nobel Prize for this. And I come away empty-handed. The more he thought about it the angrier he became. O'Toole poured him a tall glass of scotch. Then another. Then Glazer pulled his chair closer to Crocker.

"Google Pharmaceuticals has authorized us to offer you a large sum of money if you'll help us impede this clinical trial."

"What?" he said, his words slightly slurred. "I couldn't possibly do that. That would be against my principles!" Crocker said with indignation.

Glazer shrugged and said, "The money we're prepared to offer is one half million dollars. Would that make it more possible?"

Crocker was brought up short.

A half million dollars? Christ, that would give me a fresh start. I could recapture my life. I'm still young enough to rebuild my life and go on.

"Lemme thing 'bout it," he said, his speech obviously mumbly. "Call ya tomorrow."

"Just one more thing, Doctor. These conversations must remain confidential – for obvious reasons. If you tell anyone about our meetings or what we've said, there will be serious consequences."

"Whaddaya mean?"

"We got a couple of men whose job it is to make sure this kind of information stays secret."

A shudder went through Crocker. Even in his inebriated state he thought, these guys are playing hardball. What have I gotten myself into? His mind raced in circles.

He was restless in the cab going home. He couldn't go back to the Institute in his drunken state, but luckily he had no scheduled patients. The allure of a half million dollars kept him awake that night. By morning he'd made his decision. He had to have that money. It was the only way out of his jungle of problems. But he wondered what he'd have to do to get the reward. He called Glazer in the morning.

"Job, let's have lunch today. Same time, same place?"

"Love to. See you at noon."

Martin called Flannigan. "Think we got 'im. Meeting for lunch – noon at the hotel."

They met at the hotel and ordered lunch. When the waiter left the room, Crocker turned to Glazer.

"What exactly do you want me to do?"

"Does this mean you're accepting our offer?"

"I'm interested. But I need to know what you want me to do," he repeated.

O'Toole rose and came over to Crocker.

"Please stand up. I need to be sure you're not wired."

Jesus, this is like a movie, Crocker thought. He actually thinks I'd be wired? This is not my world.

O'Toole went over his body meticulously, occasionally a little too intimate for Crocker's comfort.

"He's clean."

"Okay, here's what we think will do the trick for the money we're going to give you. We need you to sabotage the trial. The way to do it is to substitute placebos for the active drug. You'll have to recruit someone in the distribution chain of the pills to help you since you don't actually handle the pills. I'll leave that to you. It could happen anywhere along the line of supply. The easiest place would be the pharmacy. You can offer a bunch of money for the help."

"What kind of money are we talking about?"

"Up to 100 grand, but don't offer that kind of money to just anyone. Be very selective, And very careful. Find someone who needs money badly and someone that can be intimidated enough so they don't squeal. Won't be easy, but with this amount of money it should be possible."

"I think I may know someone who's recently gone through a divorce – almost as nasty as mine – and has a couple of kids close to college age. We chatted at a department cocktail party a few weeks back. I know she needs money. I'll feel her out," Crocker said.

"Be careful when you approach her, or anyone, for that matter," Glazer said. "This could blow up in your face. If it does I have to say we'd leave you twisting in the wind. We'd deny everything. There's no way to trace our conversations. We'd say they never happened, that we don't even know you. Never met you. We can't be implicated in this. For obvious reasons."

"Will this payment be in cash?"

"Of course."

"When?"

"We'll give you a down payment today of $50,000," Glazer said. "You did bring the money Kevin?"

He lifted a briefcase into view and pointed to it.

"Okay, let me get to work on this." Crocker felt ill, but he knew he'd passed the point of no return.

"Oh, by the way. I mentioned those two men who like to be known as enforcers. They're very rough types but they get muscle jobs done when we need it. One is named Petrin and the other is Wayne. Here's how to get in touch with them if you need them for anything." He handed Crocker a slip of paper with phone numbers. "Memorize this number and burn this paper. And by the way – try not to use them unless you really need them. They're expensive and they're rough."

Crocker left the meeting with his brain buzzing.

I guess it's true, everyone has his price, he thought. Could I have gotten more? They seemed eager enough. Too late now. Just like my negotiations with the lawyers during the divorce. I'm too easy. Settle for the least instead of haggling. But still. A half million will do a lot for me.

What about those two enforcer guys? Jesus, I don't want to get that kind of person involved. What would I need to use them for anyway? Maybe they're warning me to stay in line. Looks like I'm really up to my ears now.

He got back to his office a little after two and started seeing his patients. He only had four appointments this afternoon. He looked up Carrie Brink's extension.

How am I going to enlist her? What motivates her? Is she a cause-oriented woman who'll be grossly offended by being offered money to cheat? Or is she as needy as I am for money? What if she rats on me? Well, I'm a gambler. That's gotten me into a lot of trouble but it's part of my personality. I'll have to take a chance on her since there doesn't seem to be an alternative.

"Carrie, how are you? This is Malcolm Crocker. Yeah, upstairs. Say, I wonder if you'd be able to have, uh, maybe coffee or a drink later this afternoon?

"Uh huh, yeah, I understand about your needing to get home for your kids. When do they need you home? How about around 4:30 then?

Would that work? Oh, just wanted to get together and discuss the study. Okay, I'll meet you at the front entrance – I'll drive – and we can go down to Starbucks. Good, See you then."

She probably wonders what the hell I'm calling her about. But she didn't seem hesitant to meet with me. Does she know I recently split up? Maybe she's lonely. I wouldn't be a bad catch. A little difference in our age, but that doesn't seem to matter anymore. Oh cut it out, Crocker. That's not on the agenda.

After seeing his patients, he headed to the lobby. Carrie was already there. After an awkward few moments, they headed to his car. Carrie seemed friendly enough so his nerves settled down. He was thinking about how to approach the big question, his reason for seeking this liaison.

Carrie Brink was in her mid-forties, still slender. Her hair looked like mahogany spring coils falling carelessly down to her shoulders. Her brown eyes were set over high cheeks; her mouth was generous and prone to ready smiles. She still turned men's heads as she walked by on slim and shapely legs. Self-assured, she didn't signal neediness, but her cheerful exterior belied the fact that she was addicted to opioids, courtesy of her ex-husband who had gotten her started on drugs. As bad as this is for an ordinary citizen, it's a fatal flaw for a pharmacist, particularly the chief pharmacist in a hospital, whose profession demanded no problem with drug addiction. No one at the Institute knew or she would have been quickly out of her job and could lose her license to boot. She was circumspect about her private life, so no one knew about her huge debts because of drugs or her divorce settlement that gave her almost nothing. She needed money desperately and turned out to be a perfect prospect for what Crocker would be offering.

Crocker wasn't sure how he'd approach this but his years as an astute clinician used to connecting dots when listening to patients would serve him well in his new role as recruiter for sabotage. He was able to learn a great deal about anyone during the first few minutes of conversation. As he listened to Carrie he was picking up clues that made him believe she would take the offer.

"Things running smoothly in the pharmacy?" Crocker asked.

"In what respect?" Carrie said, surprised that he would open their talk with this question.

"Oh, any personnel problems, space problems, you know, the usual stuff."

"Hmm, well I'd say we're under control. A little boring, since all we do is prepare the pill dispensers for distribution to the floors. But I can't complain. Better than being so crazy busy you chase your tail."

"You mentioned you had to get home for your kids. Tell me about them."

"Well, Megan is seventeen, finishing her last year of high school and eager to get away for college. Jared is fifteen, going into his junior year, so he'll be ready for college in a couple of years. A big strain on the budget. Have you looked at college costs lately?"

"Mine are all out of the nest, thank heavens. If they were younger and still at home I'd be paying big time child support to my ex in addition to all the other expenses I have. I love my kids but glad they're out on their own now."

"So you remember our talk about my divorce," Carrie said. "It's the pits. My ex was a traveling salesman and their reputation for philandering is well deserved. He was sleeping with bimbos from coast to coast. But he made out like a bandit in the divorce proceedings. His lawyer was better than mine. They dug up a bunch of dirt on me and that trumped his infidelity."

Wonder what kind of dirt that was. I'll have to circle back to that, Crocker thought.

"Ditto here. I'm a well-shorn sheep. I came out of it with my clothes and the old car I drove you here in. That's it."

"Truth be told," Carrie said, "I'm not sure I'm going to be able to stay at Zylinski unless I get a big raise. I've got debt on debt and then college expenses next fall. I may have to get a job with a pharmaceutical company. I hear they pay well and have interesting work."

Aha, Crocker thought. What a break!

"Now that you mention it, I have a side job with a pharma company. Maybe I could get you something too."

"Really? You kidding? I'd be very interested if you're serious. What kind of work are we talking about?'

"I'd have to check with them to find out what's available. Why don't we finish our coffee so you get home on time. I'll talk to them. Maybe we can get together tomorrow to talk more about it?"

The hook was set. All he had to do was be sure she didn't spit it out.

They left agreeing that he'd call her and tell her when they'd meet the next day. Crocker was curious to know what kind of "dirt" Carrie referred to. It didn't sound like an affair so the question of what it might be lingered in his mind.

The next day Crocker thought it better to meet at Starbucks rather than risk being seen walking out of the Institute together two days in a row. He didn't think anyone had seen them yesterday but couldn't be sure.

"So, did you have a chance to talk to your contact?" Carrie asked without delay, obviously eager to hear of this new possibility.

"Yes, I did."

"And?"

"Well, you'd have work with me, which I think would be a big inducement," he said with a smile. Carrie laughed.

"I could deal with that," she said.

"I'm curious about something you said yesterday about the "dirt" they found during your divorce. Are you willing to tell me about that?"

Carrie closed her eyes and then decided.

"Well, no, it's not really any of your business. I don't want to talk about it. It doesn't enter in to what we're discussing."

"Fair enough. We all have things we'd rather not get into. My dirty little secret – and what made my divorce settlement so bad for me – is that I'm a compulsive gambler and I have a ton of debts. I've had this addiction for years and it caught up with me."

Carrie looked at him for a long time without saying anything. He saw a flicker in her eyes and wondered if she had an addiction of some kind. But she didn't offer anything more.

"Our conversation from here on is strictly confidential. Understand?" he said, this time coldly serious.

"Oh, sounds intriguing. We gonna smuggle drugs?" she said, not yet realizing how earnest Crocker was.

"Not exactly. But you might consider it slightly shady. But financially very rewarding."

"Tell me more," Carrie said, clinching her fists in her lap.

He decided he'd go ahead with his gamble. It was a long shot, but he was feeling lucky, his past losing experiences having failed to disabuse him of the credibility of this impulse. He told her the details of the plan. He wondered how he'd know whether he could trust her to keep this offer confidential. He was taking a big chance, but he needed Carrie. She was in the ideal position to carry out the mission. He didn't have a backup if Carrie got up from the table in a huff, insulted that he would think she would betray the trust that had been placed in her. And if she did that, what recourse did he have? Would he have to call on Petrin and Wayne to keep her quiet? A pivotal moment.

"My role in this scheme?" Carrie asked. She didn't seem offended by the invitation to sabotage the study, but there was a hesitancy in her demeanor.

"Get rid of some of the pills and substitute placebo. Not all of them. That would be too obvious. The idea is to make the drug trial unconvincing. The drug company I'm working for is convinced the drug is bogus and they think it has too many side effects that the investigators here are ignoring and not telling the patients about. Uninformed consent, in other words."

Carrie leaned back in her chair and took a long sip of her latte.

"Okay, let's talk turkey here," Carrie said, surprising Crocker, but making him glad he'd taken the chance. "How much are they willing to pay me to do this?"

Crocker took a napkin and scribbled $100,000 on it, slid it over to Carrie.

Her mouth dropped open, her eyebrows rose, and her pupils dilated wide open. She grabbed the sides of the table and took a deep breath.

"That's unbelievable. Are you teasing me? If you are, I may have to leave right now. You better not be!" she stood up and walked to the window, looked out quickly, then came back and sat down, breathing heavily. She looked at Crocker.

"Not teasing. That's the figure," he said.

"Not to be crass, but that's a no-brainer. I need the money badly." She paused. Would she really do this? Could she do this to Akira? He was a nice man. But seriously, she could never compete with science for his heart. "I'm in.

"How dangerous is this?" she said. "This has got to be illegal, and if we're found out we'd be in big trouble."

"There's some danger, of course, but it's the old risk-to-benefit ratio. For that kind of money – high benefit – merits taking a risk, but I think it's a low one. Who could find out? You do the switch covertly in the pharmacy and no one could possibly know."

"Let me sleep on this. If I can sleep. I'll let you know tomorrow. Okay?"

"Yes, fine with me."

They left separately. Crocker smiled broadly as he walked to his car. So much easier than I thought it would be. Was it too easy? Nah, her eyes lit up when I mentioned the money. Just like mine did when I heard the figure. She's gonna do this – I'm almost positive. Manna from heaven.

28

QUESTIONING

"HAS CROCKER'S COURT–APPOINTED LAWYER – what's her name? – gotten here?" McCormick asked his secretary.

"Name is Ted Porter. Not a woman," his secretary said, with a trace of mockery. "He's been with Crocker for about an hour."

"See if they're ready for us."

McCormick knew Porter well. He'd been around the courts in Worcester County for thirty years, made a decent living by court appointments. Those who worked daily in the courts felt he wasn't the brightest attorney around but acknowledged he knew the tricks of the trade and did an acceptable job of defending his clients.

After introducing his partner Bert Williams, McCormick began questioning Malcolm Crocker.

"Dr. Crocker, we're recording this interview. Let's get right down to business. First I'd like to remind you again of your rights. You remember that?"

Crocker nodded.

"Answer yes or no for the recording."

"Yes."

"Secondly, the reason you were arrested was you ran away, then refused to talk to us during our investigation of Dr. Barrett's abduction and torture. That was dumb. Stupid. What the fuck did you think?"

"You're right. It was stupid. I was scared."

"Well, try not to be that dumb again. You saw him on the afternoon your thugs beat him up, nearly killing him. Right?"

"Yes." He looked up and frowned. "I think I have to talk with Mr. Porter before we go on."

The cops let out a disgusted sigh, but walked out and told Porter he was wanted.

"I'm gonna tell them the whole thing," Crocker said to Porter when he came in. "They've probably talked to Carrie and who knows who else. My goose is cooked. I'm too damned tired to fight. Plead me guilty. I don't care anymore."

"Hey, hold on," Porter groaned. "I know this seems discouraging but don't give up so easy. I can argue a good defense and try to get a not guilty. I'll tell 'em you're depressed, need some time to think this over."

"No," he said emphatically. "I'm decided. I'm going to tell them everything. Maybe I can make up for some damage I've done. I've betrayed so many people," he said, his voice quavering. "It's said that out of bad things some good will come. Maybe the pharmaceutical industry will see this as an object lesson. I feel terrible about Tom. They told me he's in coma, and it's because I turned him over to those two reptiles."

Porter walked out to McCormick with his head down.

"He wants to confess," he said. "I advised against it, but he's adamant."

McCormick called a stenographer. Crocker described how Tom told him about the covert video recording.

"I was in a panic. Our whole scheme was coming apart. I told those two brutes he'd be out back on Vinny's Path, to get him to turn over the video he'd taken in the pharmacy. In my wildest imagination I didn't think they'd nearly kill him," Crocker said, his regret sculpted on his face. He told them how Job Glazer and Kevin O'Toole from Google Pharmaceuticals had promised $500,000 to him if he would carry out the sabotage.

"Googles into drugs?" McCormick said.

"They're into everything. They made those thugs available to me. And I'm willing to testify to that in court to put those crooks behind bars."

McCormick leaned over to Williams. "We're about done here," he whispered. "Get Oberschmidt and Rigsby to find these two hot shot drug guys Glazer and O'Toole and bring 'em in for questioning."

Hours later, Williams reported to McCormick. "No such company as Google Pharmaceuticals."

"No kidding," McCormick said. "People are sure gullible when they want to collect the big bucks."

"But we watched surveillance tapes from the restaurant where Crocker said he met them. Put that together with information we got from the head of Zylinski, that guy Akira. He thought that Laxalta Pharmaceuticals was the likely culprit. Matched photos of the guys at the restaurant with a staff directory from Laxalta, and boom, nailed their true identities. Oberschmidt and Rigs are on their way to bring 'em in."

"Hmm. I'm surprised they have regular jobs at Laxalta. Everybody's getting entitled and sloppy. Makes our life easier," said McCormick.

Job Martin was on the phone when his secretary opened the door to his office and frantically waved her arms at him. He finished his call quickly and gestured her in.

"Close the door. What's buggin' you?" he asked.

"Two cops out here wanting to talk to you," she said in a high-pitched voice, dancing from one foot to the other.

"What do they want?"

"I have no idea. But they are very serious looking. What should I do?"

"I'll come out. Tell them to wait a minute."

He walked to the window, contemplating his next move. There was no way out of his office, no back door. If he refused to talk to them they'd just get a warrant. The news media had been all over the arrests of Mazarov and Rusker in connection with Barrett's abduction and beating. Expressions of sympathy for his condition were front page headlines. He straightened his tie, slipped on his Armani jacket and went to the door.

"Hello Officers, I'm Job Martin," he said enthusiastically. "Come on in. What can I do for you?"

"We're investigating a case and want to talk to you about it," Oberschmidt said.

"Well, come right in!" he said, brimming over with charm.

Shortly into the questioning it became clear the cops knew he was implicated in the scheme to disrupt the Zylinski trial and the beating of Barrett. He stopped talking to them abruptly.

"OK, I'm done talking to you guys without my lawyer. This interview is over."

"We'll be glad to wait until you've reached your lawyer. But then you have to come downtown with us."

Martin looked at these two rock-hard cops.

"Give me a few minutes to call my lawyer. You'll have to wait outside. Don't worry, I have no other door outta here."

When they left Martin first called his lawyer who agreed to meet him at the police station. He then called Flannigan.

"We've got big problems," he said. "I have to go downtown with a couple of cops. Talked to my lawyer. Better get in touch with yours. That chicken-shit Crocker talked, and they have photos that connect us to him."

"Jesus, the job was almost done, bonus almost in the bank. Fucking goons. I thought they might be hard to control. Well, I might be in the mood for some tequila."

"Flannigan, you better stick around. As the saying goes, "I ain't go'n down for this alone.""

29

Intensive Care

"WE PUT HIM ON TIRILIZAD," Dr. Battersby told Cynthia when she returned the next morning. She knew this drug – she'd seen it used often but didn't recall that it was very effective.

"From what I hear it isn't too great."

"We've had some success with tirilizad lessening severe outcomes in coma due to traumatic brain injuries," Battersby said. "But it's not a magic bullet by any means."

Cynthia knew that fewer than half of those treated with it had what could be considered a "good" outcome. Her friend Dr. Summer, a radiologist at Boston Medical Center, told her years earlier that people with traumatic brain injury who lapse into coma are never the same as before the injury. She hoped he was wrong.

"Any signs – you know – of him coming out of it?"

"Well, it's three days now – not too long. But nothing yet," Battersby said evenly. "He withdraws when we prick his feet and hands, a good sign. With your experience you know in coma it's devilish hard to predict what'll happen. Some take weeks or months. Some never wake up, die of infections, other complications."

Cynthia winced as she heard this bitter truth.

"I'm being brutally honest. You know too much for me to waffle. The longer in coma, it's fair to say, the worse the prognosis."

"I appreciate your being straight with me. I'd rather hear your honest opinion, not just pat my hand and give me false promises."

That's what you're supposed to say, right? Cynthia thought. Never mind you're scared out of your mind and every scrap of your professionalism doesn't change that when it's someone close to you.

Even though Tom's face was cleaned up and his lacerations sutured, she hardly recognized the expressionless mask that was now a substitute for his pleasant face. His broken jaw hung down against his chest with a sling under it for support. The tracheostomy tube wheezed with each push of air into his lungs. Cardiac monitors bleeped near his bandaged head. The oxygen sensor clamped on his finger glowed red. The life support systems were doing what normal bodies do for themselves for all the years of living.

"Tom, it's Cyn. I don't know if you can hear me or feel my hand on yours. If you can, know that I love you and want you well. You'd like the doctors and nurses taking care of you. Reminds me of how you cared for patients when you and Akira were at Boston Medical Center."

She wept, recalling the good days past when both were young, full of good feelings and dedicated to making the world better. Tears streaked down her face, followed by guttural sobs rising from deep inside.

A light touch on her shoulder made her turn. She looked up to see Akira standing next to her. She rose and Akira pulled her into his arms as tears continued to drop onto her blouse.

"Please forgive me," he said. "Getting Tom involved in this was the worst mistake of my life. I know my love for Tom can't compare with yours, but know that I love him too. I feel horrible seeing him like this. I promise I'll do everything possible to help Tom recover and I'll be there for him the rest of his life."

Cynthia slowly backed out of his embrace, took a deep breath and grabbed a tissue. Regaining her composure, she faced Akira. She couldn't address the forgiveness issue just now so she fled to ground she knew would be common to both of them.

"I haven't read his medical record. Can you tell me anything that Dr. Battersby didn't?"

On familiar terrain, Akira was relieved to talk about medical issues.

"Well, the good news first: his latest CT showed less brain swelling. But, as you know, the CT is only the shadow, not the person. We won't know how he really is until the coma lifts and we get some idea of what he can do – mentally, physically and emotionally."

"This is so much different than taking care of patients," she said, staring into the distance. "I'm not sure I ever understood how powerless you feel watching someone you love clinging to life, not having a clue about what lies ahead. We can't know how that feels until you're thrust into it." She sighed, turned to Akira.

"Have those two degenerates confessed yet that they did this to him?"

"Not to my knowledge and I'm in close touch with the police. What I can tell you is that two people who work at the Institute have confessed about their part. One of them – Dr. Crocker – implicated two executives from Laxalta Pharmaceuticals. We're getting our lawyers to explore what legal action the Institute ought to take."

"None of that makes things any better for Tom." She locked eyes with Akira. "What if he comes out of coma and doesn't know us? Or is paralyzed? Or has lost all his mental capacity? Or never comes out of it and is in a permanent vegetative state. Or dies?"

Akira put his arm around her again, struggling to keep his own emotions from spilling over. As they stood there, leaning against each other, they were startled by barely perceptible movement. They turned towards Tom. His eyes were gazing slowly around the room. His right arm was trying to break free from the cloth bindings around his wrists tethered to the bedrails. His legs were bent at the knees, tugging against the restraints. Both legs were moving. Akira swiftly pressed the call button several times. Two nurses rushed in.

"What? You buzzed three times!"

"He's moving his legs and right arm," Akira cried out. "His eyes are moving. He's out of his coma!"

One of the nurses paged the Residents, the other steadied Tom and everyone flashed broad smiles.

"Tom, can you hear me? It's Cyn. Blink your eyes if you hear me!"

Both eyes closed and opened, his slack jaw distorting his features as he struggled to focus on her face.

He was awake.

Now what? That question hung in the air while all celebrated the occasion in their own way.

30

REHABILITATION

GRADUALLY TOM GOT ORIENTED TO the sentient world. Still no food by mouth – he was being fed by infusions since his jaw fracture hadn't been repaired. The respirator tube connected to his tracheostomy was now taken away.

"If you want to talk, cover the trach opening with your finger or hand or the air won't get up to your vocal cords," the respiratory therapist told him. His initially slurred speech became more fluid and understandable as the days passed. He couldn't move his left arm but his right arm and both legs were in his control. Physical therapists worked him intensely to restore muscle tone in his legs and both arms. They reassured him he'd soon be able to sit in a chair and then they'd get him up to learn how to walk again.

Within a few days he recognized Cynthia and responded to her questions with simple answers. She held his good hand for long stretches of time, kissed him often on his forehead, the only exposed skin on his head. When the medical team asked the standard question: "On a scale of one to ten how is your pain today?" – he'd answer: "Eleven. Rib fractures – the worst!"

"Yesterday's CT scan showed an almost normal brain. I say almost because part of the right cerebral cortex that controls his left arm still shows damage," Dr. Battersby told Cynthia. "His progress is remarkable considering his initial clinical picture. Had you asked me a few days ago what his prognosis was I would've said something like 'guarded' but would have thought 'not good at all.' But now I'm much encouraged. You know,

I never fail to be surprised by how well the human brain – the whole body for that matter – sometimes responds to injury."

"Will his left arm ever come back?" Cynthia asked, knowing the answer. "One-armed surgeons aren't in great demand, you know."

"Physical therapy can do great things. Just can't predict. As I said, the area running the left arm looks gone on the CT. Frankly, I'm not optimistic about that coming back. But sometimes things work out better in the patient than on the scans."

"Any idea about what to expect," Cynthia asked, "with this combination of PTSD and physical brain damage – you know, flashbacks, nightmares, hyper-vigilance and all those things he had? Could the brain damage lessen or alter those somehow?"

"I wouldn't recommend what happened to Tom as a treatment for PTSD," Battersby chuckled. "But do they counter balance each other? Don't know, but I'd guess not.

"Your question does remind me I need to ask Dr. Patel about reinstituting nepenthe treatment while he's in rehab. Being a new drug, I've worried about how it might cross-react with recent anesthetic agents and the other meds he's on – you know – the needed pain-killers and tirilizad."

"When will you talk to her?"

"Today."

Four days after he woke up Tom's remarkable progress pleased everyone. They acknowledged his left arm wasn't improving but agreed it was too early to tell much about future improvement. His speech therapists were delighted by his daily acquisition of words and articulation. His mental capacities were better with each test but intermittently he seemed bewildered. His therapists reassured Cynthia that was not unusual.

"Dr. Patel resumed nepenthe and so far no problem with discernable drug interactions," Dr. Battersby told Cynthia when he came by for rounds the next day. "I think whenever he wants he can have visitors for short periods. Only people you think he'd like to see."

Cynthia didn't know who he'd like to see. She asked Akira who suggested Matt DiMasio and George Logan. When they walked into his room

Tom didn't immediately recognize them. Once George began talking, though, Tom smiled and held his hand out to him and then to Matt.

"Can't talk well. Broken jaw's not fixed yet. Pardon mumbling," Tom said. "Good to see you guys. Glad you weren't kidnapped, beaten up. Worried about both of you."

"So you remember that part? Too bad. Better to forget that," George said.

"Do you remember the two assholes who beat you up?" Matt asked.

"One. Big smelly guy. Weighed 250. Mean, too."

"Think you could identify him?" George asked.

"Don't know. Maybe. Bet I'd recognize his bad smell. And voice."

"When you're better the cops will want to talk. Right now you need your energy to get healthy," George said. "By the way, speaking of getting healthy, everyone in the program's getting nepenthe now. We all feel a helluva lot better."

Akira came by daily, heartened by Tom's progress. He and Cynthia worked together to arrange his transfer back to Zylinski for physical therapy and psychotherapy. Ten days after he woke up he went back to surgery to wire his jaw fracture and close his tracheotomy. He still had some word-finding problems but his familiar speech patterns returned.

"The media are clambering to talk to you," Cynthia said once she got settled next to Tom's chair. "You're a huge news story – kidnapping, assault and battery. And then there's Laxalta Pharmaceuticals being charged for corporate espionage, bribery, interference with a scientific study, and who knows what else. Several people have been arrested.

"The best news is Akira said they got permission to break the code in the study. After they analyzed the results it was abundantly clear the drug was positively correlated with improvement that they stopped the study, put everyone on the pill. He's sure this will lead to federal approval for release of the drug for production. As you can imagine, he's ecstatic about this."

"George told me about the drug good news," Tom said. "But the media? I'm still an ugly mess. I don't have anything to say they don't already know. I've watched TV and it's on ad nauseam."

"I'd say get it over with. They'll keep hounding everybody until they get their interview. They're hanging around outside – they come hoping to interview you every day."

"I want Dr. Patel here when I talk to them."

"I'll ask her."

When Dr. Patel came to his room, Tom wanted to set down guidelines.

"When I see them, tell them there's a fifteen minute limit – tell them I'm easily fatigued. Tell them anything. Tell them even before they come in. Okay?"

Dr. Patel told him to answer only questions he felt comfortable about and not to get into the police or legal issues. The hospital room contracted as reporters from television, newspapers and magazines crowded in. As they jostled for position Tom spotted Deborah Glotnik from Channel 3 muscling her way into the prime position to take charge. Her aggressive reporting was as locally famous as her repeated Botox injections and nose jobs. She skipped all semblance of courteous introductions and began questioning, or more precisely, interrogating Tom.

"You're a victim of PTSD, right?" she said, thrusting her padded microphone into his face.

Astonished by her lack of tact he could only reply, "Yes."

"And you're in this new treatment program at Zylinski?"

"Yes."

"What's that program doing?"

"You need to ask the staff at Zylinski about that. I'm only a patient."

"But you're also a doctor and a friend of Dr. Yamaguchi, the head of Zylinski, right?"

How the hell does she know that?

"True, but I'm still only a patient."

"Was the treatment helping you?"

"Yes."

"Can you elaborate?"

"No."

"Okay, Doctor Barrett, I see you want to withhold information from our viewers. What are you willing to tell us?"

"I'm tired – through an ordeal. The story will come out in due time."

"But our viewers are interested now in your story, Doctor," she said, mouthing 'doctor' as though it were some kind of pejorative. "Why can't you respect the general public by answering my questions?"

"Do any of the others in the room have questions for me?" Tom said, turning from this overbearing woman, trying not to show his irritation. She started to sputter another question, but by then the others were shouting for attention.

"You know why you were abducted and beaten?" the reporter from the Times asked, and the crowd quieted down, waiting for an answer.

"We saw some patients were relapsing. I was trying to help figure out why that was going on. That's all I can say now.

"End of press conference," he said abruptly.

The reporters talked at once, protesting that Tom wasn't giving them the story they were after. They were still chattering when Dr. Patel intervened.

"You heard him. End of press conference. No further questions."

Cries of protest rose sharply but she shooed them out of the room with such authority they knew not to challenge her.

"Thank you, Dr. Patel," Tom said when they were gone. "What a pack of jackals. Was my response unreasonable?"

"Not at all. Those people are so annoying. They try to get answers to underpin a story they've already written in their heads. However, I know a couple of trustworthy journalists. The two I have in mind have this unique quality of wanting to check facts before they rush to print. Later, if and when you want, I can arrange for you talk to them. We need to get our side of the story out, not only about the success of nepenthe but also the expose of Laxalta as a bad actor of the pharmaceutical industry. It'll help when we sue them! The public needs to know the inside of how this pharmaceutical company operates." She looked at Tom and her face softened.

"And you know, you ought to sue them for all you've gone through – I think the legal jargon is 'pain and suffering.' And I hesitate bringing this up, but if you can't recover your surgical capabilities, they should compensate you handsomely you for that."

"I don't know about all that legal stuff. Suing people isn't in my nature. As far as the media are concerned, right now I don't really feel like talking to any media, even the good ones. I suppose I'll do it if it helps nail those immoral bastards," Tom said, beginning to show some of his old spunk. Looking at his heart and blood pressure monitors he realized he was getting too excited for his own good and changed the subject.

"Any idea when they'll let me outta here?"

"I think today, but I'm not your attending doctor. By the way, Akira wants to see you but wanted to avoid the media. Can we pick a time for him to meet with you?"

"How about after lunch? That way he'll not run into any reporters. Wait. If I'm getting out of here today why not meet him back at the Institute – to avoid snoopers?"

"Okay. I'll tell him you'll call. See you later – and Tom – thanks for all you've done. Take it easy."

"I'm so glad you're doing as well as you are," Akira said once he and Tom sat down in Tom's old room at Zylinski.

"Well, I'm doing well enough. Unless some miracle happens, though, my left arm is useless. And that spells the end of my surgical career. Even though my skills were in decline before I got beaten up I hoped they'd get better. Now instead of a tremor, I have a limp arm."

He sighed.

"So I have to accommodate. I will, but I get furious and then sad. But not depressed. This was an unnecessary loss.

"I also wish now you hadn't gotten me involved, of course. But that's hindsight. On the good side, thank heaven my mind still works. At least I think it does. What do you hear about my mental functioning?"

"I'll leave that answer up to Dr. Patel and her team. From what I've heard, though, your mental acuity is good. You might not pass Board exams in surgery tomorrow but your global functioning is excellent."

"Back to the pill," Tom said. "How long before it will be available to the general public?"

"One never knows how long the Feds will take to release this to a manufacturer. I hope within months, because the results we've seen are extraordinary and the treatment should be made available quickly," Akira said. "Congress may hold hearings – that may help accelerate or delay the approval process. But even the most devious Congressman knows his constituents will press for quick release of a drug to help returning veterans, so I doubt they'll delay things."

"Will Congressional hearings address the issue of corporate espionage in the pharmaceutical industry? And, while they're at it, their obscene overcharging for drugs?"

"I doubt that. You know how politicians operate. They all get money from the drug industry so it's hard to see how they'll suddenly bite the hands that feed them." He sighed and lapsed back into his persisting guilt, apologizing again for getting Tom hurt.

"Akira, I'd still be suffering from PTSD if you hadn't persisted in helping me. So I owe you thanks for that," Tom said, knowing how responsible Akira felt for his current state.

"Without your encouragement to enter the program I'd still be out there struggling to understand what happened to me. And who knows, I might have ended up like so many others – addicted, depressed, or dead."

Akira rose from his chair and took Tom's good hand in both of his and held it for a long time. Sitting down he looked toward the future.

"In the next few months we'll watch the legal stuff unfold. I also want to see how we can formalize your relationship to Zylinski. You interested continuing to help us?"

"Yeah, but no more rough stuff, okay?" Tom said with a chuckle. "Seriously, I appreciate the offer and will be glad to continue, even though I'm not sure what kind of help I can be. We can talk more about this later."

"We will. Now I think Alicia is waiting to see you." Akira said as he rose to leave.

31

PLANNING

"SO, THE GREAT HOLMES LIVES!" Alicia exclaimed as she came into Tom's room as Akira left. She dispensed with her clinical detachment and gave him a big hug.

"I feel more like Inspector Clouseau than Sherlock," Tom said. "I survived, and now am hiding from the media, no small feat. But what happened was my own damned fault. I had to go and blab about the video to Crocker who gave me to those two goons. You know, he almost got me killed!" stoking his anger at Crocker anew. "Everyone thought he was such a good guy."

"He had us all conned. Well, he's paying for it dearly," Alicia said. "What a fool he was."

"How goes it in the courtroom drama department?"

"The legal stuff is complicated. It'll take time. Mazarov and Rusker – your good buddies – are behind bars. Last I heard Rusker turned state's evidence against Mazarov. Looks like they both will go to prison, Mazarov for a long sentence and Rusker for less. Don't know what Crocker and Carrie Brink will get for their role.

"We won't know about the big Federal case against Laxalta for a while," Alicia went on. "Their lawyers are doing everything to delay, delay, delay, but the judge told them to be ready for trial soon. Lots at stake in this one. Zylinski for sure will be compensated for its travail. Don't know how much. Laxalta may pay a hefty fine – millions of dollars – for their part. Martin and Flannigan, the two hot shots who bribed Crocker, will almost certainly go to prison. I've heard – from the horse's mouth – Crocker himself – his testimony will be damning."

"So maybe what happened to me was worth something after all. When did you talk to Crocker?"

"I talked to him soon after he'd been arraigned. He's remorseful, as you can imagine, and depressed. He's had a lot to deal with in the past year," Alicia said. "I'm disappointed in him but I also feel for him."

"He's had his share of trouble, but I can't feel sorry for him," Tom said. "How could he betray all those patients and his professional colleagues? I try to be a forgiving person but this is monstrous. No amount of money justifies what he did."

"No, nothing excuses what he did, you're right about that. I guess he felt trapped. I'm not apologizing for him. Maybe he didn't believe nepenthe was going to work anyway, that what he was doing wouldn't make any difference. I don't know, people are hard to understand. I'm a psychologist, supposed to have great insights into behavior, but I don't get this. It's a conundrum."

"Well, Alicia, you didn't get the shit kicked out of you, almost die and end up with a useless arm," Tom said irritably. Recognizing he'd been short with a person he was very fond of, he said: "Sorry to argue with you about this but Crocker turned out to be unprincipled, a coward and a weakling. I have no use for him. Ever."

"I understand, believe me.

"On to another subject. A lawyer at Zylinski –Margot Campbell – wants to talk to you about your bringing a civil suit against Laxalta."

"You know what's she has in mind?"

"She's sure you're entitled to a settlement for all the damage done to you. Laxalta's got deep pockets and they deserve to pay for that. She's waiting until you're healthy enough to discuss this with you. Think you're ready to talk?"

"Well, guess I am. Have her call me."

"Okay. The other thing is – keep coming to see me. Even though the study's over we still need to collect data so the outcome part ties up the loose ends. Sometimes when patients get better they think there's no need to keep coming. But we need to keep going so there's no doubt this treatment plan works over the long haul."

"You can count on me," Tom said giving Alicia a goodbye hug.

Margot Campbell came to see Tom the next day. In her sixties, she was short, tending towards squat. Her cropped reddish hair, surely helped with a bottle, framed a round face with blue eyes that seemed always to be about to squeeze into laughter. Her delicate nose rose from between round pink cheeks. Tom was relieved she spoke calmly in short sentences, different from his experience from other lawyers whose elliptical sentences were hard to follow. She brought Tom up to speed on the upcoming trial of Martin and Flannigan.

"The Board at Laxalta initially balked at paying for legal counsel for these two witless executives who thought they could pull off this sabotage. But the Board ultimately agreed to provide lawyers, I guess thinking throwing them under the bus would do the company no good. Laxalta lured these two hard-driving salesmen from Tamlin Corporation, a diet supplement drug manufacturer. Diet supplements are a distinctly different class of drugs than Laxalta's line and the corporate culture in that industry very different," Margot told Tom. "These two guys assumed they could use the same deceptive and borderline unethical practices they used at Tamlin. They thought by doing this they'd guarantee a bigger market for Laxalta's widely advertised and prescribed drug for PTSD."

"You know, I took that Laxalta drug when I first got back from the war. No good for lessening my symptoms but highly effective in making me lethargic. It's just another run-of-the mill tranquilizer."

"Well, it's a useless drug, but Laxalta advertised it lavishly, especially on television, and they sell a ton of it. They stood to lose big, literally billions of dollars. When this scandal broke, the President of Laxalta resigned – blazing front-page stuff, on local and later on national TV," Margot said. "He wasn't charged with Martin and Flannigan, convincing investigators he was unaware of what his two senior managers were doing. How the investigators could possibly believe he was ignorant of their actions is hard to swallow but they bought his story. When he left, he gave up his ten million dollar yearly salary and his thousands of shares of Laxalta stock lost half their value. But don't waste any pity on him. He squirreled away plenty during his seven-year tenure as President and CEO. After he resigned he repaired to his Bimini island home. Poor thing!"

"If I weren't living this I wouldn't believe what you're telling me," Tom said. "Sounds like a bad TV show with villainous unredeemable characters. But I guess these guys are real, empty suits with no moral compass. Is Zylinski gonna sue for screwing up their study?"

"Oh yes indeed. Big time. Because of all the attention the case has drawn there's strong public suspicion that drug makers are predatory. Outrageous drug prices, duplicitous advertising luring naïve patients to believe they need drugs when they don't, industry corruption – all this bad publicity has disillusioned a lot of people, made them plenty angry. People have had it with drug makers."

"Alicia said you think I should file a suit against Laxalta. Tell me about that."

"You have a right to restitution for your abduction, torture and loss of your professional life. I can refer you to one of the best firms in Boston to file a civil suit against Laxalta for you."

"Would it be worth the aggravation?"

"You bet. I'm talking about a suit asking in the millions. The firm is Rogers, Fish and Conley in Boston. Give then a call. I've alerted them that you'd be calling," Margot said.

Tom looked at Margot Campbell for several seconds. Stunned, he got up from his seat, and with his right hand pulled his limp left arm across his chest, reminding him that he had lost a lot. He took a deep breath.

"I'm flabbergasted," he said. "That's an incredible amount of money."

"Don't know what the final figure might be. There'd also be legal fees deducted but I think you should go for the max. What that should be is up to the lawyers."

"Jesus, I need to digest this, talk it over with Cynthia. Obviously a big decision. Need to figure out what to do with that kind of money. Whew!"

"Call me when you decide what you'd like to do," Margot said.

32

ALL THAT MONEY

WHEN MARGOT LEFT, TOM PACED around his room, his brain going haywire with the buzz of thousands of circuits firing all at once.

Millions of dollars, he thought. I can't even imagine that kind of money. Hold on, she said there'd be legal fees deducted. I might not get much anyhow. But still.... What would I do with all that money? If I can't do what I really love – practice medicine – being rich is kind of an empty way to live. I have to let the idea of practicing go. No one wants a one-armed surgeon. Would they? Could I learn to operate using just one hand? I'm right-handed. There are one-handed pianists, okay? But what else could I do? I'm sure Akira would give me a sinecure at Zylinski – he owes me that – but doing what? I'm not into research the way he and the others at Zylinski are – no experience and less patience. Write grants the rest of my life? No way. Teach? I could do that, but without operating room time I wouldn't be credible. I need to talk to Cynthia.

His reverie ended as he reached Cynthia.

"You coming over tonight?" he said when she came on the line.

"Yeah, around 7. Got some paperwork to finish here. What can I bring you?"

"I'd like one of those greasy pepperoni pizzas from Jack's. We can warm it up in the microwave in the rec room. Okay?"

"Sure. See you around 7."

Tom looked out at the cloud-draped city. There were milky halos around the light posts on the street. Fog gathered in the low spots near the pond. His stomach was rumbling with hunger and it was still a couple of hours before Cyn would get there with food. He walked down to the rec room where there was a drink dispenser and saw Matt jawing with one of the other patients. Matt spotted him and waved him over as he got a couple of drinks from the machine.

"Lemme have a look at you," he said. "How's the healing going?"

"You can do your inspection, but no smart ass comments."

"Turn your head sideways. Okay, turn back. Looks like your jaw is back where it belongs. The bruises on your face nearly gone. You look pretty good for a punching bag. Those plastic surgeons did as good a job as they could considering the material they had to work with." He grinned at Tom, then turned serious.

"How you feeling?"

"Okay. Pain mostly gone. Still have this useless arm. Left leg a little weaker than my right, but the good news is that I can walk without a cane. How're you?"

"Well, I'm getting outta here next week." Matt said. "Got my discharge orders, a bunch of instructions and my supply of the magic pill. Most of us leave soon. Study's over. We got clinic appointments, but the old gang's breaking up. And praise be for that, even though I'll miss some of them."

"George around?"

"Saw him at the pool earlier. He's on top of the world now that he's on the pill. Happy as a clam."

"That's great. By the way, I need your phone number when you get one."

When he got back to his room Cynthia was waiting for him, looking out the window.

"Hey, you're early. Glad to see you."

"I figured paperwork could wait. Wanted to see you."

"Just saw Matt, looked me over and declared I looked okay so it's official. You still want to hang out with me?"

"Well, we need to talk about a lot of things," she said after a long pause, turning away from the window, looking sad and troubled.

"Fact is," she began slowly, "since you went to the war we've both changed – a lot. Our relationship has changed too."

Tom looked at Cynthia. She wasn't crying. She was calm, reminding him of those days when she had bad news to tell patients. Objective. Deliberate.

"You've had experiences I can't even imagine," she said. "I've tried to understand your responses to the things that have happened to you, but I've been through the wringer watching you drop into your own private hell and claw your way out. After being with you I have to get up each day and go about my life and my work too. Since you got back, as a couple, the focus has been exclusively on your problems. Mine got ignored."

Tom looked at her, perplexed. Her recent affection and caring seemed to herald a new beginning for them. Now it seemed she was again moving away from him. He shoved his right hand into his pocket, looked at the ceiling.

"What problems? You haven't said anything."

"You've been so self-absorbed – and don't get me wrong, I understand the reasons for that – that you forgot about how I'm affected by your actions. I tried hard to help you when you got home, when you went into the program at Zylinski," she said, tearing up as she recalled those days.

"That night I came to your apartment? I woke up in the middle of the night sensing you needed me. I wanted to help you. You totally rejected me – screamed at me to go away. That hurt a lot – and was jarring. A lot of sleepless nights after that. I never could put that in perspective."

She shook her head and her eyes glistened. Her voice wavered as she continued.

"Other things are happening. For instance, I've been offered the deanship of the nursing school. This is a great opportunity and I'm excited. What I'm trying to say, I guess, is my life continues to move ahead while you've been stuck in the same place dealing with all the horrors you saw over there. I know they were devastating. I'm not minimizing them... I don't know, I'm so mixed up." She looked at Tom wanting him to understand where she was coming from.

"So the nursing school offer's one thing. I've invested a huge amount of emotional and mental energy in my career. I've centered on it for many years. I love my work." She paused. "I wonder if I want kids, a family. If I had children I'd want to take care of them myself, and that would mean giving up my life's work. I've talked so often to my therapist about this stuff, I bore myself by my own indecision. My friend Rosalie is going through a similar dilemma."

Tom sat motionless as Cynthia ran her fingers through her hair.

"I don't know whether the stress of all this is to blame, but I've also had some health issues."

"Health issues? What kind of health issues?" Tom's eyebrows were up, his head turned sharply toward Cynthia.

"Got so tired I finally saw my doctor. When it started I thought it was psychosomatic – mainly my worries about you, us, my job. But when I went – long story short – I have chronic hepatitis C. That explains my fatigue. I even had a little jaundice I thought was just tiredness showing in my eyes. So much for my nurse insight."

"My god, I'm sorry. You're right, I have been thinking only of myself. I look at you and see the Rock of Gibraltar. Never entered my mind you could ever get sick."

The doctor box in his brain immediately focused on her disease, crowding out the other issues she'd laid out.

"The hepatitis drug – get started on it right away. I've heard it's very effective."

"It's outrageously expensive."

"Get it tomorrow. Never mind the expense. We'll find a way. The longer you wait the more damage to your liver. Please, do it right away. Jesus!"

Cynthia put her head in her hands, her shoulders shaking. She could no longer hold in her gloom. Tom moved closer to her, wrapped his arms around her as she gradually regained control.

"I'm so – I don't know what to do, Tom. I do love you. But right now I'm in a quandary. As far as the cost of the drug, I can afford it and I'll get it. It'd be crazy not to. I guess I got Hep C from one of the many needle sticks I've had. I'll never know. But you'll have to give me some time to sort the rest of all this out. Please."

"Of course." Just when I thought things were starting to be okay. "You think we ought to get some counseling?"

"Maybe. Yeah, think that could help. Get this worked out."

"You know a therapist? Maybe Alicia could recommend someone," the words spilling out. "You think couples therapy or individual?"

"I have a therapist for myself already. Been seeing her for several months and it's helped some. But obviously it hasn't given me all the answers I need.

"Yes, ask Alicia, and I'll ask around too for a couples therapist. I'm so screwed up right now. Couples therapy might get stuff out there for both of us to look at."

"I need that too. I feel like a jerk. You're right. I have been completely into myself. We're both kinda in a fog. I need to listen better. Couples therapy could help me do that."

"I'm not telling you all this to make you feel guilty, that's not what this is about," she said, putting her hand on Tom's arm. "It's like I need to cleanse myself, wash all this away. I don't know – I've never had problems like this. I'm just not coping very well right now."

Silence flooded the room. For Cynthia it was painful but a relief, the first time she'd spoken to Tom about fears she'd been carrying around silently for months. She'd been so on guard since his return, not wanting to add to his misery. This was like opening the door. For Tom, this was an awakening, a call to get out of the silo he'd inhabited for so many months. It was also a new reason to be anxious.

"In the meantime," Tom asked, bewildered by this turn of events, "should I plan on going back to my apartment?"

Tears ran down her face as she crossed her arms, looked at the ceiling, struggling to untangle her thoughts.

"I need space. For now. Can you handle being at that awful box?"

"Better now than before. I'll be okay. Do what you need to do to feel better. I'm available if you need me. Just as you were to me." Then he added: "Don't worry – for once – that I'm feeling sorry for myself or depressed. I'm sad about how you're feeling, but I'm in better shape now than I've been since I left for service. My mood's good. I'll get some names of therapists, and maybe then we can move forward – in whatever direction that'll be."

Cynthia heard strength in his voice and saw traces of the Tom Barrett she remembered before this bad dream began. Maybe this will all be okay, she thought.

33

RECONSIDERING

TOM CALLED CONLEY FIRST THING in the morning.
"I wanna get going. What do you need from me?"

"I need all the details you can remember about your abduction. I got everything I need on your many years of medical training, your surgical expertise, and your exemplary military service before your – uh – medical problems. I see the bold outlines of the case we'll build. So set up a time with Monica and we'll put it together."

"Remind me of the name of the financial advisor that you mentioned the other day," Tom said.

"That's David Pomeroy. I'll arrange to have him meet with you the same day I do."

When he finished his conversation with Conley, he called Alicia.

"Hi, it's me. I had a long talk with Cynthia. She's got a bunch of problems I didn't know about. She and I are kinda on shaky ground right now. We need a recommendation for a couples therapist."

"This doesn't surprise me. You two have been through so much. So this is progress. It may not seem that way to you now, but you need to give it a chance. Robin Goodfellow is the right person, I think, for couples therapy. You have Dr. Lyon here for your individual sessions. Does Cynthia need a referral for an individual therapist?"

"No, she's been seeing someone for a while. I didn't know that until our talk, but then I haven't thought about anyone but myself for a long time."

"Of course you haven't. Don't beat yourself up about that. You haven't had the capacity to think of others. But that doesn't mean Cynthia hasn't had her share of worry. Glad she's seeing someone and Dr. Goodfellow should be ideal for the two of you."

Tom called Cynthia to tell her about Goodfellow.

"I'm good with that," she said. "I'll make the appointment since my calendar is trickier than yours. Any time you can't make it?"

"You set it up, I'll be there," Tom said. "Got some interesting news today."

"Yeah, what's that?"

"Margot Campbell, the lawyer here at the Institute, referred me to some big time legal firm in Boston. To hire them to sue Laxalta for damages."

"We can talk more about that when I see you. Any idea when you'll be discharged?"

"Deb, my nurse, was checking on it. I'll let you know."

"Just so you know, I'm feeling better today. I think just telling you that stuff was helpful. Couples therapy will move us along."

"Glad to hear you're better. You set up your Hep C treatment yet?"

"Yeah, seeing my doctor tomorrow. I can pick you up after that, late afternoon."

"Good," he said as Deb walked into his room. "Gotta go. My jailer's just come in to tell me when I get sprung."

"The good news is you can probably go home tomorrow," Deb said. "The bad news is you can't go home until tomorrow. Dr. Battersby wants to check you out in the morning."

"Well shit and double shit. I really hate being a patient."

The next morning Battersby and three other doctors examined Tom from every angle and drew some blood.

"Well, except for your arm your neuro checks are surprisingly good," Battersby said. "With the brain swelling you had I thought you'd have more cognitive deficits. But you're doing fine, and you seem to be in good spirits. You're a bloody miracle, you know. Any questions before we set you free?"

"Nope. I'm ready. Thanks for everything. Now I have to figure out what to do next," Tom said, not with bitterness, but a grin.

Cynthia picked him up in her old beat-up Honda and proceeded to gather his belongings when he stopped her.

"My left arm's no good, but the rest of me works fine. I've gotta get used to doing things for myself, okay?" He tossed his bags into the back seat and slid into the front passenger seat, looked over at Cynthia. "That sounded angrier than I intended. Sorry."

"I understand. I'm glad you're getting your motivation back. This is one of those adjustments I was talking about. Little things like that could become big things unless we work on them."

"You're right. So much stuff to take in. Guess we have to take it slow and easy."

As he settled in the passenger seat, clipped his seat belt, he looked over at Cynthia as she switched on the ignition.

"I wonder if I can get a driver's license with this limp arm."

"If you pass the driving test I think they have to give you a license. Even with your bum arm you'll drive better than most Massachusetts residents, the worst drivers on the planet outside of Rome.

"You mentioned suing Laxalta. You absolutely should do that. Employees of that company nearly killed you and you paid dearly for it. Because of those injuries it's likely you can't do what you love most because of your flaccid arm.

"Sorry, that wasn't cool. Is it any better?"

"No, it's the same. Doubt it'll ever come back. Some magical new treatment might come along, but I've resigned myself – I'll never operate again. That sucks."

"Thought about other things you could do? You still have a good brain."

He looked out the car window as the darkness settled on the road.

"I don't know. I really don't." He sighed. "I've been a one-note kind of a guy and now that one note won't play anymore. I suppose I could be one of those long-suffering people who goes around to conferences telling other sufferers how to handle it, how they've come to terms with their losses, that kind of thing. But that's not my style."

"Definitely not your style. I think you should put it away for a while, stop fretting about what you're going to do. I know, it's easy for me to say. But you're gonna need all your energy for this lawsuit. It sounds like a slam-dunk, but in damage cases you just never know. Juries are unpredictable.

"The other thing that needs attention – yours and mine – is getting used to being together. Long time since we shared space. I know you're not the jittery guy you were a few months ago, but there's going to be an adjustment period."

He looked over at her, encouraged by the prospect of getting back together, as she parked in front of her condo.

"I'm hungry," Tom said.

"Some things never change. What would you like?"

"How about take-out Chinese? I haven't had that since I went into the hospital."

"You call it in, I'll go get it. Whatever you want is fine. There's some white wine in my fridge – oh, are you allowed alcohol?"

"In moderation. They told me there's no effect on the pill from some alcohol but to go easy. I'm only gonna have one small glass."

While Cynthia went for the food, Tom wandered around the condo, looking at the familiar couch, the pictures of their trips. Sadness surged over him for reasons he couldn't understand – a vague sense of alienation. Something about Cynthia felt different. She was tender with him but it seemed perfunctory. She was right, he thought, it would take time to get back to where they'd been before. Would it ever come back?

"I'm back," she called coming through the door. After they finished eating from the containers of steaming food, Tom wiped his mouth and turned to Cynthia.

"Can we get serious for a little while?"

"Do we have to?" she said with a smile that didn't convey much humor.

Tom recounted the conversation he'd had with Margot Campbell, this time telling Cynthia the amount of money mentioned.

"Oh my God!" Cynthia cried, jumping up. "You gotta be kidding!"

"Not kidding. That's what she said. I couldn't believe it myself. If that's realistic, then the big question becomes: what to do with that kind of money?"

"You'll need some serious financial advice," Cynthia said, morphing into the pragmatist she'd always been. "I've read about people who win the lottery then fall completely apart, are targets for scam artists, get threats by phone and email. People come out of the woodwork claiming to be long lost friends or forgotten relatives."

"Whoa, hold on. You make it sound like a bad thing. This is a good thing!" Tom said.

"Well, I've seen patients come into the emergency department with mental collapses because of the stress that comes with that kind of a windfall. Couples get divorces; family members go berserk fighting over their share. It's not all roses to have big money fall in your lap."

"I've heard those stories too," Tom said. "Scary, for sure. But tomorrow I'll find out the facts. Even if millions is way out of line, I will need some source of income for who knows how many years. I have no idea what I can do to make a living. I can't stand the idea of being dependent on anyone."

Cynthia got busy and collected the empty Chinese food cartons tossing them into the trash. She moved around the kitchen in high gear, a change from her mellow mood a few moments before.

"What's up?" Tom asked, noticing her rising level of anxiety.

"I don't know. My moods swing back and forth so much these days. That money thing is upsetting, I can't figure why it bothers me so much, but it does. It seems it makes all my fears stand out like bright lights."

"You nervous about the Hep C? Have you gone for your treatment yet?"

"Not yet. Their appointments are backed up almost a month."

"This can't wait! Call that office and insist on an appointment next week!"

"Don't yell at me like that! You're starting to sound like the pre-treatment guy," she shot back.

Tom gulped in a mouthful of air, looked at the ceiling, and threw his arms up in exasperation.

"I'm sorry. It's just that..."

"I know, but I'm just drowning in all the stuff I'm dealing with. I'm irritable, on edge and scared. It's almost like I have PTSD. I think I've been trying to rush our reunion. You'll have to give me more time to figure this out."

"So it's back to the apartment for me?"

Cynthia looked at him, her expression pleading for patience. He rose from the table, got his jacket, pulled out his phone and called a cab.

"Your car open? I need to get my stuff out when the cab comes. I'll keep you posted on the legal stuff. Please see your doctor as soon as you can. I'll see you at our couples session on Thursday."

Cynthia watched him as he walked to the curb to wait for the cab then she laid down on the bed, too exhausted to cry.

Tom stepped off the elevator on the top floor of the State Street Bank building and pushed through a glass door embossed with "Rogers, Fish and Conley, Attorneys At Law."

"Hello Dr. Barrett, Mr. Conley is expecting you. I'll let him know you're here." A good beginning, he thought. I'm actually a real person to them. Get real, Tom, of course I'm real to them. I'm worth a helluva lot of money to them if this suit goes anywhere.

"Margot Campbell gave me a lot of information about your ordeal," Tim Conley said as they sat down in his office. "Wanna fill in some details so we can move ahead. Not to get your hopes up, but I think you have a strong case.

"I've worked the figures," Conley said. "The physical assault caused significant disabilities and the potential income lost over the balance of your life alone is worth somewhere in the neighborhood of fifty million dollars. Add to that pain and suffering. Bottom line: I think you should sue Laxalta for seventy million dollars," he said, arms extended.

Tom blinked his eyes, trying to grasp what Conley said.

"Seventy million dollars," he whispered. "Unbelievable. You said I have a strong case. Will this be one of those long drawn out legal battles?"

"My educated guess – and hope – is they'll settle out of court. This case is riveting. A military doctor serving his country in a foreign land returns home with PTSD and is beaten into a coma by goons hired by a pharmaceutical company. You've recovered from your coma but have a paralyzed left arm and can't pursue your career as a surgeon. This was all done to thwart the development of a breakthrough drug to help returning veterans. They sure don't want any more publicity about you. It's highly likely their wish is to let this be put to rest quietly."

34

THREE MONTHS LATER

"TIM CONLEY HERE. GOT SOME news for you. When can you come in?"

"When do you have time? I can come today!" Tom said standing up abruptly from his computer at Zylinski. "Can you give me a hint?"

"How about tomorrow? I'm booked solid today. Say 9AM? Can't really discuss this over the phone. I'm going to have Pomeroy join us."

"Be there." Having Pomeroy there sounded like this would be good news, Tom thought.

Sleep wouldn't come to him. His insomnia this time was anticipation of something good, not the old anxieties and dreams. He was up and down, punching his pillow, turning from one side to the other. He wondered why he had to pee so many times. Was he getting diabetes on top of everything else? Did he have a pituitary tumor? Stop it! All this medical over-analysis – like being back in medical school when you got all the diseases you were studying. He considered taking his blood pressure but knew it was up – he could feel the throb in his temples. He was in semi-sleep when his alarm shook him awake at six o'clock.

The train into Boston was packed at seven AM. A teenage boy actually offered Tom his seat when he saw him stumble boarding the train and noticed his limp left arm. Tom waved him off at first then reconsidered and accepted. He was fatigued from his restless night and dozed most of the way into Boston.

Conley stuck his head into the waiting room and motioned for Tom to follow him into his office. Pomeroy was already there. After shaking hands with both of them, quiet hung over the office like a pewter sky.

Is this going to be another letdown, Tom mused. Disappointing news after being led to believe this was a done deal? No one said anything for a moment. Conley was looking at papers on his desk and Pomeroy was punching the icons on his iPhone. No one seemed ready to start a conversation. Conley cleared his throat.

"I have an offer from Laxalta to settle out of court. I want to fill you in on the details," he said in a sober, restrained lawyer voice.

Conley looked over at Pomeroy who looked back and they both laughed. Tom didn't know how to react at first then realized they were in a celebratory mood. He smiled tentatively, not really understanding yet what was going on.

"Does this mean good news?"

"Not good news, Tom." He paused for effect. "GREAT News! We don't have to go to court and YOU now own an eighty million dollar nest egg!"

Tom was so stunned he couldn't immediately laugh or cry or jump up and down, but as the truth penetrated, his emotions ran away from him. He felt tears running down his cheeks as Tim and Pomeroy took turns shaking his hand and slapping him on the back.

"Congratulations, Tom. You deserve this. And by the way, that 80 mil is net – what you get – our commission has already been subtracted. We went for more than the amount I originally discussed with you. Laxalta is so cowed I think we could've gotten even more, but I tried not to get greedy. Unusual for me. Now all you have to do is decide what to do with all that money!" Tim chortled.

"That's where I come in," David Pomeroy said. "I'd like to discuss that with you if you have time."

"Are you kidding? Do I have time? I have two things: time and 80 million dollars! Wowee!" He threw his good fist into the air like an Olympian gold medalist.

Tom thanked Tim profusely. Then he and Pomeroy put their heads together to discuss the next steps of money – big money – management.

35

MONEY PROBLEMS

THE NOTION OF BEING A millionaire was sobering as Tom followed David Pomeroy into his office. Tom knew nothing about managing even normal personal finances let alone large sums. Money had never meant much to him. He'd always had enough for his simple, almost monastic, life. He couldn't have cared less about cars, houses and style. Always obsessed with surgery to the exclusion of everything else, he now had to block surgery out. He'd gradually edged toward acceptance that he'd never operate again. He had to develop new skills and interests. But what? He wondered if he's turn out to be a lonely middle-aged man slumped in a chair watching stock market numbers? His fear of loneliness rose out of his therapy with Cynthia that uncovered a thicket of conflicts he'd never dreamed were there. Would they ever get back their pre-war ardor? He took comfort that in spite of these troubles at least his PTSD symptoms hadn't returned. He credited nepenthe and ongoing therapy with keeping those demons under control.

"Had any ideas about what you'd like to do with this money?" Pomeroy asked once they were seated around a small round table. Boston Harbor was visible out the window and Tom's eyes followed a container ship as it plied its way out the channel.

"I don't have a clue. Truth is, as strange as it may seem I almost wish I didn't have it. Makes me nervous. Decisions I'm not equipped to make."

"Not unusual. I have other clients with the same confusion," Pomeroy said. "From what I've been told about you, I imagine multiplying your money is not your highest priority. Good investments are essential, don't misunderstand me, and I'll have recommendations about that. But when deciding how to put this money to good use, think about what needs to be done in the world."

I like his approach, Tom thought. But there are so many things. Some – like stopping war – are impractical. So I have to cone down.

"Before we get into the 'good works' part, it's important that you first set aside enough money for your own life, taking into consideration that you may need health care down the road secondary to your injuries. Another unknown is that we also don't know yet what kind of income you can expect from working or even what kind of work you'll be able to do. So the set-aside should insure that you have adequate annual income for the rest of your life without any additional income from whatever you do.

"Now, the good works. As a doctor your thinking probably makes a beeline to health care – HIV, malaria, disease prevention, public health. That's fine of course, but cast a broader net in your thinking. There are many things – education, art, music, literature, global warming, hunger – the list goes on and on – that could interest you. How could your money make a difference? What magic wand would you wave?"

"Boy, I'll need time to think this through. I'm a sucker for your idea of a mission though."

"A lot to think about. Tuck this thought away: create a non-profit corporation for the 'good works' part of this. Our firm can help with that – not hard to do. For now I'll need your permission to stash the money in conservative investment instruments, low risk and low yield. But safe. There are many options after that. Putting the money into a trust, for example. I won't bore you with details until after you've had time to think about this. We can talk some more then.

"Any idea how much time you'll need?"

"Well, I need to talk to some people. My mind's blank now."

On his way home Tom stared out the train window, a jumble of thoughts rattling around in his head. What matters? Pomeroy said I have a magic wand. Tom always had the "temptation to do good." He'd now been given the wherewithal. He thought of Zylinski and Akira. He could give a bunch of money to them to continue their research. He called Akira.

"Sure, come in this afternoon," Akira said. "I'd love to see you."

He called Alicia. "I need to talk to you about some things. I'm seeing Akira early afternoon. Have any time today?"

"Well, it's about time you called!" she exclaimed with a smile in her voice. "How 'bout late afternoon today?"

After lunch Tom sat with Akira in his office.

"So my lawyers came up with a big settlement." Tom told Akira the whole story. "I have to decide how to use the money. I thought of you and Zylinski. What do you think?"

"Wonderful you thought of us," he said, smiling. "You'll think I've lost my mind when I answer your question, but bear with me.

"Margot Campbell also negotiated with Laxalta and we got a bundle of money for the Institute. So – and this is why you'll think I'm nuts – I don't think you should put your money with Zylinski. Right now we have an embarrassment of riches. I'll probably regret not accepting your offer down the road, but I think there may be better ways to use your money."

Tom looked at Akira and marveled at his response. Saying no to money for his research? It was crazy. You never have enough money for research. What's motivating him?

"I'm surprised. But I'm all ears to hear what you think these 'better ways' are."

"Let me explain. What Laxalta did was unconscionable," Akira said. "But they're not the only drug company turning a blind eye to morality when greed comes calling. Lots going on out of public view in that industry. We need a bright light shone on them."

"Interesting," Tom said. "Come to think of it, Cynthia had to pay through the nose for her hepatitis C drug. Is this the sort of thing you mean? Outrageous prices for life-saving medicines?"

"Soaring drug prices are only the tip of the iceberg. There's a lot of other stuff. Enormous budgets for advertising making drugs more expensive. Mobs of drug salespeople pushing their products in doctor's offices, so-called educational cruises for doctors that are really paid vacations, subsidizing drug research investigators who have inherent conflicts of interest. Scaring customers into buying drugs they don't need. Manipulation of old formulas to fool people into thinking they're 'new, improved drugs' when in fact they're simply retreads of old drugs – a minor alteration of the old formula – with new patents and higher prices."

He's really worked up about this, Tom thought. Haven't seen Akira so passionate since he discovered the plot to undermine the nepenthe study.

"Huge salaries for executives who've never done one thing for patients," he went on. "Sparkling new buildings rivaling the buildings insurance companies have. Sweetheart deals with health plans. All the while many patients can't afford medications they need to survive."

"So what are you suggesting?"

"Shine a light on the pharmaceutical industry. Make the shadows go away."

After what he'd been through, Tom thought, this could be sweet revenge. Also a way to improve the lives of countless numbers of patients, he thought. Isn't this why he went into medicine in the first place?

"Considering my recent experience with one pharma company, if I did what you're suggesting I better spend some of my money on personal security," Tom laughed. "I'm sure there are other Mazarovs and Ruskers out there. But I do like the idea. Any other organizations doing this?"

"Lots of consumer protection groups and others who watch over a lot of businesses and governmental agencies. Some of them may be monitoring the pharmaceutical industry. But I don't know of any who are exclusively training their sights on drug houses. Even if there are, the more the better. You could lead the way.

"Give yourself time to consider this. If you need any help setting up a non-profit Board, let me know. We have a great Board here at Zylinski and I'm sure some of them could suggest solid candidates for your Board."

Akira walked him to the door.

"Thanks for coming by. Glad about your settlement. Give my love to Cynthia. How's that going?"

"A continuing saga. Let's get together sometime and talk."

"We can do that anytime you're ready. Take care, Tom."

His next stop was with Alicia.

"So great to see you Tom!" she exclaimed when he walked into her familiar den/office. "I'm intrigued by your call. Catch me up on everything."

"Where shall I begin? Well, for starters, Cynthia and I still go to therapy with Dr. Goodfellow. Thanks for referring us to her.

"My big news is I'm now a rich man." He told her about the settlement. She was not surprised about his winning a settlement but astonished at the amount.

"I just talked with Akira," Tom said. "He's thoroughly pissed off about the drug industry. He suggested I use some of the money to investigate and expose wrongdoing of some of the companies. I like this idea. But how, is another matter. My lawyer suggested the idea of a non-profit corporation. Know anything about setting up a non-profit?"

"Hmm. Interesting. You know, I'm on the Board of a non-profit called 'Grandparents Raising Grandchildren.' There are thousands of non-profits, most of them doing god's work. Monitoring what drug companies does sounds like a terrific idea, a vehicle for what Akira is advocating. The Development Officer here also might help. Deborah Rabin. Want to talk with her?"

"Can you get me into to see her?"

"Sure. I'll call her and set it up."

"What's going on with you?" Tom asked.

"Busy as hell writing about the drug trial. Are you involved in any of that?"

"No, Akira has me doing some other research. Not too exciting."

"Want to tell me about you and Cynthia?"

"Wish she could relax with me. Her major worry now is that nepenthe might stop working. That I'll relapse. Of course no one can guarantee anything," Tom said. "But I've talked with some of the guys I know in the program and so far everyone's on an even keel.

"Cynthia's Dean of the Nursing School – demanding, but she's centered on it, loves her work. Another dilemma for her – struggling with the problem a lot of high-achieving women have, that damned biological clock, wondering whether she wants a family and how long can she wait to decide. I'd love to have kids with her but I don't want to be just a sperm donor. I want us to fall back in love, get married, have a family."

"The good thing is you're still trying. Falling back in love, as you put it, may not be realistic. That kind of romance happens at the front end of a relationship when the adventure of discovery of the other person is still new, still fresh. But loving each other – in mature mutual devotion – is something the two of you can achieve, given the right circumstances."

Tom kept on learning from Alicia. He wondered why she was single herself. Had she been married? A widow? Divorced? Deserted? He knew nothing about her personal life. Why should he? But she was someone who understood so much.

"She's very tentative, making me question whether we'll ever get back together. If we're gonna have kids we should get going. Men have a different kind of biological clock – we die earlier. I don't want my kids going to college when I'm headed for the nursing home."

Tom glanced at his watch and seeing it was after six lifted himself out of his chair.

"Didn't mean to keep you so long. Thanks for your good advice, Alicia. Are you open to a dinner invitation?"

"Of course I am! Love to have time over a good dinner to catch up."

"I'll call you with a time." After a hug, Tom left. On his way home he had an epiphany. He would name his non-profit "PharmaTruth."

36

ANTICIPATION

HE WALKED INTO THE APARTMENT, flipped through his mail. There was the bill from Dr. Goodfellow. He tossed the catalogs into the trash and a small envelope fell from his hand. He picked it up, saw it was postmarked La Jolla California. He slid his finger under the flap.

Dear Tom,

Sorry it's taken so long to respond to your letter. As you can imagine life has been complicated since Danny died. Perhaps someday we can talk.

I appreciated your letter. Danny told me you had gotten to be good friends. I'm thankful he had someone like you to be with before he died.

The boys are coping. Hunter loves first grade (he started early after testing showed he was ready) and Jeff is in a wonderful Montessori preschool program close to my lab in La Jolla. We stayed in our house here. My boss understands my need for time off. I'm now back full time doing the work I love - marine biology. Of course, I miss Danny all the time.

If you are ever out our way, please give me a call. I would welcome a chance to meet you.

Warmly,

Katharine Mott

He read the letter again. Mixed emotions roiled his mind. He was glad to hear she and the boys were doing okay (at least that's what she said) but saddened, bringing Danny clearly into his mind's eye. He stared at the letter, wondering what lay between the lines. He knew all couldn't possibly be well, considering what she'd lost, but since he didn't know anything about her strengths and weaknesses, the letter didn't tell him much. Yes, her children were in school and she was back working, but that was all surface stuff. Should he call her? Maybe tomorrow. He pulled out his phone and scrolled to the pictures of Katharine and the boys Danny had sent him. Such beautiful people. Life's so unfair.

The phone began to vibrate as he held it. Who could that be, he wondered. I'm not expecting any calls.

"Tom, George Logan here. Got a minute?"

"George! Good to hear from you. Where are you?"

"At a restaurant near you. You eaten?"

"No, just thinking about it."

"Wanna join me?"

"Sure. Where?"

Within minutes he walked in the front door, found George and dropped down on the seat opposite him.

"How're ya doin'?" George said.

"Great. You?"

"Me too. Got a job in a detective agency. Good pay, good boss. Everything's copacetic."

"I've got some really great news. But I'm not telling."

"Okay, I'm not interested anyhow," George said, pretending to study the menu.

"Okay, since you insist, here's the skinny."

He told George about the settlement and his conversations with Akira and Alicia.

"Sweet Jesus in heaven!" George said. "That's just terrific news. So now what?"

"One of the lawyers in the firm suggested establishing a non-profit corporation to do something good for society. "

"You gonna get yourself in trouble again," George grinned. "Doing good always pisses someone off."

"Well, let me tell you more that will convince you I will get in trouble again. I'm starting this non-profit and calling it 'PharmaTruth.' It's object – get this – expose bad behavior in the pharmaceutical industry."

"You are one big fool of a man. You want to snoop on the drug pushers? This time get killed? And then what?"

"You seem like you're not sure this is a good idea."

"No, actually, I think it's a great idea. Why makes you think I don't like it? Just because I said you're a fool and you could die?"

"Well, those were my first clues. Remember, I'm a seasoned detective myself. Cracked that whole case at Zylinski."

"Yeah, with a little help from your friends. I need to understand how you're gonna uncover stuff inside the offices of the behemoths of drug-making. Plus I don't want to see you get hurt again. I felt I failed you when you got into that jam."

"All my own fault, George. Forget that. You weren't put on earth to take care of me. Even though you think I need a guardian angel."

George flashed his familiar smile.

"I love the name 'PharmaTruth.' But how will it ferret out wrongdoing? And then who do you tell about it? How do you get the bad guys into jail?"

"I can't answer that yet. I'm in the idea phase. Alicia is arranging a meeting with the development officer at Zylinski. I'm hoping she can explain what's involved in organizing a non-profit corporation. Then I'll get back to Pomeroy – my lawyer – who can file the paperwork to get a non-profit established."

"So what will your role be?"

"That's another question I can't answer. Not something I've ever done. But I can learn. I'll need help. After I talk to Deborah Rabin – the development officer at Zylinski – maybe I'll be able to answer questions like that."

"I finally get to meet the famous Dr. Barrett. Come sit down," Deborah Rabin smiled as she motioned toward a cluster of chairs around a small glass table. "Can I get you some coffee or tea?"

"Tea, please," Tom said, a blush rising up his neck. "I'm an unlikely celebrity."

Tom pulled his left arm into his lap as he sat down and regarded Deborah Rabin. She was about his age with shoulder length auburn hair, curvaceous with thin arms, dressed in a dark skirt and floral silk blouse. Her face was narrow, with brown eyes – a nice face, Tom thought. He saw no wedding ring, wondering why he cared.

"So Alicia tells me you want to know about setting up a non-profit."

"Yeah, and I haven't any idea about how to do it. So you need to be elementary with me."

She leaned back and told him the basics, emphasizing the need for him to be clear about the mission and vision.

"Of prime importance is recruiting a Board whose members would bring the necessary expertise to implement the mission. There's a lot of other tasks, so I've put together a bunch of references for you," she said, handing him a folder.

Leaving her office Tom knew he had the equivalent of a PhD thesis ahead of him. He relished the idea of getting started.

37

Cynthia

"TOM, CAN YOU COME HAVE dinner with me tomorrow evening?" Cynthia said when Tom picked up.

"Sure. My time's flexible. I'm working getting my non-profit set up but there's no deadline. What's the occasion? And what time?"

"Around seven. Don't like to think of it as an 'occasion' but we need to talk."

Tom didn't like the term "need to talk." It sounded heavy.

"Can I bring anything?" he asked, knowing the answer.

"No. See you then."

Shortly after seven Tom knocked and Cynthia swung open the door. After he was in the familiar living room, she put her arms around his neck, kissed him on the cheek, then went to the kitchen and handed him a glass of Pinot Noir.

"I've made some salmon and thought the Pinot was light enough for that. Have a seat. It's ready to eat.

"So tell me about the non-profit. How's it going?"

"Well, it's early and not much to tell yet," Tom said, feeling awkward and anxious.

"Don't mean to rush things, but I'm curious to know what the 'need to talk' thing is about."

Cynthia scooted her chair back from the table, crossed her legs and took a sip of wine.

"If you've been listening during our sessions with Dr. Goodfellow you should have a pretty good idea." She took another swig of wine, stood up and brought the salmon and a casserole of vegetables to the table.

"Help yourself. I recalled that salmon was your favorite fish."

Tom didn't answer but began eating, his mouth dry and his heart pounding. They ate hurriedly, reminding his dinners while on call at the hospital. When they finished, Tom looked at Cynthia.

"So, this sounds like you want out," he said.

"I can't lie to myself – and you – anymore. I can't give you what you need. This has been gnawing at me for a long while and I've tried to suppress it. We've had so many problems that have eaten away at both of us. Think of all we've been through.

"I think we both need a fresh start."

"To be honest, this isn't a big surprise. This relationship has taken so much work since I've been back. We've been swimming against the tide and it's sucked what we used to have out of us. I still love you, always will, and think you love me too, but I recognize the signs of a wilting romance. An old story of loving someone but no longer 'in love', " Tom said, looking down at his plate. In an odd way, this brings a sense of relief, he thought.

"This may seem counterintuitive, but I want very much to remain friends. Think we can do that?" Cynthia asked.

"Yes, I know we can. I want that too."

38

DETAILS

"I'VE DRAWN UP THE FORMAT for the non-profit. You need to start assembling a list of essential people needed for your Board," Pomeroy said. "I know a guy in San Francisco who's the Executive Director of a non-profit interested in exposing corporate fraud. Name's Amitav Kumar. A good person to talk to. Their mission is similar to yours, but broader."

"Can you arrange for me to see him?" Tom asked.

"Good idea. I'll do that. In the meantime, work on your mission statement. And search the Internet to see if there are other watchdog organizations already doing this."

It didn't seem there was any corrective action around high prices of drugs and the borderline unethical practices of pharmaceutical companies, Tom thought. So if there are others their effectiveness was pretty limited.

A few days later Pomeroy called.

"Tom, I talked to Amitav Kumar in Frisco. He'd welcome the chance to sit down with you to discuss your non-profit idea. Call him. You have time to go out there?"

"I have plenty of time. Give me his number and I'll get on it."

Tom called a travel agent and made airline arrangements to San Francisco. His next call was to Katharine Mott.

"Hi Katharine, this is Tom Barrett. I'm calling because I have a business trip to San Francisco next week. I was wondering if you might have time to have dinner with me. I can book a flight from San Fran to San Diego Tuesday or Wednesday, or later in the week if that doesn't work."

"Why yes, Wednesday works for me. And the boys. What time?"

ABOUT THE AUTHOR

Robert M. Reece, MD, was Clinical Professor of Pediatrics at Tufts University School of Medicine (now retired). Additionally, he served as the Director of the Child Protection Team at Tufts Medical Center and as Consultant to Child Protection Teams at the Massachusetts General Children's Hospital, University of Massachusetts Medical Center, and the Children's Hospital at Dartmouth.

Reece edited nine pediatric textbooks: three editions of Child Abuse: Medical Diagnosis and Management, and two editions of *Treatment of Child Abuse: Common Ground for Mental Health, Medical and Legal Practitioners.* Reece co-edited *Inflicted Childhood Neurotrauma* published by the American Academy of Pediatrics. He has published 48 peer-reviewed medical articles and contributed 27 book chapters. Reece edited *The Quarterly Update*, a review journal, since 1993.

He has been honored by numerous professional organizations for his contributions to the field of child abuse diagnosis and treatment. Frequently called as an expert witness, Reece has consulted and testified in countless cases of abusive head trauma and has lectured extensively nationally and internationally on the subject.

Reece's first novel, *To Tell The Truth*, is fiction based on non-fiction and focuses out abuses of criminal defense medical witnesses whose testimony is bought and sold for trial use. Reece additionally underscores that abusive head trauma is a harsh reality.

READ DR. REECE'S FIRST NOVEL
To Tell The Truth

An infant's death with evidence as high as the sky should be a slam-dunk prosecution. But what happens when the savviest defense attorney in town assists his idealistic public defender daughter? Timely in its examination of how belief in science can be manipulated, To Tell the Truth will have you questioning your own deliberations if sitting in the juror's box. A haunting expose of the clash between law and medicine, as written by a pediatrician with over 40 years' clinical and trial experience with shaken baby syndrome.

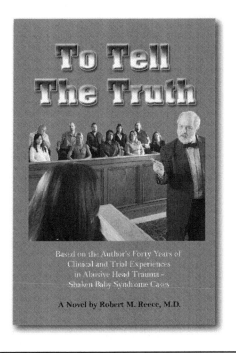

"...Reece has written a compelling story...brings the reader face-to-face with a startling reality: sometimes criminal cases are influenced by more than "the truth, the whole truth, and nothing but the truth."

Robert W. Block, MD, FAAP and Past President,
The American Academy of Pediatrics